About Brigand

The origins of Brigand Press go back to discussions at meetings of the Somers Town Writers Group on the state of contemporary publishing and its narrow focus. Members communicated their views to Scott Pearce, who has wide experience in printing and digital publishing. Subsequently discussions were initiated about the tentative concept of a micro-publisher. Impressed by the group's work, and following further talks, Scott was inspired by the writers group and thus Brigand was born. Brigand intends to expand its range in 2019, adding new voices by publishing the work of various additional new and exciting writers. It will be open for submissions in 2019, watch this space.

Brigand Press,
All contact: info@brigand.london

British Library Cataloguing-in-Publication Data
A catalogue record for this book is
available from the British Library

Printed and Bound in Great Britain by CPI
Group (UK) Ltd, Croydon CR0 4YY

ISBN 9781912978007

Neil Davies - Bio

Neil Davies left Secondary Modern School at the age of 14 without qualifications. He joined the Parachute Regiment at 17 and experienced active service in the Middle East and North Africa. Upon being discharged from the forces, suffering with PTSD, he travelled from country to country, continent to continent, job to job. He worked as a logger, steelworker, on fishing boats, building work, rank & file union organizer, outdoor pursuits instructor and lecturer.

Neil received an adult student grant and attended York University and eventually became an award winning filmmaker. His work has included Broadcast Documentary of the Year Award for "Raw Spice" (ITV), Artist of the year for two series of "Nights at the Empire" (Channel 4), as well as success with two well-regarded series, "Inside RAF Brize Norton" (Sky One), and "The Hunt" (BBC).

Neil is a member of the charity The Soldiers Arts Academy, undertakes volunteer work at the London Veterans Clinic, St Pancras Hospital, and over the past few years scratched an itch for doing stand-up comedy, and acting. He wrote and performed at Shakespeare's Globe, Remembrance Sunday performance of *Soldiers and Shakespeare*. He is also writing more fiction. *Falling Soldiers* is Neil's first published novel.

Dedication

An increasing number of veterans are facing the challenges of life after their military service. Not all of them are coping, suffering with physical and mental wounds, including PTSD, in isolation. Many turn to self-medication, such as alcohol and drugs, and become trapped in a spiral down to the streets and homelessness. An increasing and alarming number of veterans, who having survived combat, have even chosen suicide as a solution rather than reaching out for help.

The Army Covenant does not appear to be working, and therefore my novel is dedicated to the great work of people and organisations, which provide self-funded services, dealing with the many problems facing veterans. They include: Amanda Faber and the Soldiers Art Academy; Dr Sue Ferrier of The Veterans Clinic; St Pancras Hospital; former soldier Shaun Johnson of the Poppy Factory and Stoll Foundation; and Shakespeare's Globe for their production of Soldiers and Shakespeare on Remembrance Sunday. If you the reader would like to help or contribute, please find below the links to these organisations.

www.soldiersartsacademy.com

www.veteransservicelse.nhs.uk

www.stoll.org.uk

www.poppyfactory.org

www.shakespearesglobe.com

Neil Davies, 1st December 2018.

FALLING SOLDIERS

A NOVEL

NEIL DAVIES

Brigand
London

Chapter 1: Off-Duty

A drunken Eddie Conway hung from the balcony on the seventh floor by his fingertips; he took a deep breath, risked a quick glance down and laughed. The drop was dark and inviting: the urge to just let go percolated through his mind; the last fall to oblivion, the sweet seduction of release. He lowered his left arm and hanging by one hand yanked the tight green cocktail dress back down over his exposed arse, 'Geronimo' he spat, as a surge of adrenalin hit him, instinctively he threw his arm up and snatched a grip back on life. Legs dangling, heart beating furiously, he grimly hung on. Can't do it, he thought, no way I'm topping myself, not in a Mrs Shrek dress! 'Fuck.' The adrenalin rush partly sobered Eddie, a desperate desire to live swept through his body.

Furious with himself, his mind racing, this latest drunken, stunt would finish him. 'You stupid, stupid, fucker,' he whispered, 'am I really topping out?' Eddie barked a short bitter laugh, he could feel gravity pulling at his grip on the rough stone balcony wall. How long until he dropped to his death or worse end up in a hospital bed, fed by tubes. Just like Broomhill, paralyzed for life – parachute failed to deploy, candle job they called it back in the mob. It trailed behind the plummeting Broomhill, like a bridal wedding train, they'd heard his high-pitched scream all the way to impact. Broomhill had survived, a miracle and they'd all dutifully visited him in the hospital but after a couple of visits, Eddie couldn't take the sight of the poor bugger nodding like a dumb animal, which was all his sad body could do, a slow fucking nod of the head and blow into a tube to form letters. Fuck that, decided Eddie I'm not hanging here until I drop. Ha, hangar parties.

He thought back to the first time in the Mrs. Shrek green cocktail dress.

'Hey Sarge, blue boys having a cocktail and beer party in the hangar behind the shooting range, south side of the runway, be fun they got a shot bar an all.'

'You mean they're serving cocktails Gilly?'

'No way Boss, its fancy fucking dress innit, cocktail

dresses, I dunno, some go as Marilyn Monroe, wig an all.' Hangar parties were a regular item on RAF Bases. Pop-up bars in the back of huge aircraft hangars, hosted all night drink fuelled fancy dress parties in the dark cavernous interiors, no-go areas for Military police.

Gilly had got Eddie a Mrs. Shrek green cocktail dress, longer down one side but Eddie had refused the ginger wig, wearing his dessert combat boots he marched with Gilly, Mary Poppins, Beyonce and the rest. The cool night air blowing off the desert whispered up the cocktail dress. Eddie feeling a tingle of excitement, slipped through the side access door into the dark interior of the massive aircraft hanger, now used to store defunct ordinance. They stumbled between boxed crates stacked high in maze like patterns, through the gloom towards the full on party noise at the back. The pop-up bar blinking with pulsing laser lights flashing up into the dark cavernous roof. Around the bar, a mob of cross-dressing Toms, flickered through the strobe lighting yelling with life, stamping to tribal dance rhythms, drum and base, bottles in hand, swigging away the night. The lads, just back from up-country kinetic tours were still fully switched on, combat mission hyper alertness, no time to find the off-switch, just an intense testosterone fuelled, gut instinct, survival celebration off-duty rave.

Eddie felt strangely turned on in the tingling laser blinking darkness, he gulped a huge swig of the cider and cheap whiskey mix from his sports bottle and stamped his feet to the rhythm, going off-duty in a Dante-mad world. In scattered dark corners furtive mind-fragged soldiers engaged, "just helping out a mate", and the cloying fug of sex whispered on shadows, darkness cloaked inhibitions. The more Eddie drank the harder he got, a fat spliff came his way, a big toke, he was loving the fucked up lost feeling, he staggered to the thumping base line. An eternity later, dress clinging with sweat, he careened through the maze of crates trying to find the small side door, a whisper floated from the shadows, 'suckee, suckee.' Eddie peered into a well of darkness through a gap in the stacks, a mag-light switched on illuminating a drunken grinning Marilyn Monroe, wig slightly askew. Eddie mindlessly followed his swollen cock, lurched through the gap, the light went off, a hand grasped at his crutch, Marilyn sank to his knees, the wig fell off.

Eddie shivered, felt the familiar but intoxicating swell of shame rush through him. 'I want to fall,' he pleaded with himself. He'd only put the dress on for a drunken lonely laugh, but a wave of confusion and self-loathing had hit him hard and he thought the solution, was to hang over the balcony, let gravity decide his miserable fate.

Arms burning with the effort of hanging on, his mind snapped back to reality, the alcoholic fug washed away by fear. He fought to control his rising panic and peered through the darkness to the end of the balcony. In the corner, hidden in shadows, not ten feet away, a heavy-duty black drainpipe. Eddie forced himself to get a grip on his racing thoughts. 'OK I can do this . . . . Focus for fuck sake,' he spat the command to himself, concentrating desperately and carefully, ever so slowly he crabbed sideways hand by straining hand, by muscle screaming grip, inch by inch along the balcony wall. Eddie willed his body to obey, grinding his teeth fighting the fear curling in his gut, concentrating on just bloody well making it to safety.

Trembling with the effort, Eddie reached the corner of the building and pushed his right foot against the drainpipe bracket but his knee started knocking uncontrollably with nerves, his foot slipped off. He took a shuddering deep breath, pushed down the panic and screamed to himself, 'come on, by numbers. One, he scraped his knee up the brick wall, 'Two,' wedged his foot against the drainpipe bracket. Paused, breathed in slowly, held his breath and 'One,' took the weight on his right foot; the knocking slowed. He gathered his strength, "Two" and with a last shaking effort pushed down on his foot, straightened his knee and hauled himself up over the balcony wall.

A shattered Eddie slumped against the red brick, heart hammering, gulping air, he stared out over the London housing estate in the quiet dead of night. Involuntarily he started shaking; a violent delayed reaction as the tide of adrenalin receded, washing away the rush. He struggled to assemble his scrambled thoughts, 'Stupid fucking crazy stunt,' he sobbed and searched the night sky for a full moon, half convinced it would be the source of his madness but just a pale Arab crescent mocked him. Eddie feared the coming mental descent into the pit of dark thoughts, recognising the pattern, days on hyper-alert feeling invincible, then the dreaded self-loathing slide down into the bottomless well of depression. Eddie turned on trembling legs, tottered into the kitchen, desperate for any salvation, muttering angrily to the empty flat, 'what the fuck? Totally head-fragged.'

A fugue of angst scampered through his mind, a kaleidoscope of anxiety levels rising fast. 'Get a grip!' he shouted, thoughts in turmoil, spinning. Hands shaking he pulled his stash out from behind the fridge, Afghan black hash wrapped in cling film. Eddie craved the numbness that would blunt his current spiral to the bottom. He focussed his thoughts to a singularity, concentrated on rolling the moist dark lump like putty in his hands, warming it up, softening it; the faint piss-yellow threads of opium running through the liquorice hashish fanned out. Easy to get now some of the army logistics lads were moving it through Brize Norton, he thought; at least some Toms were making something out of the bloody mess of Afghan.

The hash softened, hands trembled with anticipation, he paused breathed in slow, pinching a lump off the hash, he set up his hookah, thinking back to Afghan. The lads had loved these and good shit like this kept a soldier numb-dumb-happy. Going "off-duty" they called it. But not according to the Ruperts.

'Listen in men, there are illegal drugs in the camp . . . .'

Oh yeah, give you a great fucking buzz.

'The penalty for being caught in possession will be severe . . . .'

'Fuck no, they get pissed shitless in the Officers' Mess and then take the Daily Mail stance against dope! Fuck the hell off, stupid Ruperts.' Eddie muttered to himself in anger, pulled in energy from his resentment of the Officer class and lurched down the narrow corridor, carrying a tray laden with his hookah, Zippo, tumbler and a bottle of good single malt whiskey to the living room.

He placed it carefully on the coffee table feeling light headed after his escape from a splatter, but that familiar clarity, that thrilling excitement of life in combat was revving him up.

He put a record on his mum's turntable; turned back to the tray with a trembling hands, crumbled the hash on a bed of loose rosehip, cursing his clumsy fingers as some spilled on the low coffee table. He paused to steady himself, panting in eagerness, took a deep breath, tipped the bottle, whiskey glugged into the tumbler. He lowered the needle, fumbled, tried again, and carefully placed the stylus on the edge of the record, he wished away sanity, downed the whiskey in one, flipped the silver Zippo, lit the shit, blew out his breath, paused and sucked. The bubbles purred, Eddie tasted the tang of mint and rosehip, taking the edge off the musty, sour tasting hash.

He pulled another lungful deep in his belly, the high slammed into his mind, he slumped back and drifted off-duty. The scratching of needle on vinyl, morphed into the lonely intro guitar chords of *Hotel California*, Eagles Live album. His mind drifted back, the Toms belting their version out, drunk and fucked up, high off-duty, up-country Afghan. Eddie rolled off the couch, staggered to his feet and weaved around the small living room, feeling the sensual brush of the deep-shag-pile carpet, like warm sand under bare feet. First thing he'd done when he'd taken over the top floor flat on the Camden estate after his Mum had died, was laid down deep shag pile carpet; like walking on a beach he thought. Eddie danced, shaking his hips in his tight green dirty torn cocktail dress, his lanyard holding his keys and clasp knife swaying on his chest like an Essex necklace. Eddie smiled, anticipating the cotton wool fug of staying high, banishing dread thoughts.

He grabbed the whiskey bottle; deep swigged a full mouthful, rolled it around his tongue and savoured its warm drop into his belly. 'Doo doo, doo doo, da'. Eddie strummed air guitar to the chords and came in right on the opening lines. He staggered off balance; the hash was running base guitar riffs up his spine.

Eyes shut he was back up-country, head out of the turret, whooshing through the night, he sang . . .

"*On a dark Afghan dirt track . . . Stars shine on us all.*"
"*IED's by the roadside, just waiting for the call . . .*"

Scotch John's version.

"And up in the mountains, they wait in the night . . .
My rifle felt heavy, as we rush to the fight . . ."
He was back, dry smell of goat shit and human sweat, the taste
of sand on the breeze, adrenalin surging, he flung his arms out
. . .

"I heard the radio cackle... orders clear as a bell,
'We send them to Heaven – or they send us to Hell..."
Eddie fell back on the sofa, greedily sucking another big
lungful, coughed spluttered, sucked again and hurriedly necked
more whiskey. He jumped up, copped a dizzy rush and almost
fell, staggered, hallucinating, memories fluttering in his head.
The guitar chords morphed into machine gun fire . . . dat de dat,
dat de da da. In the flickering candlelight of his fuddled foggy
mind, Eddie knew he was fucked up and laughed. What the hell,
best place, out of my box, off-duty, running from memories.
"Some smoke to remember, some drink to forget . . ."
More whisky, more minty-sour smokes slithering
snakelike down to his belly. Brooding dark images, glowing
red tracers curving dirty orange arcs through his mind. Here
it comes; that fucking reality; always that nightmare face; the
fucker being tortured; the sheer helplessness of his situation.
Eddie had looked deep into the man's yellow eyes, reflecting
fear. He was not getting out of this alive.
"They blow us to fragments . . . and we think as we fall,
We're going back in boxes for our families last call . . . ."
He had just joined the Regiment. Night patrol, they
caught this guy in the dirty Iraqi scrub wasteland, sitting by
a lonely fire with a Brit Army rifle. He was obviously special
needs, grinning like an idiot saying, "Hello, hello British." Silly
bugger. Cpl Geordie Mathews wasn't letting this one off the
hook. They'd strung him tight like a Christmas turkey, helpless,
but Geordie kept jabbing the knife in and kicking the idiot on to
the fire, then dragging him off again. The screams turned into
hopeless mewling noises. Fuckwit Johnson, the other young'n
just out of training had pissed on the guy, thinking it was funny
putting out the fire on his robes. While that big psycho fucker
Geordie laughed his head off.
Eddie had thought, all right, enough of this shit; let's

take the guy in, but he said nothing. Then Geordie Mathews picked the guy up by his feet and swung him around, the poor fucker screaming, robes smouldering, and smashed him against the tailgate of the Landrover. Snap. Broken neck. Dormouse dead. Silence, a bundle of smouldering robes.

Geordie Mathews laughing, kicking the body, shouting, 'Oh look the little fucker has lost his head. Ha, ha, ha.'

And Eddie had swallowed it, ha bloody ha. Never said what he was thinking, that this was shit, never uttered a word, not a squeak, the shame had haunted him ever since. As a newbie in the Regiment, he'd had a teenage boy crush on Geordie Mathews. A big mature strong looking soldier, handle bar moustache, a role model, a weird sexual fantasy, strong man arms that would hold him safe. But from then on, he avoided Mathews for the rest of his career, couldn't look at the sick bastard.

Another big toke filled his lungs to bursting, he spluttered it all out and desperately glugged more whiskey, wanting to kill his thoughts, freeze frame but tears trickled down his face. The room spun; a dizzy Eddie slumped onto the sofa. He curled up foetal position but slid slowly off on to his deep-shag-pile-carpet beach, head spinning, mind totally fragged, dress hitched up over his arse. No more thoughts coming in on the tide, no nightmares; but still, the tortured burnt hair; big-toothed silly fucker's grin, staring down at him with dead yellow eyes. 'Leave me alone, bloody leave me out of it,' sobbed Eddie.

"You can join Civvy Street...when they send you home
But nightmares, never leave you alone!"
...Oblivion.

Chapter 2: Dog Town

Rain riffed at acute angles along the open fifth-floor walkway on the old red brick council block. Three teenagers in hi-Viz jackets idly stared out over the housing estate, the latest in an assembly line of young gangs growing up in the inner city. They shared a joint, cupped in their hands against the wind and holding two ugly, squat, cross-breed fighting dogs on tight leashes attached to thick studded collars. The sweat-sour smell of skunk lingered in the damp air. Eddie stepped up out of the stairwell. Three synchronised heads lazily looked him over, noting the big well-balanced man, walking easy towards them. The dogs crabbed sideways blocking the walkway.

Eddie was too big to trouble, red-eyed, moody, hung-over. 'So, you guys protecting the neighbourhood?' he grunted.

The shortest of the three, a squat block of Croatian muscle, laughed. 'Yeah, we looking out for our peoples in the hood innit.' His eyes lit up with amusement.

'That so Valdrin, you left school and work for the council now?' replied Eddie; he shifted his inspection to the lanky Ethiopian kid on the right; a limp wet Afro drooped out the left side of his woolly hat framing a straight nose, large eyes and long eyelashes. The kid nervously looked down at his dog pulling the lead for reassurance, then, taking the joint from Valdrin in a display of nonchalance he sucked a big toke and mumbled.

'We're independent, know what I'm saying?'

Eddie smiled lazily, 'you're cute,' and winked at him, the kid blushed and inspected his trainers. Eddie slowly looked the others over, 'Yeah I feel safer knowing the UN is patrolling the estate.' Valdrin, the obvious leader, took the joint from the Ethiopian and offered Eddie.

'It's good stuff. I guarantee quality, my friend,' he smiled, a young kid with old eyes staring into Eddie's soul.

Eddie's smile had worn off, he gazed at the joint cautiously, felt the urge buzzing in his chest but waved his hand in refusal, 'Tell you what Valdrin, you put some weed in a bottle of rum and bring it me in six months and I'll swig bush medicine when I catch a cold.'

'My Granddad does that', announced the quiet one, a mix of all the races who end up on sinkhole estates, lightning bolt patterns shaved in his hair. He piped up again with more confidence this time, 'Yeah bro, he say smoking is gangsta bad but bush rum is medicinal, innit.' Eddie smiled to his self, the kid's father was from the Congo, a porter at Royal Free Hospital, and didn't speak like that; these kids were inventing their own integration narrative.

Valdrin sucked the last dregs and flicked the roach over the parapet. They all leaned over watching its twisting fluttering flight, the joint briefly sparking up again as it smoked down landing in the rusting children's play area. Eddie shivered; a vision of his body hurtling down in a green cocktail dress flared in his mind, stupid place to die, children's play area, everybody would think I was a pervert.

'So what brings you over this block, Eddie?'

Eddie snapped his gaze back to reality and focussed on Valdrin. 'Uh? Oh Tenants committee business; Ashok asked me to have a word with this Djokovic geezer.' Eddie made to walk by, the boys tugged the leads and the dogs waddled like steroid junky weight lifters out of his way, the Ethiopian kid's dog giving him a look that implied – so that's it I don't get to bite him and snarled in disappointment.

At the end of the walkway, Eddie turned back. 'Oi, where you get the Hi-Viz?'

'I got a job, Sports Direct, you know how it goes,' replied Valdrin.

'Sort me one out, OK?'

Valdrin smiled eagerly, 'Deliveroo soon, yeah.'

Eddie flipped a salute, turned and studied the door, its reinforced metal and spy hole screamed paranoia at him. He banged hard with the heel of his fist. The three stooges pretended to be too bored to watch but three pairs of eyes swivelled to the edges of their sockets.

No answer. Eddie, conscious that he was being watched, banged again losing his frayed red-eye temper.

'Open the fucking door Djokovic.'

Silence stretched. Eddie swore, still fragged out from last night, and started booting the door in anger, he knew he was losing it but what the fuck.

'Whoa whoa - who there?' a muffled voice behind the door, an eye flickered in the spy hole.

'It's Eddie fucking Conway . . . .' Silence stretched. Eddie booted the door again. 'I'm still here.'

Muffled shouts from inside, the rattle of chains and sliding of bolts, the door cracked open. A heavy slab face, bulging eyes, dishevelled hair above a thick neck, peered over the door chain; eyes flicked across at the three stooges.

'What you want?'

'Complaints - your Merc parked in the children's' play area.'

'Who the fuck, you not council, there no yellow lines down there. In this country, it's yellow lines no park.'

'Listen you, fucking Djokovic, or is it joke-vic? You are stopping kids from playing. So stick the Merc in bay twenty-one in the designated car park area, only cost you a fiver a week.'

'What you fucker! You don't live here.'

'Huh! I grew up here. Now I'm back!'

'You got no right, you fuck, you get plenty hurt!'

Eddie lost it, his voice quivered with boiling anger, 'I'll burn your fucking car if it's there tomorrow. You fucking hear me? That plain enough for you?'

'What you fucker, you make threat?'

'It's a fucking promise Joke-vic - move the Merc. Go pay Ashok at the office in the old air-raid shelter or woof!' Eddie threw his hands in the air, adrenaline coursing through him, lighting him up, making him tick. He smiled, cold no warmth, dialled down and in his best polite voice said, 'And let's say you owe £260, a year backdated parking rent to the tenants committee.' Eddie grinned maniacally at the face.

Djokovic slammed the door, muffled sounds of shouting. Eddie turned and walked by the gang of three. The dogs waddled around staring up at him, he paused smiling, feeling rejuvenated by the flare up.

'You think he's gonna make the right choice? Parking or burning?'

'Not much of a choice, innit Eddie?'

'S'right Valdrin, I forgot to offer him incentives like a fucking good drumming.' Eddie headed for the stairwell.

Valdrin called after him. 'He's in the bad guy business Eddie, got a crew init.'

'I been to bad guy country and back again.' Eddie nodded to Valdrin, 'but thanks for the warning.'

Valdrin nodded back and the other two joined in, enthusiastic nodding.

That meant something Eddie thought, have I won hearts and minds? Impressed the locals? He swaggered down the stairwell.

The three stooges nodded sagely. The Ethiopian kid cupped his hands, lit another joint. 'Well, he back now innit!'

Chapter 3: Down Town

If you looked hard you could see thin rain swirling above the neon-wet-night streets of Chalk Farm Road, the wet tarmac reflecting dark shimmering pools of red, yellow and blue from shop windows and traffic. Eddie stared at the pixelated scene, an impressionist painting with cars swishing through but no buses; a red bus would look good in this picture he cursed to himself. Eddie pulled his collar up, his hair was drenched, raindrops slid off his nose as he counted each breath slowly pulling the angry tide in. Fucking late bus. He felt his mind spinning off into blind anger and concentrated on the cognitive therapy exercises they drummed into him at the London Veterans' Clinic. In through the nose, out through the mouth, picture happy place, mountains, blue sky and leafy green trees; fuck it, let's 'ave a snow blizzard. What the fuck am I going doolally about the bus for?

The number 24 bus finally lurched to the stop by the Monarch Pub. A bad-tempered waiting crowd had gathered, mostly women waiting for the late bus; they swirled around forming a rough queue while the bus doors opened to a tired moan of compressed air. A big lump, shaved head, denim jacket, swore at the crowd pushing to the front barging people aside.

Eddie shouted, 'Fuck no!' grabbed shaved head by his denim collar and hauled him back. 'You, you fucker, back of the queue or I'll drum you.' Eddie tugged sharply and shaved head fell skidding on his back on the wet street, people parting around him, no sympathy expressed.

Eddie stared down at him, pumped up; just one excuse and he would drum him proper, a right military tatoo. The thrill of imminent violence flared deep in his soul, shaved head looked up at Eddie seeing madness dancing in those eyes and instinctively decided not to move. He stayed down like a subservient dog, throat bared. Eddie struggled to dial down the rush, he got a flashback of the tortured idiot, guilt flickered, he leaned over and gave shaved head a thin you-lucky-fucker smile. Eddie turned, hopped on the bus, went upstairs and took the front seat, cinemascope view. The other passengers carefully filed to seats well away from him. He sat, feeling his heartbeat still racing as he tried to get a grip on his churning thoughts. The anger from his school days flooded in; times he had fought for the front seat on the school bus to satisfy a desperate need to have that view all to himself. No fucker's pushing in front of me! Thought Eddie and looked down at the street as shaved head got up, turned in circles confused angry and scared.

'Silly cunt,' Eddie mouthed at him. Shaved head looked away and barged into the Monarch Pub. 'Yeah, get a drink and review your life,' whispered Eddie.

The bus wound its hiccupping stop-start route from Camden, down passed Euston station, muscling its way through cloying traffic towards London's West End. Eddie idly gazed down from his top deck command post at wandering tourists, lost in the wet, buying umbrellas, probably thinking they should have booked Greece, mused Eddie. The bus got held up in the Gower Street one-way system, vans blocking the bus lane, Eddie swore at them, willing the bus driver to ram the bastards, his knuckles hurt. He was gripping the seat like a hunting hawk on a leather glove, waiting to be launched at the prey. Eddie sighed ruefully and chuckled. Jesus, what the hell, stand at ease you silly fucker, he thought.

He hopped off at Foyle's bookshop on Charing Cross Road and cut through the alley by the Crown pub into Greek Street, Soho. Doorway fag-hounds loitered the pavement, staring into space, blowing smoke.

Scotch John blocked the door to 'Midnight Oasis' as only a bouncer can.

'Evening Sarge.'

'And yourself Scotch, lovely night for a stint on security duty?'

Scotch paused in thought wondering whether to laugh or not. His bushy eyebrows danced a few beats over a broken nose set in a rhubarb crumble face. 'Aye, strong as a bull so I am.' Scotch flexed a bicep.

Eddie gave a raised eyebrow-questioning look in reply but couldn't match the Scotch tango.

The smile plastered across Scotch John's face slowly

crumpled as he pleaded with Eddie, 'ah, I'm gonna fall off the wagon occasionally, I only missed the one night on the door, so I did Sarge.'

'You were fucking AWOL! It cost me,' Eddie barked, 'I had to get Jimmy Rumpunch to cover door duty for you!'

'Rumpunch is the lad so he is, eh Eddie?'

'Look Scotch, stay on the ball, door security at this club is a sweet posting, so you fucking report for duty. And don't call me Sarge, OK?'

Scotch eyebrows waltzed. 'Ach man, spent so long calling you Sarge can't drop the habit, so I can't.'

'Oh, habit eh but you can bin the duty roster. Scotch if I had you back in the Mob where would you be now?'

'Standing to attention on report facing charges Sarge.' Scotch tried a winsome smile but Eddie was in full flow.

'Fucking right, failure to report for sentry duty, its like not turning up for check point duty Scotch, serious charges in the Mob, so get a bloody grip.' Eddie glared at Scotch aware the anger was coming through. Hell he thought, Scotch was the friendly Lance- Jack who'd put a protective arm around him when he first joined the Regiment, he'd been a good soldier back then but a corporal was the highest he would ever rise to. Now, he was kipping at Stoll barracks in Fulham, a charity run place for homeless soldiers who had fallen through the gaps in societies safety net. Eddie dialled down his anger, remembering his first days in the Regiment.

'So Roger that Scotch.' Eddie still stared full on but the hard glint faded from his eyes.

Scotch twitched, lowered his eyes and shuffled in the door and nodded agreement.

'Good,' said Eddie, in a friendlier tone, 'Is Jabba in?'

'Top bar holding court.' Scotch paused, came to attention, snapped a salute and in a slow smug voice said, 'Eddie!'

Eddie snorted, shook his head and gave Scotch full marks for the come back, he flicked a salute at Scotch who stood aside. Eddie muscled in through the entrance door into Moonlight Oasis. He pushed passed the skinny-jeans-happy-hour-cocktail crowd, yaa-yaa-ing shots down their necks, climbed the round

15

stairway, opposite a pink neon-lit bar, to the upper floor where Jabba-the-Club fully inhabited his chair, in the raised section, up back by the small bar.

'Eddie, Eddie have a shot with me,' cried Jabba, half raising his immense bulk, waving at the bar. A couple of his hanger-on-shot-necking buddies were seated around him. Jabba ponderously lowered back down and with a grunt shooed the groupies away.

Eddie took a seat. 'Yeah. After you pay me. Last time I got stoned and went home with an empty pocket.'

'Ah, Eddie we have a good time eh? Boys night out like your Marines!'

'Uh? No, I told you Jabba, red beret is Paras.'

'Scotch missed a night!' complained Jabba

'I sorted it didn't I!'

'Yes and I like . . . how you say, Rumpunch, he keep things mellow.'

'You can't have Rumpunch, he's expensive cavalry.'

'Pity,' Jabba grunted and pulled a wad out of his bulging cargo-pants side pocket, where he kept the Club's spare cash. He peeled off a bunch of fifties, snapping each note with his chubby, gold-ringed fingers.

Eddie separated the notes into different pockets, an army thing, each pocket a function. He patted his breast pocket that was designated for Scotch's cash payment; it felt light, this week.

A tray of Jägermeister shots carried by a thin blonde with unnaturally large tits halted at the table. Jabba patted her bum. 'Good girl Adyta.' His hand stayed on her bum. She gently, purposely slid away. Jabba raised his drink with a grin and knocked it back, wiped his mouth and nodded to Eddie and his shot.

'Guy wants you to meet him, Eddie.'

Eddie rolled his eyes in surrender, necked the Jager and grimaced. 'Shit. Tastes like cough medicine. Jesus, you sick Jabba?'

'Never had a cold in my life, Eddie,' wheezed Jabba.

'What guy Jabba?'

'Well-heeled guy, had a P.A. with him.'

'OK, a very solvent guy.'

'So, bit of business for you eh. I told him you'll give him a ring.' Jabba pushed a gold-embossed card across the table. 'I promised him, Eddie.'

Eddie looked down at the card. 'Arabs sure love gold Jabba.'

Chapter 4: Keep On Running

Eddie liked rain on Hampstead Heath; it kept the "Ruperts" indoors. In good weather, they strolled the woods wearing outdoor Himalaya green Barbour expedition gear, clutching take-away lidded coffee. He always ran the back trails to avoid them. The endorphins were just kicking in when a dog bowled out of the bushes, got tangled up between his legs, he tripped, did a tap dance, regained his balance and sharp eyed the dog barking at him like it was his fault.

'Don't worry, he won't bite you,' shouted a Barbour jacket twenty yards away.

'Oh, but I bite lady,' growled Eddie

'Here Dolphus, here boy, come to mummy,' she pleaded.

Eddie pushed on a few yards, the dog barking and leaping alongside him, the woman shouting, worried now, 'Dolphus . . . Dolphus . . .'

Eddie mumbling, 'Fuck off dog...' Then he stopped suddenly and glared at the dog. Dog stared back.

The owner nervously called. 'Oh Dolphus come here, come, come on.'

Eddie couldn't believe the bloody dog was wearing a blue and white polka dot bandana round its neck. He waited for the dog to make its move, felt the anger bubbling up, wanting to hurt it. The dog broke eye contact and paced a figure of eight before him. Eddie thought, smart dog. The owner stayed where she was, obviously very nervous of Eddie. He turned towards the woman wanting to curse her but could see her fear, he recognised the up-country look, villagers staring at the troops wondering if they were going to be hurt, he thought, what-the-fuck, doolally frag- head again, and jogged on.

Dog lolloped beside him, the owner's pleadings for Dolphus to come back fading out behind them. Eddie ran a trail through the woods, up hill towards Spaniard's Inn. After five minutes Dolphus the dog was still with him.

Eddie paused at a water fountain and slurped water; the dog lapped at pooled water by his feet. Eddie wiped his lips and looked at Dolphus. The dog wagged its tail waiting for the next move. He bent down removed the bandana and hung it from a low branch.

'Dolphus, you look like a dog now - fuck off and enjoy yourself, OK?' Eddie ran on. The dog stayed and watched him as he disappeared up the trail.

Eddie settled back into the rhythm of the run, letting ever more endorphins flow, he tried to build a mental picture from the scattered jigsaw pieces of his life, searching through faded dreams and broken aspirations for some purpose. This current existence could not be his totality, he thought, his whole army life had ticked along, working out mission parameters, deployment of men, preparing for action and then the sweet heady rush of combat. But now, he was empty of purpose, life cast adrift. He growled in frustration and sprinted the last two hundred metres up the steep path to the top of Parliament Hill, burning regrets from his mind and sank onto one of the dark wet wooden park benches. Head between his hands, panting furiously, he read the inscription, donated in memory of some "Friend-of-the-Heath," etched onto the back of the bench, he worked out the guy had lived eighty-three years. Fuck last night he thought, I'll not even make fifty-three, no way. Feel sick. The sweat and rain coursed down his face and trickled down his back. The six-mile run over Hampstead Heath had been hard and muddy; but the combat wound hardly bothered him these days, as long as he kept fit. His feet were soaking but the effort had damped the anger down like smouldering coals, he started to feel better.

Looking up, he stared out across the London skyline, the old docklands covered in huge construction cranes, giant reptiles rearing up in the sky, building new financial nests for the City. He felt chilled out, calm, happy even and pulled his phone out his tracksuit pocket, plugged earphones in and dialled the number from the embossed gold card. Beep, beep. Eddie's mind drifted. He heard sounds from a far away country, a different world, harsh echoes of life and death. The smells came back.

'Good day, Mithras Investments, April Bentley-Forbes here, how may I help you this morning?'

Eddie shook off melancholy; the throaty gargle of a posh

female voice snapped him back.

'You what?'

'I'm April and you rang us.'

'A lovely wet morning it is, April showers.' Eddie smiled wondering where his banter had come from.

'Sorry . . . Oh yes,' sounding bored now, 'is that supposed to be funny?'

'I was thinking poetically on top of a hill, gazing at far horizons.'

'Yes indeed Mr err . . . '

'Conway and the Bossman wanted to talk to me.'

'Oh, and what matter is it concerning Mr Conway?'

'No idea April, the sun has just broke through and a rainbow has appeared over the city cranes. You think that means more pots of gold in the city? You ask him eh?'

'Ah, yes one minute. Please hold.'

Eddie put the phone on his lap, taking in the rainbow.

'Mr Conway, Hello Mr Conway'. A thin well-educated tinny voice squeaked from his lap.

Eddie jerked back and lifted the phone. 'Sure, I'm here.'

'Ah Mr Conway, I'm reliably informed you may be the right man for a certain type of service, so to speak.'

The guy sounded like an oil-rich Sandhurst Arab. 'Reliable eh? Sounds like something with a bit of difficulty and decorum attached.'

'Ah, well put, precisely Mr Conway. Could I hand you back to my PA?'

April came back on. 'Mr Conway, would it be convenient for you to meet at 8 pm tonight?'

'Meet you April,' he whispered, smiling now, feeling some control over his life.

'Are you on medication Mr Conway? No, meet Sir Omar al-Khayyami Agassi at his club.'

'OK, his club eh. Where?' April recited a very swanky area address. Eddie replied, 'sure April over the rainbow bridge into Asgard, home-of-the-gods.'

'Ha, yes, well ask for me at reception and they'll bring you to us Mr Conway.'

'Will do, Roger that.' He clicked off. Screw my old boots, mused Eddie, anyone for cricket. He stood up and jogged easy down Parliament Hill towards rainbow city.

Chapter 5: City Folk

Eddie took the Northern Line tube from Chalk Farm to Euston and cut through the narrow tiled tunnel to the Victoria Line. He exited at Green Park, counting the steps as he jogged up to the surface. The drizzle was making a comeback. He pulled his collar up and walked towards Piccadilly, past shops dripping in luxury, cut a left into the solid posh but sleazy Mayfair, through Burlington Square a short hop and he was standing in front of the "Alexandrian Private Members Club." Big solid doors protected the paranoid rich and influential from any pleb incursion.

A sallow-faced man looked up from the front desk, immediate concern writ large across his well-manicured face.

'Yes sir, might I help you?' Which Eddie took by its tone to mean, 'What the fuck d'you think you're doing here?'

Eddie reacted against the opulence decided to play it swagger mode, he flipped the gold card on to the front desk.

'Just tell April Mr Conway is here will you and don't get your knickers in a twist mate.'

The mannequin sniffed and adjusted his cufflinks in a gesture of defiance, flipped a page of the heavy leather bound appointments book, ran his finger down the guest list and looked up at Eddie, thinking, you're just hired help and beckoned a well-built suited and booted lump. Mannequin flicked his fingers at the heavy doors, the lump led, Eddie followed through two opulent open rooms of rich deep purple carpet. He felt the old anger as he resisted a strange urge to walk on tip-toes, passed the scattering of old suits in old brown leather armchairs gathered around log fires. Newspapers dipped as bored grey-haired heads peered over the top at him. Jesus, thought Eddie its like a first class waiting room for the graveyard. The lump ushered him up a set of curved stairs to double doors. Eddie felt the old deep-seated resentment of Officers' Mess bubble inside him. The air was thick with money, privilege and self-entitlement.

The high double mahogany doors opened and the silent lump ushered Eddie in. By now Eddie had decided to bin the job out of sheer resentment. Then April Bentley-Forbes sashayed forward in a languid hi-heel-slow-mo-saunter, a merlot wine red polished fingernail hand floated out to greet him. She was tall, shapely, deep chest with horse riders' thighs', a hard fit body with a handshake that could take the reins of a stampeding horse. Not what Eddie was expecting, he swallowed a wise crack. April kept hold of his hand, tightened her grip and pulled him close. Eddie thought she would throw a saddle on him next but she inhaled deeply, looked him in the eyes and twitched him a good day for a gallop smile. Eddie felt the pull of the bit in his mouth and swallowed.

'Mr Conway I presume.' Easy upper-class tones, still holding his hand she led him like a horse to auction, deeper into the room, past ornate chintzy screens. 'Good of you to come, Mr Conway,' April released his hand and ushered him to the far corner.

Eddie made a late recovery from April's spell and quipped, 'that so Showers. You just galloped up here from Home Counties?'

'Oh, how do you know I ride?'

Eddie paused, gesturing behind him at the room's expanse, 'Looks to me, like most people in here would ride a bit.'

April dipped her shoulder and carried on to the far corner, 'You have a certain oblique way of speaking Mr Conway.'

Eddie hurried after her, 'Call me Eddie,' he offered. April chuckled as if she had won the first round.

Ornate dresser screens in different colonial motifs divided the room. They rounded one, showing a turbaned man and boy with muskets hunting mountain lions, into a large space with yet another smouldering log fire. Didn't we have a clean air act in this town? Mused Eddie? Sitting in a wingback chair by several leather seats circling a low table, a man around fifty years old, grey at the temple, impeccably suited and booted.

Showers introduced him. 'Mr Conway please meet Sir Omar al-Khayyami Agassi.'

Eddie thought smoothy Omar Sharif. Sir Omar stood up, took Eddie's hand in both his but again held on too long, what was it with these people. He indicated the chair opposite.

'Please be seated Mr Eddie Conway.' He waved a finger in the air and a flunky hurried forward. 'Would you like a whisky perhaps?' Eddie thought yeah, Jabba's favourite trick, stick em with shots and wipe the floor with em.

'No thanks, last night I, *"drowned my Honour in a shallow cup, and sold my reputation for a Song."* Eddie spoke slowly, knowing Rupert's hated plebs quoting poems. 'So a glass of water is fine.'

Sir Omar shifted in his big leather chair, a slight cough and adjusted the crease on his trousers. 'Goodness, quoting Shakespeare! Ah, I do so like polite English chit-chat.'

Eddie rolled his eyes. 'Where I come from we cut out the chit. So what's the deal?'

'Yes of course. So. Ah straight to the point then. I have a proposition. It's ah, how shall we say, personal and how did you put it? Calls for some decorum Mr Conway.'

'And you think I can help? Must be down dirty work amongst the proles.'

Sir Omar curled his top lip and took one of the glasses next to an ornate decanter on a silver tray, that Eddie hadn't even noticed arriving and sipped his whisky. OK, that's a touch of class admitted Eddie.

'Yes. Well put. You see I have a young daughter, unexpected really, a liaison that bore fruit but none the less, my daughter is very precious to me, do you see?'

'Yes, I can see fine.' Eddie replied curtly.

April Showers moved into Eddie's eye line, carrying a folder suppressing a smile.

'My daughter Rainya, Mr Conway, is a student here in London but we had, ah how shall I say . . . a disagreement about the company she was keeping and now she has been out of touch for some days.'

Eddie felt himself becoming impatient with the long-winded delivery. 'So she's missing. You call Plod?'

'Plod?' Sir Omar asked, confused.

April leant in, explaining. 'It's a local colloquial term for the constabulary sir.'

'Ah. Oh no, that would be embarrassing, repercussions

25

back home don't you know and I hate all publicity, of any sort. No, I think she has debunked with some of her, how shall we say, radical save-the-world friends, you know Green Peace types and . . .'

Eddie cut in, 'Yeah, the green ones. So why not contact them?'

'Well yes Mr Conway, an excellent question. You have been recommended. Let's see now.' He beckoned to April who bent over the low table, raising an eyebrow at Eddie and handed the file to Sir Omar, who nodded his thanks and opened the file.

'Sgt Conway retired from the Regiment with multiple wounds on a disability pension. Service record shows excellent work, even a stint with UN in difficult situations. Now medically recovered fit and able, making a living supplying various security personnel and skills to London night-clubs.' Sir Omar looked up, smiled politely. 'Just what I need, ah how shall we say, someone flying under the radar.'

Eddie's eyebrow rose without any effort, Scotch John style. OK, now I'm starting to really dislike you Sir school-tie-fucking-repercussions-back-home-Omar, with an elaborate need for status and a bloody file-on-me for Christ's sake.

'Not sure I want to be under the radar Mr Agassi. I like flying above it. Less chance of crashing.'

Sir Omar showed just a hint of displeasure at the Mr, but Eddie smiled in that openly innocent way the ranks used to insult army officers, and get away with it.

April stepped forward opening her notebook. 'May I Sir?' Sir Omar mollified by the curtsey held out the palm of his right hand in answer.

April dipped her head slightly. 'Thank you, Sir.' Eddie thought this girl is riding her Boss and he doesn't even know she's saddled him. April smiled, arched an eyebrow at Eddie as if reading his thoughts and said. 'Well, Mr Conway, the rate for under the radar work is one thousand pounds a day plus expenses.'

Eddie taken by surprise whistled the opening bars to the Dambusters.

Sir Omar nodded, pursed his lips, feeling the mention

of money had restored his equilibrium and status. 'Yes, you will report to Mrs Bentley-Forbes, there may very well be a substantial bonus for you. I want to know where my daughter is, that she is safe, so I may unobtrusively keep an eye on her while she plays out her romantic ideals. Ah yes, youth, dreams and romance, not to be stepped on and crushed. The English way don't you think Mr Conway?'

'Yes, I think,' answered Eddie looking at April, who arched one delicately plucked eyebrow.

'Excellent.' Sir Omar turned his head slightly to take in both April and Eddie, wondering if he was missing something. 'Ah yes well, most importantly it is very crucial that my daughter does not know I'm checking on her.' He looked at the ceiling and steepled his fingers, Eddie and April waited patiently, knowing there was more to come.

Sir Omar lowered his hands as if he had deeply contemplated the issue. 'Rainya may resent my parental concern and do something foolish, as young people often do.' He wafted a hand towards April, 'Mrs Bentley-Forbes will provide you with all the details Mr Conway. I'm sure you will do a sterling good job.'

Eddie wondered about the Mrs, and imagined the usual Rupert's formality of married relationships.

Sir Omar stood slowly, aiming for dignity and proffered a well-manicured hand enclosed in a crisp white gold-cuffed shirt for Eddie to shake. Eddie rose thinking what's the worst can happen? A grand a day and I get to talk to Showers not Mr gold-monogrammed-cuff-linked Sir Omar. Roll on. Eddie gripped the limp hand and squeezed, Sir Omar suppressed a wince.

April led Eddie out of the plush suffocating rooms to an office. She opened a drawer of an old oak desk and pulled out a vanilla folder tied in green ribbon. 'Photos of Rainya Agassi, a list of known friends and known places she frequented. Find her, ascertain her health and report back.'

Eddie untied the green ribbon, pulled the photos out of the folder and thumbed through them. 'Good looking girl, must take after her mother.' April rolled her eyes. Eddie suppressed another quip and continued, 'any boyfriends she could be staying with?'

'Not the sort of information I have at present, Mr Conway, and, she certainly wouldn't tell her father. He might not look it but he is a fairly conservative Eastern gentleman.'

'Yeah sure, aren't they all, and you? Fairly conservative as well are you Showers?'

'That wasn't Shakespeare you quoted was it. I'm fairly sure it was Omar Khayyam. Learn that in the middle-east Mr Conway?'

'Sergeants' Mess quiz night Showers. Thought Mr Agassi might appreciate it.'

April gave him the "naughty horse" look. 'He's a businessman, not a poet. Goodness what sort of questions do they ask at the Sergeants' Mess Mr Conway'

'Ones Rupert's can't answer.'

'How intriguing a night in the Sergeants Mess must be Mr Conway.'

'Ever had a night out at a Sergeants Mess then, Showers?'

'No, but I have heard the boisterous noise of fun when walking past to the Officers Mess Mr Conway.'

Eddie chuckled, nice try Showers he thought. 'Call me Eddie.'

'When you stop calling me Showers.'

'That'll be in May then.'

Chapter 6: Rumpunch

The phone answered, 'Yeah.'

    'Rumpunch?'

    'Yo, Eddie.'

    'Need an hour of your time.'

    'What you got Eds? Quick dusting job?'

    'No. Just OP work.'

    'You want me to be witness

    'That's all Rum.'

    'Hostiles?'

    'Maybe a couple – low-grade lumps'

    'OK Ed's but if it turns into a dusting . . . that's extra you know that, right? Don't be getting me up on a cheapo and then. "Oh fuck sorry Rumpunch it looks like it's a dustup." Cos' much as I like you, I'm not no cheap deal . . . Comprende?'

    'Come-the-fuck-what?

    'Yeah, been on holiday Eddie, Costa del Crim.'

    'OK enough on your time-share. My yard two pm.'

    'Yo. I'll swing by.'

    'Swing low. Cheers Rum'

Chapter 7: Burn Up

Eddie wore his brand new Hi-Vis jacket; he looked at the arms admiring the glow, then put his rucksack down near Djokovic's Merc, undid the drawstring, pulled out a plastic container, a megaphone and a towel. Held the megaphone in his right hand, tapped it with his left. Megaphone squawked.

He placed the plastic container on the roof of the brand new midnight blue Mercedes-Benz saloon. The towel he placed on top of the rucksack.

Eddie waited. It was five-to-two, a wine-red 4x4 vehicle glided onto the estate. A large black guy stepped out, expensive suit, silk tie, brown brogues, top pocket wine red handkerchief matching the 4x4. He leant back against the 4x4, nodded at Eddie and folded his arms.

Eddie squawked the megaphone, three blasts echoed around the estate, bouncing off the red brick blocks, circling the children's dilapidated play area. People shuffled out onto balconies and walkways. The three stooges and their dogs appeared at the far corner. They stood off.

Eddie raised the megaphone. 'Mr Joker-vic. Calling the Joker-vic. Your times up.'

On the fifth floor a flurry of movement. Two lumps came out followed by Djokovic.

'This very nice brand new Merc is parked in the children's play area, on the roof is a plastic container of petrol. I'm going to take the top off and pour it over your expensive car and then set light to it.'

The black guy by the 4x4 refolded his arms with a smile.

On the fifth floor, there was shouting. Two lumps scurried to the lift. Eddie twisted the top from the plastic container.

From the fifth floor, Djokovic shouted, 'Fucker,' and marched along the walkway, wiping his forehead with a handkerchief. The two lumps appeared on the ground floor, shoulders swinging, muscling towards Eddie, he placed the megaphone on the roof of the Merc. When the lumps got within striking distance Eddie leapt into a crouching Kung Fu fighting stance. The lumps put up their guard, bent their knees and crabbed forward. Eddie stood upright with a smile on his face and laughed. The lumps paused; confused, the first one began to straighten up. Eddie kicked him an inch below the extended kneecap right on the soft patella. Crack, the knee gave way, lump one unbalanced, crying in pain, keeled over, slo-mo fashion.

Lump two looked at Eddie as if he had cheated. Eddie walked right up to him, smiling, hands out, palms up, a conciliatory gesture. Lump two uttered threats, 'you fucker you going to get f . . .' Eddie slapped him hard across his Adam's apple. Lump two gargled, 'f . . . aaaahhhgggg . . . ' bent over with his hands around his throat. Eddie took one step forward and elbowed him, side of the head, bang on the temple. Lump two took up the same position as his compadre, on the deck, in pain.

Eddie strolled back to the Merc and held the container over the bonnet of the car. In the other hand, he held his Zippo lighter.

Djokovic scuttled out the ground floor entrance and came to a dead stop. The picture didn't look right. His guys were maimed and the Fucker was still standing.

'What you do? You crazy? You don't know who I am, you fuck.'

'I know where you live, I know your business and I know I explained yesterday, face to face very nicely I thought, at your door.'

Djokovic looked around, people on the balconies, this was a big loss of face moment. He pulled himself together, a big man beginning to run to fat, used to getting his way by intimidation. He switched to the confident big man, let's work this out approach.

'Look, my friend, we have miss-understanding here. Come up my place, I give you drink we settle this like two big men eh?'

The black guy leaning against the 4x4 laughed out loud. Djokovic looked at him.

'Who he?'

'Oh, he's like a UN observer.'

'You fucker, think this game huh?'

'The rules. I burn your car, or you go to the old air-raid shelter pay the two hundred and sixty pounds plus one pound twenty for petrol and five pounds for the container, cash, to Ashok. Now.'

'This you do for two hundred and sixty pounds for play area that children no play in.'

'It's two hundred and sixty-six pounds and twenty pence now.' Eddie flicked his Zippo open and twirled the cog, the Zippo lit up. 'OK, one Merc, retail price what forty K on the road, worth zilch when burnt out. Your choice?'

Djokovic felt like his world had turned, he'd been on the estate two years, just a bunch of offal lived here, frightened people, immigrants who wouldn't look at you twice. Now this crazy fucker! Djokovic was screaming in his head, this fucker will die for this. He looked up at the audience of this theatre of the absurd. 'OK, OK. Hey.' He forced a chuckle. 'I got that much in my pocket, it small change, it fucking nothing. OK. I give to community eh.' He shouted up at the audience hoping to save face.

'Good we got plans for the play area.' Eddie packed his megaphone away and wiped his hands on the towel, he nodded at the container and spoke pleasantly to Djokovic, 'that's yours, you paying for it right?' And walked over to the smart Black guy leaning on the 4x4, who nodded appreciatively at him.

'I'd say lot of social damage has been done to that man today Eddie, here certifications for your boys.' Rum handed over a manila envelope.

'Cheers.' Eddie took the envelope and waved it at the estate. 'You think they got the message Rumpunch?'

'Oh, they got the message but what's your end game Eddie?'

Eddie looked around. Even the three fucking stooges were laughing. 'I don't like the way the old place smells, like Basra in the early days.'

'And is this what your mob did in Basra?'

'No, we didn't and it was a fucking big mistake!'

Chapter 8: Street Life

Red, yellow and orange colours swam before Lofty's eyes, he squinted trying to focus, to make sense of the swirling patterns. He was mind fragged, thoughts dripped like cold treacle onto thin porridge.

He started drifting away, Maria? Wasn't he supposed to be at Maria's? He clutched at a memory - moving in with Maria and her three kids but when did that happen? He felt a numbing cold seeping through his body and something tugging at his hand. He couldn't get a grip on his thoughts, they were spiralling down a dark well, he closed his eyes, drifting away again.

Later, the low hum of nagging thoughts pricked him back into consciousness, he forced his eyes open, slowly the colours came into focus. He wasn't at Maria's. He was sprawled in a city centre doorway, late at night. He was cold, there was a dog on the other end of the string wrapped round his wrist. The dog shuffled up and began licking his hands.

Where the fuck did I get a dog from? Thought Lofty. He tried to stand, discovered his prosthetic leg was missing, swore at himself and fell back onto the cardboard boxes in the shop doorway. He screwed his eyes shut fighting the pain, panting for breath, the pain receded but the dog was still there and he dimly became aware of lying in a doorway on a ripped smelly sleeping bag, amongst squashed cardboard boxes and newspapers. He felt around him searching for his leg, 'fuck,' he swore, 'lost me bloody leg.' Slumped back and drifted away again, the usual dream of running in swirling oily waters claimed him.

He felt a warm gush of liquid and heard laughter, forced his eyes open again and looked up. There were faces above him, backlit by streetlights, creating fuzzy yellow halos around their heads. Lofty stared in confused wonder, was he dreaming and slowly realized somebody was pissing on him. Three laughing faces stared down at him, one pissing on him, one filming on a mobile phone and the third bent over with laughter. Lofty screamed in futile rage, the dog whimpered and sidled behind him. The drunken young men hooted with laughter and careered off down the street. Lofty stared after them, the rage hurting him, he shut his eyes, keeled over, started crying, and prayed for revenge or oblivion.

Somebody was shaking Lofty's shoulder; a nasal scouse whine penetrated the fog of his brain. 'Alright there youse' de ya miss me eh?' Lofty stared; a man he vaguely recognized was patting the dog.

'Here got some scram for yeh.' A warm yellow polystyrene container was shoved into his hands. 'Back door Burger King, the lad there is alright like, he's proper scouse, Evertonian, so he stashes some scram in the back alley for us!'

Lofty smelt warm meat, tore open the container and wolfed the patties down.

'Eh, feck sake, youse stink - ye pissed ya sel?'

Lofty tried to speak, he croaked, coughed, cleared his throat, a baritone E flat cello brummie voice rolled out. Maria said she had loved his voice, he thought. 'I lost me leg. Some bastards pissed on me for fun! Who are you?'

'Ah compos mentis now eh. I'm Stevie, youse been on some bender der lad, what was ya on?'

'Dunno, pills, meth, smoked something, crack. I dunno, just wanted out me head.'

'Well youse ended up in me doorway like, us soldiers has see to each other!'

'How you know?'

'Cos youse ranted a bit about yer old Mob eh. Me, I was Rifles like, up and at em, swift and bold that's the Rifles motto. Anyway me dog liked youse.'

'Lost me leg, I'm fucked!'

'No, I got it, here.' Stevie thrust the prosthetic into Lofty's lap.

'What the fuck you doing with me leg.'

'Lad at Burger King wanted to see it like, he, em, gave me extra burgers for ya!'

Lofty grabbed the prosthetic, rolled up his pants, started lashing it on, his leg was raw and it hurt like hell. The prosthetic never did fit that well, wasn't he supposed to go back for another fitting. But where was that? He thought and gave up thinking. After struggling and cursing, he was able to stand up, leaning in the doorway, panting from the effort and pain.

'Where youse off then?' asked Stevie.

'Revenge matey, those bastards went in there.' Lofty pointed at a Hotel entrance and staggered away.

Stevie sat down and cuddled his dog muttering, 'fecking eejit.'

Lofty picked up speed, rolling his hips and swinging his prosthetic leg through a short arc, the faster he went the less pain, as long as he kept a balanced rhythm. The doorman was busy loading an elderly couple in a taxi, so he rolled straight through the hotel door into a plush foyer, dark polished wood, leather couches, low coffee tables, a murmur of hushed voices. Lofty scanned, three young men sitting around a bucket of champagne on a low table, looking at a phone laughing loudly, dominating the foyer with an air of entitlement.

Lofty stood there blinking, then the rage erupted and he lost it and charged, bellowing like a wounded bear, people looked up in astonishment. The three chaps stared at the charging Lofty, frozen in incomprehension. Lofty pivoted on his prosthetic and backhanded the nearest to him, grabbed a bottle with his free hand, smashed it against the table, then grabbed the one with most hair yanked him off the seat and held the broken bottle, hovering over long hairs face.

'Piss on me would you, you cunt, now you'll pay, fucker.'

People started screaming in fear. The one Lofty held started crying for mercy. The adrenaline rush emptied, Lofty felt his face flush, the light a diminishing halo around him. He started to pass out and fought the blackness, desperately hanging on to long hair but slowly he keeled over and for the third time that night sunk into oblivion. As he faded, he thought he heard the whimpering of a wounded animal, it was himself. He crumpled to the floor.

Chapter 9: Therapy

Eddie stepped from the single deck C46 Bus near St Pancras Hospital. The bus had been rammed; ethnic women heading to shit jobs, to feed their families, a couple of irate white pensioners and a wino talking to himself. The C46 bus, always full of passengers in terminal decline.

When the fuck will it stop raining? He thought as he slouched through the main gates of St Pancras Hospital, like a gothic red brick Victorian Hammer Horror film set. Eddie followed the signs "London Veterans' Clinic", signed in at reception ignored the lift and made his way to the fourth floor, taking the stairs two at a time. By the time he pressed the buzzer of the double door security entry system on the fourth floor he was panting hard; that's, ninety-six steps, thought Eddie.

The plumb friendly receptionist gave him the usual look of - why jog upstairs?

Eddie shrugged his shoulders thinking, why not, she could lose a bit of weight. 'Hello, here for Dr Vaughan.'

'OK, take a seat,' she replied, concerned.

'Sure, I'm early, always early for parade, you know.'

She ignored him. He sat in one of the blue IKEA minimalist armchairs, picked up the Outdoors magazine but ending up staring at the Armed Forces PTSD poster on the wall opposite. "Do you have these symptoms, ring . . ." Fuck me thought Eddie, you climb these stairs, you must know something's wrong with your wiring by now, bit like horses bolted isn't. First time here, he had the shakes just walking through the gates. He'd asked his doctor for sleeping pills, desperate, he wasn't sleeping at night. The doctor had just been to a PTSD briefing that month, saw his service medical record on file and made an appointment for him.

The first session was with a big, soft-eyed therapist with distracting cleavage. Ten minutes in Eddie had made an excuse and hid in the toilet trying to get back control of himself, shit he had broken down and cried. What the fuck was that all about? fuck that; get a grip. But over the next few weeks, he had come to realise that talking to her was actually helping him sleep, she put all the nightmares, the hyper alertness, and urge to commit violence, in context. The first six months out of the mob he'd gone drinking, done drugs, got into fights, stupid brawls for no reason. Eddie had actually gone looking for any excuse to rear up at someone.

Doctor Vaughan poked his head around the corridor doors.

'Hello Eddie.'

Shake of the hands, big smile, always forced, made him look like a silly fucker, pulling his mouth up at the corners like that. Eddie just stared back at him. Dr Vaughan led down the corridor, Eddie looking at the doctor's little cut-off large buckle cowboy boots, his tight pants crumpled up on top of the boot. Doctor Vaughan was wearing an M&S cardigan: top half middle-class doctor; bottom half gay disco.

The therapy session usually lasted an hour but Eddie was thinking of binning this treatment. Doctor Vaughan did most of the talking, wearing a saintly I'm doing good but isn't it exciting smile. The only time he listened was when he got Eddie yakking on about gruesome combat episodes. Doctor Vaughan always re-crossing his legs during those times, the buckles on his boots reflecting the light from the standard lamp, it all felt a little off. Eddie wanted soft-eyes back. He could look into her eyes and pour it all out, getting all misty-eyed and tearful. I suppose I want a mother figure, lay my head on her breasts. But Mum was a drunken whore, out most nights on the game and me getting up to no good on the estate. He had joined the army as soon as he was of age. Doctor Vaughan was yapping on about hippocampus response patterns and drawing a diagram of the fucking brain to show how clever he was. Eddie stared out the window, Fuck this I'm binning it, doing me no good at all, so what I'm a frag-head. He turned his head; zoned back in connected the words he was hearing.

'So it's another job another challenge but I'm sure you'll get on with Christine. Although my junior, she will be supervised by the head of the clinic.'

Then it was all shake hands and goodbyes, Eddie

thinking, OK, maybe I won't bin it if he's off the map. Lay my head on Christine. He pictured a nurse in uniform, with big tits at a Hangar Party.

Chapter 10: Squat Eviction

There were one hundred and thirty-six steps ascending a tight tiled dirty stairwell. Eddie had started taking them two at a time but binned that as his heart was doing a Geiger-counter ticker panic. So he just concentrated on jogging up one by one. He paused at the gantry to get his ticket out and nipped in front of the crowd coming out of the lift, heading to the ticket barriers of Goodge Street tube. He'd counted every step, an army habit - long miles tabbing, count something, trees you pass, big rocks, anything to keep your mind ticking along and ignore the effort.

OK, now it was fucking drizzling again, he nearly screamed in anger. On tour he'd dreamt of rain, now he dreamt of desert nights, lit by the red glow of tracer fire, rat-a-tat, screams, rat-a-tat. He weaved across the traffic lanes of Tottenham Court Road, through Russell Square into Woburn Place. He couldn't work out why people bimbled in front of him, heads stuck in mobile phones, no sense of being alert, it's a dangerous world, fuck's sake you people, scope your environment. Turning a corner, a wall of sound, angry chanting, sirens and loudspeakers playing classical music greeted him.

Earlier in the day, Eddie had chased down various leads to a squat in Hackney. He managed to get the name of Rainya's possible boyfriend, from a very stoned guy at the door of a dilapidated three-storey townhouse, a bed sheet hanging out the top window inscribed "Stop Private Landlord Evictions of Council Property" in red paint. Yeah, I'll make a note of that, Eddie thought. Wearing his old combat jacket, beanie hat, tracksuit bottoms and old army boots. Stoner thought he was a dope dealer. Eddie had given him the "been travelling schpiel" and asked for Rainya, the guy didn't know where she was but suggested he check her boyfriend.

Stoner babbled, 'at the Bloomsbury thing man, fighting Tandem Properties, tell Fitz I'm there for him man, yeah?'

Fitz, he found out, was Everett Fitzwilliam, the dynamic dude leader of Radical Housing Network, Eviction Resistance Movement. Sounded like a Rupert to Eddie.

The chants and noise intensified as he rounded the

corner. Police vans parked up in the Holiday Inn entrance bay, chocker full of Plod. A few hundred motley crew, marshalled by uniformed Plod, were chanting their anger at the bailiff lumps. A court order was being read over a loudspeaker but drowned out by wailing baby noises and classical music, booming from speakers sticking out the upper windows of the squat. The crowd chanting, "Squat the Rich," "Our Prediction No Eviction." "Only war - class war." The building was festooned with banners and slogans. Bunches of hoodies, scarves covering their faces, leaned out the windows and balconies giving it the clenched fist salute. Passing cars were blowing horns, no one sure who they were supporting. A heavy wet tapestry of noise enveloped the street.

Eddie clocked the chief bailiff, wearing a red body-armour vest, for fuck's sake. He was waving some paper, shouting something about a court order. Plod looked distinctly uncomfortable at Mr Fucking-redbreast-body-armour, desperate to rule the roost. Eddie slipped into the crowd, worked his way to the front edge and listened in. The protesters were alternately shouting and talking to each other.

OK, Eddie thought, I'm not getting in here anytime soon. He turned to the woman beside him, purple jacket, purple scarf and thick dark hair poking out the front.

'How long's this going on for then?'

'That pig of a man,' she nodded at Mr Robin-red-breast, 'will want to break down the doors.'

'Jobs-worth type of fella is he?'

'Oh yes. He was the bailiff geezer in charge at the Newham Eviction,' she replied. 'Were you at that?' He detected slight posh Indian overtones in the accent, especially on geezaaaa . . .

'No, just back from Holland.' Eddie fell back on the "been-travelling" tale.

'Oh, the squatting movement is really strong there.' More Indian accent leaked out.

The police, led by Robin-red-breast-bailiff, fanned out either side of the front doors. Shields went up as a couple of bailiff lumps bashed at the door lock, using a Fire fighters forcible entry Halligan-Tool. Eddie laughed, same battering tool his mob had used, on late night house-to-house raids in the townships.

The crowd surged forward, anger bubbling over, loud shouting and shoving. Eddie was propelled to the edge of the steps pressed up against Purple girl on the railings. More Plod boiled out of parked vans; riot shields up, a news camera crew set up on the steps next door. Three man teams of Plod began pulling protesters away from the steps. A very keen young looking Plod, grabbed Purple. Eddie was on her inside.

She screamed, 'Police protecting the rich.'

It didn't go down well with young Plod holding onto her, he locked a chokehold around her neck. Eddie stepped in, hooked his foot around Plod's ankle and reached over twisting his thumb back. Plod cried in pain, jerked backwards and let go of Purple as he fell over. Eddie pulled Purple away into the swirling chaos of the mini-riot, funnelled her across to the far side of the street.

A line of Plod now stood between the crowd and the bailiffs on the steps, shields up, blocking anyone from interfering. A film news crew was getting excited; a smoking flare had been thrown on the road, protesters chanting loudly. The young presenter doing her piece, 'This riot broke out as bailiffs attempted to seize the property blah, blah . . .'

Purple was massaging her neck, torn scarf hanging from her right shoulder, front of her coat ripped and necklace undone. A rich dollop of dark hair fell over a forehead above an intense face, strong nose framed by trendy glasses.

She put her hand out and shook Eddies very formally.

'Thank you I owe you, getting arrested wasn't on my agenda today, I'm Jassi Singh,' she said and stared intensely at Eddie.

'Yeah, look don't put your scarf back on and turn your jacket inside out. Plods out there looking for the one that got away. I'm Eddie.' He let go of her hand awkwardly.

'Oh yes, good idea.' Jassi busied herself reversing the jacket and fishing the broken necklace out from inside her top, she wrapped the necklace in the ripped scarf and stuffed it in her bag.

The front door was forced open, revealing a barrier of double plywood sheets and two-by-four batons nailed across the entrance hallway. The occupiers were shouting and laughing at the bailiffs and Police. The bailiffs held a hurried confab; Robin-red-breast was fuming, the top Plod almost looked relieved and waved half his troop back to the vans. The others took up guard around the entrance. The bailiffs sloped off to their cars.

From a windowed balcony, an occupier was giving it the big speech. "Victory to the dispossessed, a defeat for agents of the state controlled by the rich, blah, blah."

Jassi was waving her fist in the air, the crowd started chanting, "What did we predict, you can't evict . . ."

She turned to Eddie, face aglow with passion. 'That will be a blow to them, the eviction notice only stands for a finite period.'

'Yeah, fuck em,' said Eddie, thinking well that blows it. I'll not get in there today.

'They'll try to starve the comrades out now.'

'Tell 'em ring Deliveroo.'

'Oh, very funny Eddie, err look, this is my card,' she said hesitantly, 'Keep in touch yeah? You know, once you save someone you're responsible for them.'

'Plod was only trying to arrest you, not kill you.'

Jassi lowered her eyes, 'Ha ha, am I being overly dramatic.'

Eddie shook his head looking at the guarded entrance. 'Well I'm not getting in to see Fitz today am I!'

'Fitz?' said Jassi looking at Eddie curiously.

Eddie turned to her hopefully. 'Yeah, you know him?'

'Of course, don't worry, he'll be at the anniversary gig Friday night, at least I owe you a drink.'

Eddie looked at the card, black on red. Jassi Singh. "Radical Housing Network. Legal Team." 'So you're a Team?'

'Not really, I work in a solicitors office, it's my voluntary work, the fight against fascism goes on Eddie.'

A skinny black guy rushed up, panting. 'Oi Jassi, you OK dear? We got to go innit, over Ealing.'

'Oh god, is that the time Shania. Eddie, I got to dash, Ealing council eviction hearing. But maybe I'll see you at the gig, ya?'

Eddie held the card. 'You singing?'

'That's an old joke Eddie. No, it's short for Jasveer.'

'OK, fair enough. Where's the gig Jassi?'

Shania the skinny black guy piped up, 'Occupation year one Grosvenor Square Belgravia, enemy territory innit. The AAM do cool gigs man. So who are you?' He reached out and stroked Eddie's arm.

'Shania, say hello to Eddie my guardian angel today, he stopped the police arresting me.'

'Really? Cool man, you wanna save me?' Eddie gave him a thoughtful look.

Jassi bustled Shania away in the direction of the Tube and looked back over her shoulder and shouted. 'Friday Eddie?'

'Yeah, I'll bring a six-pack.'

Shania waved, a cheeky grin.

Eddie rolled a smoke. Fucking flirty lot these Radical Housing Network squatters. Wonder what AAM is?

Chapter 11: Banged Up

His defence told him he was lucky, a very clever but geeky short sighted young lawyer doing a bit of legal aide for her CV. She had managed to convince the court to look at the phone video the three men had taken of them pissing on Lofty. The judge had been outraged and rattled on about the army covenant and duty to veteran soldiers and then given Lofty two years, minimum sentence.

He had a new prosthetic fitted but every time he put it on he felt the ghost leg, still itching, it drove him mad, nothing to scratch, pain was much easier to take. His lawyer, Emma, was astonished when Lofty explained that he had moved in with Maria and her three young girls because Freddy Roberts, the Dad, had died dragging a wounded bleeding Lofty, under heavy incoming fire to a drainage ditch but had been hit and collapsed over Lofty's body and bled out. So when Lofty came out of UK hospital, he went to see Maria, pay his respects like. Lofty felt guilty. She was the lonely wife of a dead mate who had saved his life.

Lofty had stayed the night and moved in to the marriage quarters with Maria and her kids. Lofty had no idea how to raise kids. The girls were demanding and clever. He was a man of few words, out of his depth, so like a typical Tom, started drinking heavy. Days of moody silence followed as he tried unsuccessfully to blot out Afghan. It only took a few months before Maria and the kids had had enough of a one legged moody man suffering with PTSD and guilt. So, as soon as Maria got access to his bank account, she emptied it, why not? A drunken Lofty had repeatedly told her it was his fault her husband died, he was just drinking his money away. Maria took off back to Manila. Lofty came back from a two-day drinking session, walked in to an empty house, broke down sobbed. Washed his face and went back out on a huge bender. He ran out of money, was evicted and hitched down to London, the last place he heard the Sarge was. It was all blurry dreamtime, scattered carelessly on a froth of alcohol and nightmares, the real world a distant shimmering mirage, out of reach.

Lofty kept to himself in prison but he was on a wing run by a psycho body builder, Gorgeous George and his pals. George was in for a "Passover", he'd waved his gun in a bank and shouted, "Pass the fucking money over," but had lifted his balaclava up checking they'd given him all the fifties, it was all on CCTV. The old lags laughed about it on the wing, when George was elsewhere. He was a mean nasty type who needed a patsy to elevate his place in the world, a real narcissist who pumped iron lovingly in front of a mirror. And the hollow men collected around him, feeding off his physical menace and bullying threats to others on the wing.

Gorgeous George was nervous of the veteran soldier, but took every opportunity to take the piss, peg leg, hop-a-long; George wasn't very original.

Lofty did what he did well, nodding, saying nothing, but stoking up his rage until the moment the pressure could erupt in sudden violence. One day after a bad night of sober nightmares, he got to the canteen late, just the leftovers. He hefted his tray, a plate of congealed beans and eggs and looked for a space to sit as he wobbled down the central aisle. He heard one of George's hollow men crowing, 'hey ho peg leg to starboard.' George's table guffawing and George shouting in forced mirth. 'Fucking gimp, maybe we'll shove his leg up is arse tonight eh, and we can watch him hop it.' The table rattled with the hollow men's hollow laughter.

The bubble of white heat rage was ready to burst, the cork near to popping. Lofty swayed over to George's table, he stared down at the hollow little men clustered around their big bully shield.

'You ever killed anyone George?'

George stared back, open mouth, confused. This was not how it went at all, something wrong in his domain. Lofty bent in low, peering in into his eyes.

'Thought not!' and let the rage erupt.

He threw the trays congealed contents over the hollow men and back swung the tray with all his might, right into George's confused face. George flipped backwards off his bench. Lofty on pure hi-octane fuel stamped down with his prosthetic leg, right on George's balls. George screamed like a stuck pig. Lofty knew the fucker had just lost face with that feminine scream. Lofty went after the hollow men, his rage fuelling strength to the violence of his attack. Lashing out, kicking snarling hitting biting, mob training, immediate maximum force applied directly with anything at hand. The hollow Gorgeous George hangers-on felt their deep well of emptiness and scattered in fear, desperate to get away from the righteous berserker rage. The old lags looked on, nodding sagely as another wing tyrant's reign ended in a severe drumming. Lofty got a last stamp on George's head before prison officers, in anti riot gear, charged in and swamped him.

Lofty was escorted to an interview room, the door opened and Emma was sitting reading his case file, Lofty sat opposite.

Emma looked up, 'How was solitary confinement Mr. Lewis?'

'Seems to me like it should be a reward not punishment.'

'This is serious,' Emma shook her head, 'assault and damage to five other prisoners.'

Lofty smiled. 'Five eh, not bad, now I got my own room and room service.'

Emma adjusted her reading glasses. 'You're there to prevent prisoners attacking you in revenge, apparently. Anyway, I'm going down the mental instability PTSD route for your defence. It's your only bloody hope.' Emma pushed her glasses back up her nose. 'Get you transferred to a psychiatric unit?'

'What? You think I'm a nutter?' Lofty looked worried.

Emma swallowed. 'Well you're not exactly sane are you, Mr. Lewis?' She blinked at him nervously, her eyes looked large behind the lenses.

Lofty felt the anxiety and blew out his cheeks. 'Call me Lofty, Mr. Lewis feels odd.'

Emma regained her confidence and shook her head in despair. 'This is the last time for me Mr. Lewis. I'm moving Chambers, managing my career, thinking ahead. Why don't you try thinking ahead, you know managing your life? I mean where is this going to end up Mr. Lewis? As far as I can see it's a pretty depressing downward spiral.'

They marched Lofty back to his grey cell, he lay down trying to shut out the artificial light. His head was chattering again, his leg hurt, he sat up took the prosthetic off and suddenly in a mindless rage, repeatedly smashed the leg against the wall roaring incoherently. The leg broke apart, Lofty nutted the wall until he slumped over senselessly.

Chapter 12: Three Amigos

It was dark when he came out of Chalk Farm tube. Only fifty-nine steps, easy, up a steep and draughty circular stairwell. Eddie wasn't even puffed, getting fitter but it was like fighting a gale force wind up the last steps. He wondered if they couldn't harness all that spare energy of trains rattling around underground creating vortex-like winds? Then he wondered who they were, oh yeah, they don't travel by tube.

He stopped at Sainsbury's, bought cider, a piece of chicken, broccoli, tomatoes, onions and olive oil. Stir-fry tonight, he thought, slung his backpack over his shoulder and walked down Chalk Farm Road to Marine Ices, he got a one-scoop cone of mint choc chip for two quid. A treat he thought, for battling Plod and saving a damsel in distress. He was happily licking ice cream, thinking, do cops call themselves iPlod? He wandered through the back of the Estate.

Valdrin hailed him, 'Yo, Eddie my friend,' from the bench under the two scraggly trees in front of his block.

The Hi-Vis posse, when the fuck did these kids, a Croatian, Ethiopian, and the quiet Congolese, become Yardy gangsta, thought Eddie! A sick smell of skunk wafted over him.

'So, Guardians of the Galaxy, what's up?'

Valdrin smiled, stood up. Eddie had to admit the kid had a way with him. The dogs were sitting content, probably stoned of their nuts. Valdrin offered the spliff to Eddie. Eddie reached out for the joint and before he could resist the temptation took a toke.

'Phew, tastes rancid.' He licked his ice cream to drown the sour taste. 'Forget putting this shit in a bottle of rum. Ain't you got some old style natural sensei?'

Valdrin looked upset. 'But I already put some in a bottle of rum for you. Skunk, what the market want innit, Eddie.'

Eddie pulled a face. 'Yeah, good fucking luck to the market then.'

The other two grinned like giggling fools, on a daft high.

Valdrin wiped his grin. 'The Joke-vic putting it about he

gonna teach you manners innit.'

'That so? You letting me know, or are you passing on his message?'

'No Eddie, we don't run with him.'

The quite Ethiopian murmured shyly, 'we indie outfit you get it?' He gave Eddie a half smile.

Eddie smiled back and slowly licked the mint choc chip, no one spoke for a while.

'You guys, Three Amigos eh?' Eddie broke the silence.

'Band of brothers, you know it.' The Ethiopian kid licked his lips, eyeing the ice cream.

Eddie slurped the runny stuff collecting on the rim of his cone, 'wanna lick my cone?' The Ethiopian blushed and looked away.

Eddie chuckled, 'Lads when I was your age, did the same shit but I signed up army style. Some of the gang ended up doing time, some never made it.'

Valdrin flicked the roach away. 'Well we're starting-up in business Eddie but I'll look after the citizens here.' Valdrin waved his hand around the estate. 'London been good to us.'

Eddie caught off guard, blurted, 'really? That's good. Lads this is where we live, no shitting on our doorstep eh.'

'Yeah we hear you. Innit bros,' said the quiet one, the other two nodded like it was a pledge. Eddie thought - this is a solemn moment and slurped.

'Guys, that's an oath of honourable men you giving me.'

The lanky Ethiopian pushed his fist out to Eddie. 'We hear you. Word innit.' The other two joined in fists out. Eddie touched his knuckles to the three fists, while ice cream ran over his other hand but he managed to look serious, nodding to each of them.

'Robin Hood and his merry men.'

'Who that?' The Ethiopian, kid getting really chatty now.

Needs new terms of reference, thought Eddie, as he walked to the entrance of his block pushing the top of the ice cream down into the cone with his tongue. Was that a moment back there, a coming of age thing, rites of passage, making a choice of who they want to be? Eddie was impressed. He turned and placed his entry fob on the metal plate by the door, gave the kids an ice cream cone salute, they raised fists in return. The door beeped and let him in.

Chapter 13: Awakening

Lofty stirred slowly, waking, he tried to scratch his head but his arms were clamped.

'What the fuck,' he said but it came out as "Whafffuk".

A male nurse swam into vision, stuck a thermometer in his mouth. 'You waking up, nod if you understand me. OK good. You're in J-ward, contusions to the head.' Lofty just stared in silence.

'We drugged you up dear; you're labelled as prone to violent outbursts. Doctor will assess you later.' The nurse shook the thermometer, scribbled on a pad, hooked it back on the end of the bed and flipped the curtain aside and walked away. Lofty peered through the gap in the curtains, he could just about make out three other beds, he tried to think, he wasn't on the street, thank god but the drugs dulled him, he could not think any further and drifted off.

He'd been here a month now, they put him on a course of cognitive talking therapy and anti depressants but Lofty had never been one for talking,

'I want you to relax Mr. Lewis,' asked a young female therapist who chewed on her pencil.

'What's this for?' Lofty picked up the small brown bottle on the table between them.

'It's lavender oil Mr. Lewis, helps centre you if the memories are too much.'

'Smells like a bazaar.'

'OK, interesting. Now let's try again, you're on patrol, what were you thinking, just cast your mind back to that day.'

Lofty sniffed the bottle and put it down. 'It was fucking hot and dusty. I felt like a moving target.'

'Yes but can we get in to your mind at the time.'

'No fucking way.' Lofty was suspicious, not telling this young girl anything, she'd probably scream in disgust.

'This isn't helping Mr. Lewis, for cognitive therapy to work, we must re-experience the moment and contextualize the experience.'

'Oh yeah,' Lofty laughed, 'my left leg flew over my right shoulder, I thought fuck, that's me ticket home.'

The therapist scribbled in her note pad, 'So you had a sense of relief as well as loss?'

Lofty shook his head, 'No, I didn't want to go home, I'm a soldier.'

The therapist leaned forward. 'Interesting you should say that. Let's explore that thought, shall we?' She leaned back waiting.

'Fuck you, sorry didn't mean to swear love. Eh sorry, Miss.' Lofty hauled himself up and opened the door, 'its meal time.' He walked out heading for the day room.

The library trolley fella ambled around the day room, a lifer, in for murder had the job and the clever fucker was working the nutter system, one of the big bastards. Another pumping iron career criminal, called CJ.

'Oi Lofty my son,' he strolled over, pushing the trolley across in front of him. Lofty was sat looking out the window at the hospital grounds, concentrating on not thinking, keeping his thoughts away from the deep abyss in back of his mind, threatening to bubble over with dark thoughts. Since they had started him on therapy he was suffering nightmares while awake and most nights waking up in a hot sticky sweat.

'What you want?' said Lofty harshly, meaning leave me alone.

CJ paused took a deep breath and decided to ignore the insult, 'I got you a book my son, right up your little dark alley.'

'Don't read books CJ.' Lofty looked up. 'What you mean dark alley?'

'Look son, you're stuck in here with your terrors, but books can set your mind free, a fucking route march beyond the wall you're gawping at.'

Lofty swivelled his head, looked CJ full on. 'So, that what you do then?'

CJ flicked his nose with a thumb, 'Fucking too right son, don't do time angry, afraid of looking back, scared of looking forward. You wont survive mate, they'll drug you up.'

'Who cares? I don't.' Lofty turned away.

CJ wondered why he had a soft spot for soldiers. 'Yeah, who cares? Listen you silly fucker do the time chilled, don't let it do you. Know what I mean? What else you got going for yourself? Think of it as a mission.'

Lofty jerked upright at the word mission, a light flickered in his head. 'What's the book CJ?' he asked in a respectful tone.

CJ smiled, he was getting through, 'Its Jap stuff, way of the warrior. Bushido code, something you soldier boys might recognize son.' CJ tossed the book at Lofty, who caught it one handed.

'Bit thin isn't it?'

'Fuck me son, small steps, small steps.' Lofty glanced at his prosthetic, CJ laughed, 'OK, didn't mean it like that son,' and ambled away pushing the trolley across the day room.

Lofty sat back and opened the book. **Bushido: The Way of the Samurai.**

CJ called back over his shoulder, 'It's in big print son.' Lofty gave him two fingers, smiled and started reading slowly.

Chapter 14: Down Again

Eddie had aimed to get out of bed early and go for a run. He felt very confident that he would do this. The alarm went off at half six, but at eight he was still in bed feeling a total failure. The day had started as a fuck up, so why bother? Eddie knew he was in a big downward spiral after the adrenalin-fuelled last few days. He had been all action, invulnerable, take 'em all on - fight the world. Now he couldn't even get out of fucking bed. He threw the covers over his head and buried himself in sleep, the radio was on, the sports results, Spurs had won, and he didn't give a fuck, blackout.

In the back of his mind, he knew this'd take a while to work its way through. Stupid mind exercises of doctor gay-disco-Vaughan were shit, shit, and shit. Fuck it. He stretched his arm down beside his bed, fingers curled around the whisky bottle, big swig and fuck you, back under the safety of the covers. Fuck-off world.

It was two in the afternoon before he got out of bed and staggered to the bathroom, still signs of where he puked into the toilet bowl last night.

'Aaghh feel like crap, I am crap.'

He forced himself to take a hot shower, get dressed and get out. Need a fry-up. 'Fucks sake you pitiful idiot get moving. Fuck, fuck, fuck.' He was talking to him self and didn't care.

Showered, he padded naked down the corridor. As he passed the kitchen a cold draught hit him. The kitchen window was wide open. Did I open that last night he thought. The window opened on to the balcony seven floors up. Eddie went to close the window and noticed that the flowerpots were scattered. Realisation hit him.

'Fuck me someone's been in here,' he cried. They would have to had come over the roof and shinned down the drainpipe.

Edie felt that ice-cold sweaty feeling people have when they realise they have been burgled. He searched the flat to see what had been taken. Cash gone, medals hanging on the living room wall, gone.

'Fuck, fuck, fuck, while I was out of it,' anger bubbled, 'what a useless fucker I am.' He jerked his head up, dread hitting him and dashed into the other bedroom, his Mum's walnut Victorian dresser, her pride and joy. Pulled open the top drawer, jewellery box gone. Eddie sat on his Mum's bed, tears and anger coursing through him scouring the hangover in a rush. He pounded the floor with his fists.

'Jesus fucking cunting hell, I'll kill 'em I'll kill the fuckers,' he cried and walked out on the balcony and screamed at the estate, 'Whoever done my place, you're dead. Do you fucking hear me?' He stood there in the weak early afternoon sun, naked, trembling with anger, tears running down his face.

Chapter 15: Lofty On Guard

Eddie shuffled his feet in the doorway of Moonlight Oasis; it was a bit nippy tonight, punters wearing coats made it difficult for him to pat them down for knives or drugs. He let two guys in, looked up and spotted the tall, thin, wide shoulders silhouette, at the end of the street. Lofty Lewis and that walk, big slo-mo ostrich stepping style, all his one-legged own. He wore shorts, even on a cold night, proudly displaying his prosthetic from knee down.

Lofty halted in front of him at attention, 'Reporting for duty Sarge.'

'Right you are – Good to see you on the outside, suits you. I'm having a bad day Lofty, me gaff got done last night.'

'Fuck! Bad luck Sarge, toe-rags take a lot then?'

'My Mum's stuff, her jewellery box.'

'The Fuckers, the stuff you got her in Kabul.'

Eddie patted a nervous young punter down, he pulled a zippy bag of pills out of the inside coat pocket. Eddie gave the kid a look, 'You wanna get rid of this and come back, we'll try again eh?'

The kid nodded and sloped away. Eddie turned to Lofty. 'They think we never lived. Yeah, it's all I ever got her. Now it's been half-inched by some little toe-rags.'

'Not right Sarge. Not your Mam's'

'I got an old mate on the job.'

'Oh? Plod is he?'

'No he's a crim, Lofty.'

'Ah well, you'll be all right there then Sarge, bit of local criminal Intel. Sound move.'

'I'm Eddie now we in Civvy Street!'

Lofty gave it some thought and answered, 'Yeah, Boss.'

'Here's your security certificate and security radio, stash em' in my locker downstairs when you're done, security code same as our Afghan call sign, OK?'

'Roger that Boss.'

They stood for a while in silence, Lofty reading his certificate, Eddie staring at people walking passed Moonlight

Oasis. Thinking of Afghan. Then a rush of micro-skirted girls traipsed across the street, wobbling on hi-heels, fully pre-drinking fuelled up. A bunch, tottered up to Lofty, he bowed.

'Just need to check your bags ladies.'

'All right love,' said the leader of the pack. She looked at his leg, 'I'd do you, darling,' and turned screaming with laughter at her mates, 'Help a hero innit!'

Her friends cracked up. 'Oh, Emma you're a scream I tell ya.'

The name Emma made Lofty uncomfortable, thinking of the young lawyer who tried to help him, so he moved aside to let them walk passed into the club. Emma paused at his shoulder, 'Really it turns me on,' she pointed at his prosthetic and walked on waving her hand, wankers style.

Eddie shook his head, chuckling, 'Never thought your leg would be a pulling card Lofty. Look, just think of the job as check-point duty back in the mob.' He gave Lofty a quick rundown on Club door etiquette as they worked. After an hour there was a lull in clubber traffic.

'Listen Sar . . . eh Boss, I want to say something.'

'Spill it out, Lofty.'

'It's like this'n; I want to thank you for this chance. Don't want to go back.'

'So, why didn't you get in touch?'

'Cos, well you know, only had a little bit of pride left somewhere inside me, not enough to call out, you know how it is.' Lofty squared his shoulders. 'Took three Plods to pull me mind'

'Yeah, we all sing that song.'

'Well I was out of tune Boss but stir-time pulled my shit together, read a lot. Been sticking to the code, want you to know that.'

Eddie looked surprised. 'You sure you off the juice then?'

'Yeah, they put me in a hostel. It's OK. I march five miles every morning now.'

'Fuck you do! How's the leg?'

'Plastic and metal chaffs and blisters, bit like having

64

new boots innit.'

Eddie looked down at Lofty's left leg. 'Can't tell when you standing still.'

'I'm into meditation you knows. Puts me right so I won't let you down, Boss.'

Eddie put his hands in his pockets and looked up and down the street, 'Look mate it's only door work, not much to it.'

'So where is Scotch John, Boss?'

Eddie blew into his cupped hands, 'Yeah well, when I find the fucker he's gonna get a rocket.'

Lofty looked up at the sky as if he was in meditation. 'What did we fight for, Boss? We were good at that but Civvy Street is shit.'

Eddie gave him a startled look. 'What . . .? Listen Lofty, I got some business to attend to if Scotch turns up.'

'Yeah, Boss, I'll sort him.'

'OK, doors all yours, OK with you?' Eddie patted Lofty on the shoulder and turned to go.

Lofty bowed his head 'Katajikenai Eddie san.'

'You what Lofty?'

'Samurai greeting, "Way of the warrior".'

Eddie chuckled and walked to Leicester Square tube thinking, back in the Regiment Lofty was the quiet one, now he's talking Japanese Zen at me. Do all the lads get fucked up on Civvy Street? You got your work cut out for you with my mob, Dr Dancing Boots.

Chapter 16: Squatters Party

Eddie jumped tube from Northern Line through the short tiled tunnel to Victoria Line, exit at Victoria Station, hardly any steps, brisk walk to Eaton Square, Belgravia. The squat, an imposing detached mansion, a dozen steps leading to an impressive entrance, Greek pillars, big balcony above. A plethora of protest banners draped over the front. Eddie walked up smiling at the people running the door. He was the punter now.

'You got your invite code?' asked a tall skinny longhaired Scooby-Doo guy. Eddie fished in his pocket. He showed Jassi's card. Scooby-Doo turned to the big guy next to him.

'What you think?'

Big Guy looked like a rugby front row, peered down at Eddie from the top step and scowled. 'Looks like he could be a copper.'

Eddie snarled, 'Now you just insulted me, big fella.'

'Oh, and what the fuck are you going to do about it then, copper?'

Eddie weighed up the options, enjoying the pumping thrill of adrenalin. Big Fella three steps above him, Eddie stepped up one and mentally measured the distance between them. Big Fella would have to punch downwards, losing force but Eddie was just out of reach, so the big fella might realise this and try a kick. Eddie placed his weight on his left foot, ready for a sweep kick at Big Fella's ankle, that should put him down, or at least off balance. Then Eddie could swivel on to his right and snap kick Big Fella in the bollocks, and if that didn't finish him, he had plenty more to dish out. Although Eddie thought, it's not the way to slip quietly into a party is it? Just as he was tensing, a black guy bounced up all youthful energy, short locks dyed green and red, baggy denim bib and brace, Dr Martin boots.

'All right, Eddie, cool, Jassi be pleased to see you handsome fella.' Shania greeted him with a Jamaican accent, gave him a hug and grabbed his hand.

Scooby-Doo interrupted. 'Got to be careful, we had a bunch of fascist goons attack us yesterday.'

'Yeah, we set the fire extinguishers on em,' boasted Shania posing hand on hip with a swagger. Eddie smiled and lifted his six-pack of cider out of the carrier bag. The Big Fella leaned over and peeled a can from Eddie's six-pack.

Eddie thought, fuck-me I'm being hassled by crap door security. He dialled his temper back down with an effort, stared Big Fella in the eye, wanting to communicate to him how close he had come to being hurt.

'You sure? Drinking on duty!'

Big fella took a swig, wiped his mouth, burped, 'Yeah, well I'm watching you.' He did that thing with his two fingers, pointed at his eyes and then at Eddie.

Eddie shrugged, what the fuck and postponed the urge to punch the daft fucker. Shania dragged him up the steps by the hand, laughing in party mode. The squatters had built a zigzag entrance out of industrial plywood. Smart, Eddie thought, no one charging in here.

Inside it opened up into a large domed vestibule, lit by hanging mini solar lights, a curved marble stairway in the middle. How the Ruperts live! Thought Eddie as he automatically checked the exits. Then he checked the crowd, no obvious danger here he thought, not a hangar party full of switched-on Toms. He turned to Shania releasing his hand in a slow friendly way.

'So you got some Jamaican heritage, or was that just yard talk?'

Shania reached out stroking Eddie's arm, 'I'm touchy feely, how about you?

Eddie snorted ignoring the question.

'Well I'm third generation Eddie; Granddad on the buses, my Dad was born here, works in a bank, hates it, comes home to his garden shed pretending to re-build an old BMW, smokes homegrown weed he grew from seeds his Granny gave him in Jamaica.'

Eddie laughed, 'Home-grown heritage uh. Is it any good?'

'Oh yeah man, I suppose so but I don't smoke heritage. My Dad's stoned most nights yakking patois, demanding I give him grandchildren even if I batty boy.' Shania giggled hysterically.

Resistance slogans were spray painted on the walls. They walked upstairs where the party was full on. Shania linked his arm through Eddie's. Eddie looked around the human zoo, checking, new crowd new dangers. White, brown, yellow and thin, would they be vegans? He thought. All sorts of costumes from boring black to riotous colours dancing to drum and base with red, blue and green laser beams playing over them, a lot like a hangar party. In the left corner, a group sat cross-legged spraying stencils on a large white sheet. Shania guided him to what looked like the bar area, a trestle table set up at the far wall under another spiral stairway. They walked through clouds of dope smoke getting buzzed. Eddie put his five-pack cider on the table, unhooked from Shania, ripped a cider off, put his back against the wall and took a gargle, while still scoping the scene for danger.

A woman appeared in front of him. Sexy black cocktail dress over tight leopard skin leggings, high heels, short dark hair, Elvis-style, big drunken mascara eyes, maroon lipstick and big earrings. She stared at Eddie as if expecting him to say something. Eddie tried playing it cool, took another sip from his can.

'Yo Jassi, look who I got.' Shania all cockney accent now.

Eddie did a double take at leopard girl. 'Shit Jassi, sorry, I mean didn't recognise you love, you look . . . you're not wearing . . .'

'Contact lenses, party time, I'm off-duty Eddie.'

Eddie chuckled, thinking "Off-duty" the mob's name for smoking Afghan Hash.

'What's funny?' Jassi laughed slightly slurring her words, 'tits not perky enough?' She pushed her breasts up. 'That's quality cleavage right there.'

Eddie's attempt at playing it cool ended spluttering cider, froth landed on Jassi.

'Coming already big boy,' Jassi winked, Shania giggled up a storm. Jassi burbled throaty laughter.

Eddie was off balance. 'Uh, fancy a cider?'

Shania took a can, 'sure ting man I swallow yo brew,' back to Jamaican accent again, like a one-man *Carry On* film.

Jassi reached for Eddie's can, took it gently from his hand, touching fingers, sipped slowly while looking Eddie in the eyes, 'All by yourself? Isn't there a Missus, girlfriend, long lost love, then Eddie?'

Shania leaned in and stroked his arm, 'Or a nice guy like me?'

Eddie felt deep waters closing around him. He tried to be cool. 'No I'm flying solo.'

'Not good for you Eddie,' said Jassi, 'But then me? A string of wrong choices, one doomed flight after another.'

Shania fluttered his eyelashes, 'Tell me girlfriend.'

'Oh.' Eddie tried to regain his composure, eyes locked on Jassi. 'Who you been flying with?' And thought why the hell did I ask her that.

'Oh you know,' Jassi half smiled with a slo-mo eye lashes flutter, 'the useless type who can only fly charter. Maybe I should try the gallant knight-errant, you know when one pops up and rescues me.'

Shania laughed, 'You two sparking on each other, well Eddie I'm off for a dance, laters.' He kissed Eddie on the cheek and twirled away dancing on his toes. Eddie jerked his head in surprise.

Jassi reached out and held his hand. 'Come on Galahad,' she whispered and pulled Eddie into the middle of the dancing throng.

Eddies gave it a go but Drum n' Base took him back to the hangar party. He felt anxious, couldn't lose himself in the music, too many people, seemed like an eternity, shuffling around, eyes peeled for danger. Jassi swayed to the music eyes half closed, oblivious. Eddie tapped her on the shoulder.

'I've had enough, I'm more rock 'n roll.'

Jassi opened her eyes and smiled slowly. 'OK, you like Elvis, Eddie?'

'Sure.'

They shared a moment gazing at each other. She knew what was going on but Eddie didn't have a clue and she knew that as well.

Eddie rolled on his feet breaking the spell, regaining balance. 'So is Fitz here?'

'Oh he'll be up in HQ.' Jassi gestured up another marble staircase curling up to the next floor. 'Come on I'll take you upstairs Eddie.' Jassi winked at him.

Eddie smiled. 'Blimey, girl you got some front when you're off-duty.'

'Rock 'n' Roll, Eddie.'

Upstairs HQ was like a scruffy ops-room, laptops on a paste table against a wall, above, black and red anarchist banner with clenched fist. People sitting on beanie bags chatting, in the middle a group of people, all jeans and long pullovers, were having a heated discussion, ponytail guy yelling, 'No! No! I tell you we fight this one, mobilise support grab the headlines, force the issues on the public.'

Lots of nods, thin intense guy short curly hair, spectacles on top of his head, waved for silence, 'OK, OK if we're all agreed, maybe this time it will get headlines, after all we are in Belgravia!' They laughed.

The group broke up. Jassi led Eddie over. 'Hey, Fitz meet my friend Eddie, he's been looking for you.' The intense guy examined Eddie. 'Oh?'

Then Big Fella strides up like he can handle trouble and stands next to Fitz. 'I think he's a cop.'

Jassi laughed at him. 'So silly; he saved me from the cops at the Bloomsbury squat demo?'

Fitz looked Eddie over carefully. 'So why you looking for me?'

Eddie gave the Big Fella a cold smile, postponed the urge to hurt him for the second time and stuck his hand out to Fitz.

'Yeah well, I'm not interested in any of your plots.' He'd prepared a cover story about his own estate, as close to the truth as possible. 'Just that people over Hackney squat said talk to you, man with ideas at ERM.'

Fitz looked interested, 'Am I now?'

'Well you could be,' Eddie said, thinking this guy is no fool. 'We got some housing issues on our estate in north London.'

'Oh yeah?' Fitz's interest perked up a notch.

'Sure, we got different languages, different religions and cultures, need some community building stuff.'

Fitz visibly relaxed. 'Sure that sounds great, real housing estate eh, yeah. Maybe some public graffiti art or a gardening club, or . . . Have you got a community centre?' Fitz was speeding up, talking in clipped Rupert tones, tossing ideas out.

Despite himself, Eddie was impressed with Fitz's energy, like an alternative Rupert. Eddie held up his hand. 'OK, whoa there, hold up mate, how about we have a chat, when I haven't been drinking.'

'Yeah sure take my number, in a few days, OK?' He handed over a card, "ERM: Eviction Resistance Movement".

Eddie looked, Red on Black this time, really, and shoved the card into his back pocket, 'Good on ya mate, will do.' Well, that wasn't hard thought Eddie, boyfriend in the bag, Rainya bound to show up soon.

Chapter 17: The Fence

Eddie was very comfy sitting front seat in the big four by four, after a late night at the party. Slightly pissed he somehow had agreed to Jassi cooking him dinner. 'You bring your nice bottle of wine and I'll cook my meat,' she said. What the fuck, everything was *Carry On* double entendre.

Rumpunch parked on Brecknock Road, a one-way leading to Camden Road. It had a small shopping parade, of second-hand furniture, kebab shop, organic hippy food shop and pawnbrokers. Eddie looked at the parking sign.

'You'll get a ticket.'

'It don't come my yard,' Rumpunch smiled as if to a child, 'I got a parking protection policy.'

Eddie wondered what that really meant, 'Oh that's handy. So maybe third time lucky with this place eh?'

Rumpunch and Eddie got out the car, Eddie automatically scanned the street for threats. Rumpunch gave him that smile again. 'Come on Eddie, the guy's called Izzy, medium level fence but an intellectual type, thinks he knows about antiques.'

They crossed the road, Rumpunch pushed the heavy front door open, inside they faced an iron grill over a counter with jewellery and gold on display, rest of the place assorted jumble of semi-expensive priced clutter, musical instruments hanging on walls. Izzy looked up from the counter, shiny head, tufts of grey hair stuck out at angles, half-glasses perched on his nose, a wrinkled parchment face. Not a man who enjoyed sunlight.

'Ah, oh, Mr Preston, ahem - nice of you to visit.'

Rumpunch nodded. 'Looking for some old style jewellery Izzy, what you got?'

Izzy came out from behind the grilled counter, his grey cardigan buttoned up unevenly, rubbing hands together as if it had suddenly turned cold and stuttered nervously, 'A, . . . a, .. . gift?'

Eddie was staring at a heavy ornate necklace. 'What's this worth?'

Izzy got his mojo back and went into sales pitch mode.

'Ah, a fine example, late Edwardian, German-crafted, has antique value, to a friend of Mr Preston.' Izzy paused, face wrinkles flickering showing computations going on in his mind.

Eddie looked up. 'It's Afghan gold with Indian ruby.'

'Ah ha, really my friend! Mr Preston your friend thinks he knows jewellery?'

Eddie walked over in a threatening manner. Izzy took a nervous step backwards.

'No, I obtained it in Afghan for me Mum's fiftieth.' Izzy laughed very nervously. 'Your friend joking?'

Eddie grabbed Izzy around the throat. 'How about I choke you, you fucker.' Rumpunch put his hand in front of Eddie's face.

'Easy, take it easy.'

Eddie let go, Izzy staggered back rubbing his throat, gasping. Rumpunch moved to the entrance locked the door and hung "Gone for Lunch" sign in the window, it was four p.m.

Izzy was sitting down now scowling at Eddie, who was scanning the rest of the jewellery on display. Rumpunch pulled up a matching antique oak chair and sat facing Izzy.

Eddie stood over them. 'It was in a jewellery box. Dark blue velvet, lid opens upwards, mirror on the inside.'

Izzy groaned, looking at Eddie over Rumpunch's shoulder, and decided his fate rested with Rumpunch. He held his hands up and shrugged. 'Look, Mr Preston, it was just business. He had paperwork OK? You can't expect me to . . .' Izzy snatched a quick glance at Eddie to see if this was going down OK. It wasn't.

'Listen, you fucker . . .' snarled Eddie. Rumpunch interrupted.

'Leave it Eddie.' He turned to a shaking Izzy, 'You had no idea it was knocked off, right?'

Eddie paced away, fists clenched, taking in deep breaths, no happy place left. Try this for a happy place Doctor buckle-me-shoe Vaughan.

Izzy and Rumpunch stared at him for a moment. Rumpunch tapped Izzy on the shoulder. 'So, Izzy, look at me. Let's get passed this awkward moment. You can see the extent of my friend's anger; he recently left the Armed Forces, decorated as a hero for killing our enemies overseas. But his Mother passed away recently, lots of deep-seated anger. So, if I walk out of here? Rumpunch held his hands out. 'Believe me, you're toast.'

Izzy made another attempt to protest at the inevitable. 'Look, look, let's be reasonable, people bring me family items. I'll certainly consider a purchase back at cost. How's that?' Izzy pleaded, he made his way to the grilled counter and slipped inside but Eddie squeezed right behind him, pushed Izzy into the backroom. Rumpunch got up shaking his head and followed. There was a narrow workbench next to a desk with a big stuffed bear opposite.

Eddie picked up a soldering iron and plugged it in and laid a cold stare on Izzy. Rumpunch walked in shaking his head.

'Izzy just get the box, we're not here for anything else.'

Izzy gave Eddie a shuddering look and went to the stuffed bear, glancing nervously over his shoulder; he pulled the bear's belly away on Velcro fastenings, revealing a safe. He unlocked the safe and from the middle shelf pulled out a jewellery box and placed it on the workbench. Eddie switched on the desk light opened the box, examined the contents. Izzy stood back, nervously glancing at Rumpunch for support.

Eddie looked up. 'Her fucking ring is missing, big vulgar thing three red stones, she loved shiny red stones and my medals.'

Izzy pleaded, 'all I got. Honest Mr Preston.'

Eddie laughed at the honest but Rumpunch was running the show. 'Names Izzy.'

Izzy rubbed at his forehead. 'You didn't get this from me, OK? Very bad for business.'

'Agreed' said Rumpunch in a civil tone. Eddie rolled his eyes.

'Young mixed race kid. Said it was his dead Aunt's. Had receipts with him, eh handwritten,' he shrugged apologetically at Rumpunch, 'you know the business.'
Rumpunch snorted, 'Give him up Izzy, my friend has developed a habit of setting light to people's property.'

Izzy looked like a beaten man and sunk back on a chair, rubbing his forehead, 'The name's Marlon, lives over Kilburn next to . . .'

Chapter 18: Jassi G&T

Jassi shrugged her arms out of the coat and let it fall to the floor on top of her bag.

'I need a bloody drink!' she shouted at the empty flat, stepped out of her shoes walked to the kitchen and reached up for the bottles of gin and tonic on the top shelf. Clutching them awkwardly Jassi slumped on the chair by the window and poured a large slug into the half pint glass on the table, knocking back a mouthful she stared out of her only window at the twinkling red crane lights, sighed and took another large swig.

Images of her day replayed in her head, three court cases lost, two families evicted and a very vulnerable lonely man out on the streets. Could I have won against those eviction notices, she pondered, going over the arguments, feeling the weight of her own guilt and angry at the blatant hostility of the judge and the opposing briefs.

'Damn landlords' rights – oh hell,' she muttered and again saw the sad eyes of the little girl, youngest of a single parent family with three kids out on the streets, after just less than thirty minutes in court.

Jassi had handed them over to the council housing officer, who would lodge them in a run-down dirty and dangerous converted pub B&B. The other family in the second court case, in South London, blamed her for running late from the court in Ealing. Her apologies to the court were swept aside; being late meant she was flustered and lost the case at the start. Another family evicted so the landlord could raise the rent and pile a load of young people in, sharing rooms, working in coffee shops while applying for graduate jobs. My god she thought, more baristas, is that what society needs, coffee the one constant in graduate lives.

Jassi sighed again, lifted the glass, surprised it was empty, poured another big G&T with determination. The last one had been gulped down in a cold misery, now she felt angry and the alcohol warmed her insides. The last case – she could clearly picture the face of that single lonely incoherent man, a former soldier, scared stiff just kept saying 'Yes sir, no sir,' all the time and stuttering red in the face when the posh brief went on and on about his lapse in rent and car payments. They'd won an immediate eviction against him and Jassi had tried her best to get him into social services, but he refused, broke down crying and swearing loudly at her on the steps of the court. Clutching his carrier bag of worldly possessions, he staggered lurching down the street hollering like a mad man.

By now Jassi had knocked back four big glasses of G&T. The tonic was empty, she slipped off the chair, clutching the bottle of gin she crawled over to her futon sofa. Lying back she thought of Eddie and took a big gurgle of gin straight from the bottle. He had undoubtedly saved her from arrest; she smiled thinking of his strong arms and physical confidence he showed in pulling her away from the cop. A rather old fashioned chivalry, but was it verging on sexist she wondered, yet somehow attractive when slightly out of his depth at the party.

'Bloody hell, I invited him to dinner must have been pissed,' Jassi slurred and lifted the bottle, it was empty, she swore and dropped it on the floor. 'Bet he is sexist . . .' more slurring and giggling, 'but my god if he walked in the door now I'd jump his bones.' Jassi collapsed in a fit of giggles, lay her head down, pulled the futon throw over her and drifted into a deep drunken sleep.

Chapter 19: Report Back

Eddie came out of Marble Arch Tube made his way through the bustle of shoppers on the fag end of Oxford Street and slipped across into Hyde Park. The parks were the green lungs of London and you could slow down enough from the city rush to dawdle. He strolled across the grassy green undulating folds to the Serpentine Lake, sun out, smell of spring in the air. He emerged south side of the park onto Kensington Gore and walked passed the Albert Hall. Different class of people on show, affluent rich foreigners and country set English up in town.

He found the gaff up a well-heeled side street, little fusion food place with a high priced menu on a plinth at the entrance, very Gucci Eddie thought. April sat in the back, big wooden table high backed chairs, thick Persian carpets on the walls. She wore a midnight blue business suit, pencil skirt, white shirt top two buttons undone, pearl necklace, very alarm-bells-ringing sexy.

'What'll you have Eddie?'

'Whatever you're having Showers. We on first names now, are we?'

'That could be dangerous,' April flashed a naughty girl smile and waved a hand, a waitress busied over. 'Two builders teas please.'

Eddie sniffed. 'That what you call a cup of tea in the posh part of town, is it?'

April mock-frowned at him. 'Builders tea is very trendy lately, must be all the house renovation going on around here. Anyway, green tea tastes so bloody awful,' she pointed her chin at him. 'So, how's progress, Eddie?'

'Yeah well, I'm in amongst the alternative lifestyle set, nice squat in Belgravia.'

'God, they should try working, get a proper job.'

Eddie laughed. 'Ha, like the one you have me doing?'

'Now, now, Eddie,' she gently admonished.

Eddie scanned the room's clientele, a mixture of young lady housewives lunching on plates of green nothings and trendy digital execs, long-sleeved shirts flopping over wrists and cord pants. He began to feel nostalgic for army Ruperts.

'Yeah, anyway should get sight of her soon, taken a while to chase down, they're a paranoid lot.'

'Oh, that's very good work Eddie, so are you undercover then?'

'Hardly a behind enemy lines op, is it?'

The tea came over on a thick round wooden tray, large pot, two very elegant mugs, silver bowl of sugar, little blue jar of milk, and long handle teaspoons on the side.

'Looks farmhouse tea to me, Showers.'

'Yes. The posh set has a very baroque way of appropriating the lower orders culture. Shall I be Mother?'

'Whatever turns you on girl.'

April smiled and poured the milk first, then tea and passed a mug to Eddie. 'Well, that's good news Eddie, Sir Omar will be so pleased. So who are these squatters?'

'Bunch of anarchists fighting a class war, whole bunch of different outfits the ERM seem the most sensible.'

'Music band?'

'No, Eviction Resistance Movement, led by one of your lot, a class traitor and boyfriend of your boss's daughter. She's really rebelling against the old man isn't she?'

'Yes, that's Rainya for you. Very high spirited; attended all the best English schools you know.'

'Yeah, don't they all in Rupert land?'

'That a big chip on your shoulder, Eddie?'

'And the Ruperts have pips but doesn't make them any smarter, it's us NCOs who run the bloody show.'

'Well, you're getting officer style pay now, Eddie.' April took little sips of her tea.

'And yourself, Mrs April Showers, working for the money, or is it a hobby?'

'No Eddie, I have bills to pay and no family trust fund to live off, so I'm a working girl, a hard working girl in fact.'

Eddie raised his mug in a toast.

"The toiling classes sweat and strive,
While them above, us do drive.

So they may live in sweet existence.

Thus we survive on mere sustenance."

April clinked mugs. 'Which poet you quoting now Eddie.'

'No idea Showers, one of my Dad's sayings.'

'And where is he now?'

'On a high hill in Wales looking after sheep, haven't seen him, since my Mum's funeral.'

'Sorry to hear that.'

'Don't be, he's a right hard bastard, feel sorry for the sheep.'

Chapter 20: Kidnap

'Leave it out, Eddie. I do the "runnings" on this one, black on black thing, know what I mean?'

Eddie was agitated, 'I'll break the fucker's arms.'

'There you go again, all army-barmy attack shit.'

'C'mon Rumpunch what's the sit-rep then?'

'Wow, my man, what the fuck is sit-rep?'

'Yeah sorry mate, means situation report, we got loads of it in the Mob, SNAFU was my favourite.'

'OK, do tell me, Eddie.'

'Situation Normal All Fucked Up.'

'Ha, yeah my man I like that one, SNAFU, very good, kind of tells you about the Army, eh?'

Eddie nodded and stared out the window. Rumpunch drove a Jaguar today. He hung a left onto a housing estate west of Kilburn High Road and parked up.

'Our friend Marlon is kipping at his granny's place. She big-feather-in-hat-church-going Caribbean lady, probably praying for the little fucker's soul, so she's not the enemy, got it?'

Eddie nodded. 'Ok, I get it - not the enemy,' he said.

They climbed out of the Jag and walked up the steps of a long row of council houses set on top of underground parking, facing a narrow strip of green, an abandoned supermarket trolley with missing wheels leaning drunkenly against a lonely stunted tree. The row was a mirror image of four others facing the same green strip. Down the concrete walkway to number eighty-three, a "Jesus Loves You" sign above the frosted window on the front door.

'OK, Eddie stand to one side like an important white man but come in after me, OK?' Eddie rolled his eyes.

Rumpunch held the brass knocker thumb and index finger, a polite rat-a-tat-tat, waited and repeated. A hollow sounding 'Who dat?' came from inside.

Rum leaned in to the front door, 'Youth service Mrs Benson.'

The door pulled slightly ajar, a matronly black woman

peered out, gave Rum a hard suspicious stare but relaxed a tad when she spotted white Eddie.

'Marlon in no trouble, he bin behaving himself.' Rumpunch shoved the door open. Mrs Benson clattered against the wall. 'Lord me God,' she shrieked, 'Lord me God save me.'

Rumpunch dashed upstairs shouting to Eddie, 'Be nice to Mother Benson!'

Eddie approached her slowly hands out palms up, 'Sorry, Mrs Benson we just need a word with him.' Mrs Benson sat down on the stairs.

'I knew it, knew it, him up to no good again. I tell his mother you must beat him, beat him good when im bad, put fear of God to im.' Mrs Benson had a hanky out now blowing her nose. 'But im mother silly white girl and won't beat im, spoil im rotten, rotten I say.'

Rumpunch peered over the bannister top of stairs. 'It's OK, Mother Benson. Eddie come up.'

Mrs Benson peered up at Rum, 'Don't you touch my grandson, it's family must beat im.'

Rum gave her a big reassuring smile, 'We won't beat him, Grandma, OK.'

Mrs Benson sniffled then started praying. 'Lord Jesus, hear me I say you . . .'

Eddie walked into the bedroom. Rumpunch had his phone out taking a photo of Marlon sitting in front of a laptop, underpants down watching porn.

'Caught the little fucker on the job, whacking one out in his grandma's house. Just got no respect this generation.'

Marlon looked terrified, hugging his knees Y-fronts still around his ankles. Rumpunch indicated his Y-fronts. 'Pull em' up, got nuff pics of you to put out large, whacking off to gay porn.'

Eddie snorted. 'Really?'

'By time I go photoshop on it - who believe, when him deny dirty deed, eh.'

Marlon pulled his Y-fronts up. 'No man, that's not right, doing that.'

Eddie stood over Marlon, who cowered against the

radiator. 'Listen, you little fuck, robbing my mum's shit is not right.'

Marlon visibly paled; he tried defiance. 'You taking me to the Feds, you got no evidence.'

Rumpunch grabbed a parka out of a dirty white plywood cupboard. 'Put this on.'

Marlon shook his head. 'Can't make me.' Eddie lunged at him.

'You little fuck where's my medals? I'll fucking rip you...!' Rumpunch grabbed Eddie's shoulder.

'Leave this be man, I told you it black-on-black.' He slapped Marlon hard across the face. Marlon toppled back over the bed hitting his head against the windowsill.

'Eddie, hold his legs.' Rumpunch pulled a staple gun and a silk cord out of his pocket, leaned over, placed the silk cord along Marlon's chest and snapped staples over it lashing the cord to his chest. Marlon screamed.

'Put on the coat pussy, next one in your eye.' Marlon whimpered and put on the parka. Rumpunch led a barefoot Marlon by the cord down the stairs. At the bottom, he handed the cord to Eddie, fished in his pocket peeled off a fifty-pound note and handed to Mrs Benson.

'It's for your church grandma, put some flowers on the altar, light a candle and pray for him.'

'Oh Lord Jesus, hear me now - hear I say you . . .' Mrs Benson carried on mouthing her prayers silently.

Rumpunch nodded at Marlon shaking with fear, tears rolling down his cheeks. 'Come on.' He tugged the cord; Marlon stumbled after Rum out the door along the walkway down the dirty concrete grey steps to the car. Rumpunch ripped the parka off Marlon and popped open the boot. Marlon stood shivering in his Y-fronts sobbing. Estate youth gathered. Rumpunch turned to them.

'This here little fucker thought he could rob my friend, not a good idea.' He shoved him inside the boot. 'This what happen to dem who transgress.' He and Eddie got in the Jag and drove away.

Chapter 21: Lofty Meditates

Lofty lit the second candle and carefully placed it three foot at right angles from the first candle. With an effort he pulled his leg into some sort of Lotus position over what was left of his amputated limb. Lofty grunted and toppled over, he swore, pushed himself back onto his arse and shifted about for balance. He sat midway between the candles facing a six-foot blow-up Michelin man propped in the corner of his room. Lofty had bought it at a car-boot sale for seven pounds fifty. To him, it looked like a fat Japanese Buddhist monk.

He tried to banish the discomfort of the Lotus position, it was only a few months since his self-conversion to Bushido. According to a sensei on YouTube, a seventeen-year-old kid in Milwaukee, he was a Samurai gone Ronin, so he must find his centre first before seeking a new Daimyo to serve. When Eddie gave him the door job he took that as karma, his Daimyo. Lofty felt comfortable serving, it had been all he knew in the army, kept him together. Since medical discharge from the Mob he had plummeted, rudderless lost in confusion, depression, alcoholism, which in short order led to homelessness, drugs and the spiral down to prison. He had to battle to survive against other prisoners who thought nicking and hiding his leg was funny and it had shocked him deeply how low he'd sunk. After the lifer gave him the Bushido book Lofty had searched for a way back, to what he had been best at, a soldier with a mission. He had devoured books on Japanese culture and philosophy in the prison library.

He tried again to empty his mind but the meditation would not happen. He picked up a deck of cards and tried the card tricks he had learnt in prison but combat memories churned in his mind, memories of fire-fights, and after, nights waking sweating, panting, a warning too late. Fragments of a helicopter ride screaming in pain, a medic leaning over his face shouting hold on, injecting morphine and tightening the tourniquet. Night ambush dreams of Afghan, lying face up in the scrub staring at the stars. Bleeding out.

Lofty drifted off, finally sleep. But he hears screaming, sounds are distorted. He tries to get up and realises it is him screaming, he falls back down and the first taste of pain washes over him like raw chillies. He bites down on his lip, just a thin mewling escaping his throat. Hands grab him; he is dragged through the dust. He stares up at the sky, a lonely cloud hangs in the blue, dust devils swirl around him, he sees a trail of blood in the dirt and realises it's his blood. A man is talking to him but his hearing is blocked. It's a mate, he's sure, then he's thrown in to a ditch, a body collapses on top of him and again he thinks he is dying.

Lofty jerks awake and shakes himself, his leg aches, he readjusts his semi Lotus position and thinks about Eddie, a good leader who looked after them and stood up to glory-seeking Ruperts. Lofty decides he has his mission, serve and protect Eddie. He picked up the cards and flicked the top card over, Ace of Spades, shook his head, what the fuck does that mean?

He reached for his laptop and clicked on YouTube, the sensei kid from Milwaukee was in full flow, 'Picture the ocean at night under a full moon, now float on the surface and empty your mind . . . breathe out . . .' Lofty breathed in and then out through his nose, he went very still . . . As his mind emptied his last thoughts were, 'Fuck it's working this time.'

Chapter 22: Educating Marlon

The Jag parked in the old docks area east of Canning Town on the bank of the Thames. Rumpunch and Eddie sat on the boot smoking a draw, sharing a bottle of cider, watching evening shadows play on the river.

'So Eddie, tell me again, in the army, you tied dem up and chucked dem out the helicopter.'

'Yeah, we called it "chopper-one-out."' They both sniggered enjoying the play-acting.

Rumpunch pulled a toke. 'Does dumping the little fuck in the Thames count then?'

'Dunno, maybe if we shackle a weight to his neck, grab him by legs and arms, toss the fucker face first out in the river from top of the dock. Yeah that would count.' They could hear Marlon's muffled pleading and sobbing coming from the boot.

'How far you think we throw him?' Rumpunch banged on the boot, 'Shut your noise in there or I'll staple your mouth up . . . How about we wrap him in barb wire roll him down a hill, that count as chopper-one-out?' The noise lowered to snuffling mewling sobs. Rumpunch had to step away from the car, hand over mouth to cover his laughing. He and Eddie walked out of Marlon's hearing.

Rumpunch whispered, 'think he's frightened enough now?'

'Little fucker's shit himself Rumpunch. I can smell it.'

'Yeah, I laid tarpaulin down, knew he would. In our day we were tougher.'

'I was in the army then, mate, didn't see myself as a career crim.'

'You know Eddie, neither did I.' Rumpunch flicked the dog end out over the Thames. A tugboat sailed past, upriver, red and green lights reflecting on the water. 'Just kind of drifted into it, started earning decent wads and then, well not many other options for us was there. And I got baby mothers to take care of.'

'Kids, yeah, how many you got Rum?'

'One boy, two girls and the girls with the same mother.

Well she was the only one waiting for me when I got out of nick. But the boy, him going to Uni now, eh, think on that. You should have kids.'

'Huh. I was too busy surviving wars to think of having kids. Anyway, it takes two, right? I never really met a woman who interested me.'

Rumpunch took another joint out of his silver ciggie case, one-paper joints with a menthol tip, carefully rolled every morning. He offered one to Eddie who shook his head Rumpunch shrugged and lit up. 'Its I-tal Eddie, no tobacco, straight homegrown old fashioned weed, none of that skunk shit.' A police cruiser rushed upriver, blue lights flashing.

Eddie shouted, 'Plod up the river!' Rumpunch laughed. 'What we gonna do about the kid?' Eddie gestured at the Jag. 'I lost my appetite for revenge, he's cried me out.'

'Hop in the motor; I show you the "runnings wid de yoot".'

They walked to the Jag, Rumpunch banged on the boot and shouted, 'We have decided the river's a no-no, don't want to pollute.' More wailing from inside the boot 'And shut the fuck up.'

They drove north for twenty minutes towards Enfield. Another industrial estate, old engineering buildings, they rolled to a halt. Rumpunch unlocked big double steel roller doors, drove inside, opened the boot and dragged Marlon out. He was snotty faced, whimpering, fear filled pleading eyes.

Eddie looked around. A couple of Jags were jacked up and what looked like Bentleys with dustsheets over them.

Rumpunch pressed a red button by a car lift; it ascended revealing a metal-hatched floor, which rolled back, revealing a pit. 'In.' He waved at Marlon who started begging for his life again. 'Get the fuck in.' Rumpunch shoved him down the steps and rolled the metal shutter back over, pressed the red button, the lift came down on top of the hatch. He and Eddie walked back to the car.

'What's all this, you in the luxury car business?'

'Yeah, we export 'em. This is where they get a new identity; you know re-spray, number plates and chassis numbers.

The Iranians are mad for luxury Brit cars.'

'I thought there was an embargo.'

'Exactly why business is so good, bang the cars in a container and they find their way around the Middle East.'

Eddie shook his head in amazement. 'What the fuck were we fighting for?'

'Didn't I keep telling you Eddie, fool game?' They drove out, the metal roller doors slowly grated down behind them.

'I'll leave him in there overnight, give him time to reflect on his sins.'

'What about Granny, she gonna worry.'

'She'll spend the night praying for him. And tomorrow Marlon can confess his sins to me and go church with Granny and thank the fucking lord him still alive. Black on black ting, know what I mean.'

Chapter 23: Piccadilly Patrol

Scotch John hopped off the bus at Piccadilly. He was wearing grey slacks, blazer with Regimental badge and black polo neck. He'd had a haircut that morning the smell of the aftershave he'd plastered on his red shaved and scrubbed face, was killing flowers. It was 12.30 in the afternoon and Scotch John would not admit to himself but he had gone to all this trouble to impress the lads. He felt good for the first time in days and in that moment, the terrible anxieties that plagued him receded as he marched up Brewer Street, to the Glasshouse pub. He paused, checked his reflection in the glass door, smoothed his polo-neck jumper, put on a cheerful face and walked inside the dark wood, glass and more wood, interior of the Pub. He immediately felt at home, spotted his veteran mates at the back, all spruced up, sitting round the far table, ready for the Sam Smiths Piccadilly Patrol, a pub-crawl tradition amongst the lads when up in London.

They cheered as Scotch walked in, and broke into casual banter about being late for the Piccadilly parade. Three pints glistened on the table, dewdrops of condensation trickled down the sides of tall glasses. Scotch hurriedly knocked back his pint of lager top in one go, wiped his lips and with a big grin let out a long slow controlled belch.

'Nothing like the first one o' the day, come on my round, ye ken?'

'Fuck sake, Scotch, what's your hurry? The day is young,' replied Uncle Ben as he leant his crutch up against the mock fireplace mantle.

A middle-aged man, military haircut, regulation badge, blazer and tie, hesitantly walked up and stood over them. 'Excuse me lads is one of you called Uncle Ben?' They all looked up recognizing a toy soldier but fellow veteran instantly. A quick glance between them confirmed they had all marked this one, as head still back in the military. Scotch scowled irritated at the interruption to his drinking and by a veteran wearing a similar Blazer.

Aye up, lad, that'll be me,' said Uncle Ben, a kinder soul

than Scotch John, he smiled, 'what's up then?'

Blazer guy smiled back in relief. 'Me case worker like, said this is a regular meet up, I'm to ask for Uncle Ben. I just got a billet at Stoll barracks.'

'Oh aye, who's your caseworker son? Uncle Ben gave a knowing look.

'Amanda Foster at Stoll, Acton barracks office.' The Sir Edward Stoll foundation had been set up as a registered charity at the end of World War One, and still provided housing and support services to look after vulnerable veterans.

Uncle Ben rubbed his chin and spoke to the others, 'Aye she's ok, comes from an army family, means well.' He looked back at blazer guy, who was standing, uncomfortable, awkward. 'Aye, sit down then.' Uncle Ben waved him to a seat. 'Have a beer, what's your name son?' Blazer sat down, smiled at the lads, still awkward, but relieved.

'They call me Doughnut, me real name is Harry Dunking like. But its Dunking Doughnuts, you get it?' The lads all nodded, you get a nickname in the Military, it sticks for life.

'So Doughnut, what's you story then?' asked Uncle Ben.

'Green Jackets, lost me house, got divorced like.' The lads all chuckled in recognition, the same old story. You come out, experienced marital difficulties, split up and end up on your own.

'How did you get in Stoll son? Long waiting list,' inquired a sympathetic Uncle Ben.

'Visited me in jail, offered place to live like.'

Uncle Ben sighed. 'So what happened?'

'I was having a drink like, up in Leeds, that's where I'm from. Was minding me own self you know.

'No wife with you,' asked Uncle Ben

'Ah no. We had words like, you know. Anyhow there was all this smashing noise and shouting. It were me, smashing the bar up, didn't even know I was at it. Judge said £2,080 damages, basically pay up or go to prison.'

Chorus around the table, 'so you went inside.'

'Aye.'

'Many a Tom has been there, done that,' replied Uncle

Ben. 'Well Doughnut this fellow opposite is Larry the Claw.' Doughnut looked at Larry quizzically, Larry held up his right hand, three fingers and much of the hand missing, just his thumb and index finger left. Doughnut nodded recognising an IED wound.

'You can call me Claw, everyone else does now, better than my last moniker anyway.' He leaned, back to the wall, the shoulder of the injured hand twitched from time to time and he blinked every time. 'It were Ba Ba.'

Doughnut looked confused, Uncle Ben butted in, 'Larry the Lamb, thus Ba Ba, get it?'

The Claw ignoring another twitching spell, reached carefully for his pint, clutching it with his thumb and index finger, he concentrated on setting the grip and lifted the pint glass slowly to his lips and paused.

'Physio said to keep exercising the hand or lose functionality, so.' He saluted Doughnut with his pint and took a long drink.

'Next,' Uncle Ben indicated Scotch. 'This here is Scotch John.' Scotch growled a greeting and waved at the barman for refills. Doughnut nodded to the two of them, raised his glass in a mock toast and turned to Uncle Ben.

'How come people call you Uncle Ben?'

Scotch laughed as he spoke, 'Ach man, he was the regimental quartermaster and fucked up an order, five tons of rice were delivered to the cookhouse door, so it did.'

The Claw chimed, 'and in a hot dry land, it bloody well rained, the rice got wet, swelled up like, took all day to clear it. He got called Uncle Ben ever since.' Group chuckling broke out.

'That's funny, so what's your real name then?' asked Doughnut.

'Ben,' answered Uncle, straight-faced. They all laughed again.

'Let me buy the round lads,' Doughnut suggested, he got up happy to find some mates. They all gave him their orders and he went to the bar.

'Behave yourself, Scotch, the lads just out.' Uncle Ben tapped Scotch on the arm. 'He's a vet down on his luck, like the bloody rest of us.'

'We've all been there,' whispered Claw, leaning in over the table. Scotch looked to the bar. Doughnut was clutching pints in two hands.

'Ach, OK, suppose so, at least he's getting the bevies' in,' said Scotch.

Doughnut came back and carefully lowered the drinks on the table. The four of them leaned conspiratorially over their pints and sipped.

'We'll go up to the White Horse next, do a lovely chocolate stout so they do,' Scotch grinned as he worked out four in a round meant more drinks and began to warm to the comfort of an old military camaraderie piss up. He'd suffered another bad night, only getting to sleep in the early hours and waking with a befuddled head. But now the warm alcoholic fuzz of drink kicked in and turned back time, a soldier on the lash with his mates.

The tide of alcoholic happiness washed up against the shoreline of his unnamed anxieties. Since de-mob Scotch couldn't sleep more than two hours at a time, constantly waking, sweating, confused by bad dreams that faded like morning mist, as he struggled to remember. Scotch John, a product of Army drinking culture, took to self-medicating with drink to blot out the fears lurking below the surface.

Today, right now, he was back in the company of veteran soldiers who shared the scars of combat, never to be spoken but by a nod of the head and banter. Scotch felt the joy of belonging, one of the lads again, safe from the deep fears that alone at night threatened to overwhelm him.

A crutch slid along the fireplace plinth and landed on Uncle Ben's drinking arm, just as he raised his glass to his lips.

Scotch laughed. 'Your crutch wants to go walkies Uncle.' Uncle grabbed the crutch, propped it back up against the fireplace and resumed his drink without a pause.

'It's a well trained crutch that one, heard about Hathaway?'

'Isn't Hath RSM at Sandhurst now?' said Claw. Uncle took a careful sip and looked over the top of his pint at his drinking pals in turn, they all paused, waiting for a typical Uncle bit of barracks gossip.

'Yeah . . . he was Claw, But.' Uncle put his pint down slowly and puffed his chest out indicating the seriousness of the news. 'He topped himself. On the rife range. Blew his bloody head off in front of a bunch of young Ruperts!'

Claw hit the blink button and Doughnut, who like Uncle was a 22 year served Veteran cursed in a throaty whisper, 'Fuck's sake, what's going on Uncle? Is everybody fucking topping out.'

'Christ on a biscuit, that bit of news deserves a bloody drink, so it does.' Scotch John shivered as the anxieties bubbled back up and waved hurriedly at the barman, indicating another round. They sat in silence for a while, none of them sure what to say, until Uncle started telling them of banter with Hathaway at a reunion last year. It was about him being a strict by numbers NCO, climbing up the ladder to RSM by the book.

'You're a typical army barmy RSM at Sandhurst, I pity the young Ruperts.' Uncle paused, sipped his beer, 'I told him straight, we had a laugh about it, me and Hath. He tells me he loves driving around Sandhurst in an open top Landrover, yelling at all the Officer recruits.' His voice lowered, 'said he loves it, putting a rocket up their arses.' The awkward silence lingered and he felt the need to explain.

'You can't tell anymore lads, like swans it is, all smooth on the surface but lots of stuff going on out of sight.'

Scotch waved at the regular barman again, desperate for more medication but a tour group walked in, shaking the rain off plastic macs. The tour leader was lecturing about UK Pubs history and Sam Smiths traditional eighteenth century roots. The barman started pulling the pre-bought traditional ale for the tourists, who tasted the brew and pulled sour faces. They peered around the old Pub, looking at the veterans as if they were Disney characters.

'It's not good lads,' said Claw worriedly, 'we can't have the lads falling apart as soon as they hit Civvy Street, it's not right.'

'Topping out is a waste of drinking time,' replied Scotch, relieved that the barman had nodded back acknowledgement of the drinks order. The other three shook their heads at him.

China Lil walked in, dressed in pink pushing her pram, working the tourists for handouts. The tourists were mugs for London characters and handed over spare change, thinking it was part of a London tradition. China spotted the veterans and wobbled over on high heels, wearing a jet-black wig, which sat askew above a late night lipstick face. 'Ha, you drunk already, bad Scotch man and Uncle Ben, no walk anymore without crutch, ha?'

Uncle greeted her with a smile, 'Hello Lil. Want a quick drink?' A dog poked its head out of the pram, wearing a pink baby bonnet and yipped weakly. Lil slapped the dog, it shrunk back into the pram.

'No time Uncle, tourists only out till four o' clock,' Lil replied, turning her gaze on Scotch who had his head down ignoring her. 'Give money you owe me,' she stood hovering over him, he looked sheepishly at his drinking mates, the lads hooted.

The Claw blinking back tears of laughter, patted Scotch on the shoulder. 'Lil sorted you out did she?' He turned to Lil, 'still a regular then?'

Lil held her hand out to Scotch, 'who else going to do him, ha?' Scotch dug in his pockets and pulled out a few crumpled notes. Lil snatched the notes from his hand, 'Pay as you go from now on, ha.' Lil turned and pushed her pram past the staring tourists gaggle at the bar and out the entrance, the lads still in fits of giggles.

'So any of us thinking of topping ourselves?' A red-faced Scotch John tried to shift attention away from himself. They all shook their heads at him in pity.

Milos, the regular barman carried a tray of drinks to their table, 'Ya soldier boys, you patrolling the rest of our pubs today.' Uncle still laughing at Scotch pulled himself together.

'Yeah we'll be back here by dark, what's in the kitchen today?'

Milos finished placing the last drink, "Oh yeah for sure, English favourites, Shepherd's Pie and chips boys.'

'That will do us nicely.' Scotch rubbed his hands. 'OK

lets get the drinks down then.'

'Smashing bit of scram at the end of a session, nice one,' said Doughnut, nodding.

'How's it with Eddie's door mob Scotch?' the Claw said, addressing Scotch, thinking the humiliation had gone on long enough.

'Oh aye fair enough, you know Eddie runs a tight ship.' Scotch still looked slightly guilty but pleased to be off the hook.

'Here's to Eddie Conway,' Uncle lifted his drink, 'a fucking one-off, who seems to be employing most of the nutters in your mob Scotch.'

'He is that right enough,' Scotch nodded, 'and I'm on door duty twenty hundred hours at Midnight Oasis, but I'll need a bit of a kip before that, so we need to get a move on, so we do lads.' They all lifted their glasses in a toast to Eddie Conway.

'Guess who starts tonight with me?' Scotch licked his lips, looking around the table. The lads shrugged 'Fucking Lofty hop-along Lewis.'

Uncle looked surprised he hadn't heard that bit of gossip. 'Lofty Lewis, last I heard that mad fuck was banged up for terrorizing a hotel with a broken bottle,' said Uncle.

'Well he's on duty with me,' Scotch smiled at getting one over Uncle. 'Eddie got him a security work ticket somehow and I'm teaching him the ropes . . .' They all burst out laughing, the thought of Scotch John teaching anything to anybody.

'Learnt a few rope tricks from China Lil then, eh Scotch . . .' said Doughnut, breaking through the laughter.

Scotch was on the verge of slagging Doughnut but realized he was one of the lads now. They all burst out laughing again, well into a session of banter and booze; the warm feeling of alcohol-fuelled comradeship enveloped them. They were the boys in the mob again on the Piccadilly Patrol. Scotch downed his beer, another few pints he thought, will numb the bloody memories, so it will.

Chapter 24: Moonlighting

Scotch John turned up looking messy. Lofty rang Eddie. 'Sit-rep Boss; he's just showed at Midnight Oasis.'

'OK Lofty, what state is he in?'

Lofty looked at Scotch leaning crookedly against the wall in the doorway, head down mumbling.

'Well, it's Scotch init, so you never know. He, ah, bit messy Boss, been on a bender.'

'Ahh, bloody hell Lofty, Saturday nights are two-hander's dealing with a pissed-up crowd. You're in charge, what you think?'

'Well Boss, it's quiet now. How about I give him an hour, see if he can pull it together.'

'Lofty it's your shift but tell the fucker in no uncertain terms he's after getting a rocket from me, ok?'

'Roger that, and Boss permission to induct Scotch to Bushido?'

'Fuck me Lofty, what's this more "way of the wanker" shit?'

'We both know he's lost his way, like a Ronin?'

'Say again Lofty, what's a Ronin?'

'Jap samurai thing,' Lofty watched Scotch trying to straighten up, 'when a warrior loses his command structure, kind of goes to shit until he can find another mission or commander.'

'Lofty we both know mostly the only thing Scotch can find is a drink, he's got a talent in that department.'

'Right enough Boss but I wanna try, he's not been the same since we lost Dinger Bell.'

'OK Lofty, good luck with your Jap therapy on the ugly fucker.'

'Roger that Boss and listen in, my thanks for bringing me on the firm, beats being Ronin.'

'Yeah whatever - over and out.'

'Attention soldier!' Lofty said, putting the phone in his pocket as he took Scotch by the elbow, Scotch shook himself, hearing the old command and looked up trying to focus. Lofty slapped him across the face.

'Whaaaa' Scotch roared in pain, and recognised Lofty, 'the fuck . . .' Scotch tried to swing a punch, Lofty parried and slapped him again.

'You're in a right state Scotch, can't even defend you self.'

'Fuck you Lewis,' slurred Scotch, as he fell back in the doorway, Lofty followed him squeezing him up against the door jam.

'You're in a right fucking state.'

'Bollocks bastard Lewis . . . bollocks you . . .' Scotch tried to push him off.

'Listen up you bag of shite.' Lofty held Scotch's chin between thumb and index finger and glared in his face. Scotch tried to shake Lofty loose but couldn't coordinate and gave up, breathing heavy, glassy eyed.

'Whaaa . . . you . . . always hated me you did . . . bastard,' the words tumbled out in a throaty protest. Lofty shook his head releasing his grip on Scotch's chin and laughed.

'What you gonna do about it Scotch?'

'Wait till I'm sober, bastard, so you are,' Scotch rubbed his face as he mumbled in a rush between his fingers.

'Listen in Scotch you got an hour. March up the park, stick your fingers down your throat, chuck up, then get coffee down you.'

Scotch mumbled and nodded his head defeated, accepting the orders. Lofty slapped him again but not as hard, 'Ok, you good to go?'

'Aaghh . . . aye, I ah, am aye,' Scotch tried a defiant smile.

'OK you ugly fuck,' Lofty smiled back, 'I'm covering for you but need you back on duty, ASAP, got it?'

'Aye ok . . . Will do.' Scotch peered with relief through red-rimmed eyes and took deep breaths. He lurched out of the doorway, paused to straighten himself, 'Owe you one Lofty, so I do,' and marched clockwork soldier style to do his duty in Soho square park.

Lofty watched him wobble up the street, thinking he

either means a thumping or he'll buy me a beer, you never know
with Scotch.

Chapter 25: House of Fitz

Eddie put the phone down and stared at his reflection in the train window for a long time. Are all my old-comrades fucked up? He laughed, got up, stood next to the train door. Of course, they are. Who am I kidding, we're all fucked up, that's the starting point for recovery innit Dr twinkle-boots Vaughan?

The Docklands Light Railway train glided over the rooftops of former east-end docklands. Regeneration they called it, new housing, looked like Tonka Town in primary colours bathed in orange streetlights. The Isle of Dogs, an area stuffed down a southern loop of the Thames with the river on three sides, felt like an island.

Eddie got off at Mudchute Station, a lonely little Lego place next to an inner city farm under the long shadows of tall financial skyscrapers. A big illuminated sign asked people not to chase the sheep during lambing, "Stress may cause miscarriage". Me old man would be at home here then, he chuckled. Mudchute didn't have any steps. He felt cheated, the exit streetlight flickered, he walked around the farm fence to a new-build hipster toy-town estate. He pressed for number nineteen at the redbrick townhouse type block, was buzzed in, up a flight of stairs, Rainya holding an open door.

'Hello, you must be Eddie.'.

'Yeah, that's me love,' Bingo, bulls-eye thought Eddie.

'This Fitz's place then?'

'I'm his partner Rainya.'

Eddie smiled at her thinking, partner? So that's what they call it now. He was ushered into an open-plan kitchen diner come office. Fitz was sitting headphones on, typing on a laptop and chatting on the phone sounding very important, organising the struggle.

'Good of you to come to us Eddie,' said Rainya, 'Fitz is so busy with the evictions and dealing with the councils, he hasn't had a break all day. Coffee or tea?'

"Yeah, nice cup of tea please, one sugar.'

Rainya switched the kettle on, Eddie took in the space,

wasn't that big, obviously not a squat. Posters on the walls, decent IKEA type furniture, not what he expected, almost domestic.

'So you part of the movement then love?'

'Yes, we work together, it's really, really important to raise the housing issues, it strikes at the heart of the system, don't you think?'

'Ah, yeah I think.' Talks like her Dad he thought and took the mug of tea from her hand. 'Thanks.'

'We're hoping to have a proper office soon and get some staff to take on the workload,' Rainya looked at Fitz, 'He can't keep working like this you know.'

'Yeah I know, err, Rainya, you do your bit then?'

Rainya got serious, 'Yes, I'm changing my degree to law you see. Fitz says we have to fight them with their own tools as well as organise on the streets. I want to be an advocate.' Her eyes lit up with zeal. Eddie decided this girl was on a "save the masses" mission and having a romantic Bonny and Clyde thing with alternative Rupert, Fitz.

'Sorry, Tower Hamlets occupation people threatened with bailiffs again,' said Fitz as he removed his headphones, reaching out a hand to Eddie. They shook. 'Rainya we need people up there for a leafleting blitz next weekend.' Rainya zoomed in total attention on Fitz, nodding enthusiastically as he rolled off a series of organisational duties while sipping his tea.

Ruperts taking on their own system, how long will that last Eddie thought cynically. Her Dad should be pleased she's not squatting or dropping out. Let the passion run its course, anyway what's the harm, they're trying to help people, more than her up his own arse Dad's doing.

The two of them finally turned to him after their little rev-up of direct action passion.

'So Eddie, your estate?'

Eddie reeled off the diverse collection of people living on the estate and the fact that hardly anyone talked to each other, not like his childhood days when most people knew each other. The Irish and the West Indians had got along, some English were racist but they soon learned not to bother the Blacks. But the newcomers seemed frightened of their own shadow. Ruled by fear and intimidation. Fitz and Rainya come up with a load of bollocks about street art as a first step in changing perceptions. Lots of highfaluting called "externalising through art in shared spaces".

Never had that in the barracks, sounded hippy shit to Eddie but he played along. Fitz gushed about this Brazilian artist in town, who wanted to do some public places, he was after big walls. Eddie told them he had plenty of big walls with rubbish graffiti all over them. He accepted another cuppa, while Fitz made roll-ups and got all excited ranting about the struggle.

Eddie zoned out of the buzz-chat on crimes of the ruling classes and watched them both. Fitz was all nervous energy bubbling with passion, nicotine-stained fingers always on the go, rolling one ciggie after another or just twitching, pulling at hair, earlobes, adjusting the horn-rimmed specs, which conveyed a Trotskyite image. Maybe that was the idea.

Rainya got a ciggie going but she was just blowing smoke, defiantly off the family leash. She kept flipping her long dark hair over her shoulders gazing at Fitz through rose-tinted glasses, lapping him up, intoxicated on dollops of class crusade passion. The struggle seemed a religion to Fitz and Rainya had caught the bug. In the old days the family would have bunged him in a monastery.

Eddie came back online. Fitz had asked him a question something about the army.

'Say again mate?'

'The army Eddie, how long you been out now?

'A while mate.' Eddie wondered how did he know that, must be gossip flying around already, probably Jassi, he'd let it slip at the party.

'So you decided not to fight their imperialist wars for them?'

'Yeah, something like that, old men start wars, young men die in them.'

Rainya and Fitz nodded in sympathy.

'You'd be really useful on our demos Eddie. Help organise our stewards,' Fitz beamed at Eddie. Oh yeah thought Eddie, get the lower orders do all your heavy lifting, bloody

Ruperts all the same everywhere, they just assume that us idiots need them to lead us.

Eddie checked his wristwatch. 'That the time? Look, I got to go to work.'

'Oh, what do you do Eddie?' Rainya even sounded interested. Oh yeah, I work for your Dad spying on you, he thought.

'Nightclub work,' Eddie said instead. 'I run a couple of doors. Anyway got to dash for cash.'

'See you at your Estate,' Fitz got up to shake his hand in a very formal manner, 'I'll bell you mate.'

Blimey, a Rupert talking like a ranker. Rainya gave him a big squeeze hug. Bloody hell mused Eddie, gone well so far.

Chapter 26: April Rings

Eddie's phone rang. He tugged it out of his pocket as he marched through Soho, dodging through the annoying meandering crowds. The early rush of punters flooded the streets, clumping in hungry bunches searching for good food venues before hitting the good time bars.

'Hello, Eddie here.'

'Good evening Eddie.' April's posh purring earthy tones filled his mind with images of feline-sharp-claw sexuality.

'Yeah Showers, you OK?'

'Oh yes Eddie, Splendid, and yourself, did you find our little Miss Rebellion?'

'Sure, you want the address? I'm just on my way to sort a little bit of business at one of the clubs.'

'No Eddie why don't you come over later, report in person and I'll decide if you have been a good boy?'

'Ha, been a long time since I was a good boy.'

'Come to The Waldorf, the Astor Suite, ring when you're on your way.'

'Err, Waldorf, that on the Aldwych, off the Strand?'

'That's the one Eddie, you're a regular GPS aren't you.'

'Yeah Showers, I like to know where I'm landing.'

'I'm sure you do.'

April rang off with a throaty chuckle, leaving Eddie with the impression of claws being sheathed reluctantly. He stuffed the phone away, turned off Compton Street into Greek Street. There were roadwork signs up, blocking cars from driving through.

Early night Saturday crowds spilt onto the street revelling in the extra space. Outside the Moonlight Oasis, Lofty and Scotch John wearing the black bomber uniform of downtown doormen were checking punters for knives and drugs at the door.

'How's it going guys?' When you spoke to Lofty - usually you had to wait while he chewed it over. Unlike Scotch, who responded straight off, like he had worked everything out.

But of course you knew Scotch was full of shit. Lofty turned to face Eddie, paused and gave a little bow.

'Konnichiwa Oyadama.'

Scotch John danced his bushy eyebrows. 'He's trying to teach me Jappo, Eddie.'

'You still able to learn then Scotch?'

'I been learning card tricks,' said Lofty and produced a deck of cards. 'Take a card Eddie.' Eddie took one.

'OK, memorise it and put it back,' Lofty shuffled the cards. Scotch was watching intently. Lofty turned the top card over, 'Is that the one?'

'No,' replied Eddie.

'Ha, ya fucked it up, knew it.' Scotch laughed.

Lofty grinned back at the two of them. 'OK Scotch, reach around me and pull the card out of my back pocket.' Scotch did so and showed the card to Eddie.

'Jesus Lofty, that's my card, how you do it?'

'Zen and the art of magic Boss, sharpens the focus.' Scotch looked incredulous.

'I never saw his hand go behind his back, do it again Lofty?'

'Hold up with the magic circle, Scotch,' Eddie butted in, 'I want a word with you.' Eddie beckoned Scotch to the empty doorway next to the Club. 'So what the fuck happened to you? If it wasn't for Lofty this job was down the river for all of us.' Scotch fidgeted adjusting his collar.

'Ah well, err Eddie, it was uh like this, I went to see Uncle Ben, ya ken?'

'Uncle Ben, didn't he get slung out for selling gear out the Quartermaster's back door?'

'No, no, his years came up. Retirement. They never nailed him on that, ya ken. Anyway, he runs this house down Kings Cross and we did the Sam Smiths and got into a wee bottle at his gaff, so we did, chatting to the girls, ya know, in between punters like. Ah one thing led to another, ach Eddie, I was too pissed.'

'Fucking hold up Scotch, you're out of order and you know it, snarled' Eddie, and pulled an envelope out of his breast pocket, handed it to Scotch. 'Open it and read Scotch.' Scotch John angled the letter to the streetlight.

'Och Eddie man, this is a formal warning.'

'Yeah, wrote it myself.'

'Don't ya supposed to get a verbal or something first like?' Scotch said, looking up hopefully.

'Scotch I been verbal'ing you and you ain't listening. You putting this kushty little business in danger here and that means the rest of the lads being out of pocket.'

'Ach man, away with you.'

'No, it's away with you if you fuck up one more time. You were solid back in the mob, fucking good trooper, dependable but now you gone to shit Scotch.'

There was a lull at the club door. Lofty stepped over to them. Eddie was glaring full on in Scotch's face trying to get a grip on his anger. Scotch uncomfortable at the dressing down was avoiding eye contact.

'Can I make a suggestion Eddie?'

'What the fuck Lofty, yeah what?' Eddie still full on in Scotch John's face.

'I'll go two-hander's with Scotch rest of the month, you'll always have cover.' Eddie broke contact with Scotch shook his head at Lofty.

'I can't ask Jabba for more bunce; there's firms out there who'll undercut what we're getting now!'

'Pardon me Boss, same price, call it work experience, call it learning on the job, what you think?' Eddie rubbed his jaw, thinking it through.

'OK, I'll talk to Jabba, two for one deal.' Eddie nodded at the club entrance to Scotch who took up his post. 'Why Lofty, why the fuck you taking a hit?'

'Like you said the other night boss, no one else will, we're, us, Scotch, all military surplus, remember Jebal Whalfi.'

Eddie nodded remembering the engagement. Scotch had been cool when first contact had happened; caught in a deadly ambush; he'd been lead man on the patrol probably saved many of them but not Dinger Bell, his best oppo.

'Ah fuck it, see how we go eh Lofty but you let me know

if he starts dossing off.'

'Arigatou gozaimasu, Eddie.'

'Whatever the fuck that means, Lofty.' Eddie walked up to Scotch, thinking Lofty was going samurai and Scotch going south of reliable.

'Get a fucking grip Scotch, OK?' he whispered in Scotch's ear. Scotch snapped a salute as Eddie went into the club to find Jabba.

Lofty stood next to Scotch staring out at the crowd, micro-skirt girls tottering alongside bearded hipster guys, playing it casual under the piss orange glare of street lights.

'I dinna ken the matter with me,' Scotch John spoke in a low voice out of the corner of his mouth, 'I keep trying to fuck meself up, so I do, eh Lofty.'

'I been there Scotch, we Ronin got to find our way back from lost, start with doing little things as well as we can, OK.'

A giggling flock rolled up, faces flush with night on the town anticipation. Lofty leant forward. 'Evening Ladies, Welcome to Midnight Oasis, may we just check your bags . . .'

Chapter 27: The Waldorf

Funnily enough, Jabba had been impressed, getting a two for one deal on the door. Eddie had blagged the on-the-job orientation line. He'd refused the offer of doing shots but listened to Jabba wax on about his plan for a fine-dining gaff in the city area, uniformed doormen, proper Italian waiters, top young chef, blah, blah, moving up into Toff-land, feeding the Ruperts. He got away after a couple of hours, checked on Lofty and Scotch at the door, they were doing an over the top polite greeting style with punters, Scotch looked like he'd pulled at least one bootstrap up.

Lofty asked Eddie if they could wear Tweed jackets instead of black bombers. 'Be more friendly and very classy Eddie, like a signature eh.'

Eddie thought he was joking and walked off laughing and texted April, "On My Way" and headed through Covent Garden. The bar flies flowed out on the cobbles, crowds well into jolly up time now. Text alert. "I'll be ready for you." Which, could mean a whole bundle of things.

Eddie hurried trying to shake off unnamed anxieties, why was he rushing, what's the urgency, he forced himself to walk slow, saunter. It was hard, he was so used to quick marching everywhere, keeping thoughts at bay. He concentrated on slowing down, being calm, afraid he was slipping into the dark well. Think of a happy place, how? He caught his reflection in a street window, big guy, jean jacket, hair falling over his ears, must get a haircut. No uniform he thought, who the hell am I? Just another soul lost in the crowd, I'm a bloody Civvy now. The refection shimmered away in the passing lights of traffic. At the next window he stopped, ignoring passers who stepped around him and studied his reflection, trying to pin down an idea of self. His image stared back, and raised an eyebrow. A door opened, his image swung away, a parting stranger. Eddie shrugged his shoulder. What the fuck Dr Vaughan all this introspection crap is confusing the hell out of me. He turned and stepped into a quick march.

He passed the Theatres on the Strand, different buzz

here, well-heeled old style English theatre supper crowd. He paused in the Waldorf atrium looking up at the high glass ceiling. A piano player was knocking out safe jazz. In the lift, a sign had the Astor suite on the top floor. A couple, dinner suit and gown strolled in, braying loudly with moneyed confidence, they got out on the top floor. Eddie stalked behind them, the woman cast nervous glances over her shoulder. Dinner suite fumbled with his key card. Eddie prowled past whistling the regimental marching tune, "Ride of the Valkyries". At the end of corridor, a big door, Astor Suite in gold lettering. Eddie knocked to the Valkyries rhythm, da da da, durum dum.

A long pause before the door swung slowly open, low-mood lights, strong whiff of expensive perfume. April, in a black leather bolero jacket, tight leather skirt and thigh high boots, looking like a female cavalier or someone in Panto.

'Hello, Eddie.'

April thrust a glass of bubbly at him. Eddie took it from her and padded in. Big couch leather armchairs, low table, bucket of Champers next to a make-up mirror, face up.

'Let me take your coat Eddie. Sit down, relax.' Her voice was purring an octave lower than usual. Eddie put the glass on the table, noting the coke line smears on the mirror. April came behind him and rolled his coat slowly of his shoulders. She sashayed across the room but just threw the coat on the floor; turned and posed in the bay window area, bent her knee, tilted her hips and pouted, thick red lipstick Marilyn Monroe style. Eddie flashed on a hangar party memory. Behind her the red glow of crane lights floated above the rooftops of London, a cinematic scene, as if set up, staged. Eddie felt off balance and decided to inspect the suite. He prowled the sitting room area tugging the heavy drape curtains, running his finger along the top of mahogany furniture checking for dust and moving the expensively ornate chair that blocked a straight line from window to door. April lifted her glass to her lips and sipped very slowly watching how he rolled on his feet, a growling predator prowling a cage, dangerous to be provoked and shivered in anticipation of doing just that.

Eddie padded up the four steps through the archway to

the purple four-poster bed area, he picked up the chocolate on the pillow, popped it into his mouth and finished his inspection, logging the topography of the open plan rooms. He walked back to April, she was still posing but amused, the ready to rumble signs coming over loud and clear. It was like being at officers mess Ruperts' functions, and he not sure of the form, an etiquette hidden from him.

'OK, now you know the lay of the land, did you think it was an ambush?' April knocked back her bubbly and glided over to Eddie.

'Am I in bandit country, Showers?'

'Silly,' she replied, tapping him on the nose with a long red fingernail, 'Freshen it up will you.' Casually she handed her empty glass to Eddie, he hauled the champers out of the ice bucket, bottle dripping. April sat down and cut lines of coke, a sliver snorting tube appeared in her hand. She did one up each nose, throwing her head back with a sigh of satisfaction. Cut another couple of lines, winked at Eddie and reached behind her for a leather notebook, crossed her stocking and booted legs, perched the notebook on her knee.

'So give me your report Eddie, let's see if you've been a good boy.'

'Huh?' Eddie looked cautiously at April and sat down, 'you planning on having a party Showers?'

'Business first, party later . . .' April purred, low tones.

'If you're a good boy.'

Chapter 28: Call for Sir Omar

Just off the Strand in a small intimate office block, with paranoid tight security on the fourth floor, Sir Omar was sweating in his large leather chair; hunched over his large oak office desk, phone to his ear.

'Of course, they are safe, perfectly in a safe place. No need to be worried. On the twenty-third, yes, of course, I'll have a car to meet you . . . same hotel . . . What sorry, which club?. . Yes, I'll book a table.'

Sir Omar switched the phone off dabbed his face with a handkerchief and locked the phone back in his top drawer.

Chapter 29: Morning Blues

'Where the fuck am I?' Eddie surfaced, disoriented. The phone was ringing. He slapped his own face, trying to wake up, croaking, 'Fuck me, I'm feeling rough.' Saying the words made him feel better, he laughed in a pitying tone and tried to find the phone, his pants were on the floor, he made a couple of grabs before he snagged them and fished the phone out. The screen said Rumpunch - he clicked on.

'Eddie listen, the little fucker . . .' Long beep tone then nothing, battery dead. Eddie cursed and flopped out of bed and threw a towel around his waist. He was home, morning time. He splashed cold water on his face, went back to the bedroom picked up the phone and plugged in the charger. Eddie sat massaging his temples. I'm totally fucked he thought, what a night. April had written down his report uncrossed her legs and told Eddie to have a snort; he'd earned a bonus.

He went into the kitchen, opened the fridge. It'll have to be a WIF "What's in Fridge" meal, he thought, He cracked three eggs in a bowl and whipped them with butter, milk and black pepper. Last night he had resolved that whatever happened he wasn't getting into any sex with April. That lasted as long as the first snort, then April lit a joint. Leaned into him blowing smoke in his mouth. Fuck, game over. Well, it had been a while.

Eddie chopped, sprouts, a red onion, celery and tomato, threw them in the frying pan with a glob of crunchy peanut butter, rapeseed oil, easy garlic and chillies. When the onions started frying he sprinkled balsamic vinegar on top, it swirled around the pan like black ink. The onions and celery sizzled, the rest joined in and the balsamic smoked its pungent smell, he started salivating.

They had fucked their way around the ornate furniture in the glow of the red crane lights, took a break for Prosecco and more coke, then started again moving from the couch to the four-poster, April calling him dirty names.

'You're a dirty oik bastard, can't come till I say, ha, ha, ha.' She'd clasped her legs around him and ridden him moon-walking backwards to the four-poster, April shouting 'Giddyup!' laughing like a maniac. They got into it in a big way then, April slapped him in the face swearing he was a rough bastard, crying 'I've been a naughty bitch spank my arse you fucker.'

'Christ almighty,' he muttered, shaking his head in disbelief while he poured the egg mixture into the pan, turning the heat up. Soon the mixture solidified, he cut slices of Feta cheese and placed them on top. Eddie was so gone on the coke he'd spanked her arse red. What was it with these Rupert women? Posh Totty and rough sex equals banging the lower ranks. Hell, he'd even heard that Scotch John was a regular bit of rough for officer's wives when hubbies were away on tour.

Eddie stuck the frying pan under the grill and ground some coffee beans, clicked the kettle on and checked the omelette. Looking good, the feta cheese bubbling. He poured boiling water on the ground coffee the smell teased his senses. A night of coke-fuelled down dirty sex. No chat, just get-the-fuck at it. In the early hours, April had passed out, too much champers, coke and weed. He pulled the pan out flipped the omelette, gave it a quick blast on full gas and slid it on a plate, grabbed a bottle of HP sauce, squirted a figure eight infinity on the omelette and started spooning lumps into his mouth. Always have a spoon in the field, he chewed and swallowed furiously.

He'd put her in the recovery position on the four-poster, thrown the duvet over her and had a hot shower. Eddie didn't want to wake up with her and try making conversation, way out of his depth. Intimacy frightened him, and she was to smart upper class, anyway he felt like a male escort. In the bathroom he found men's toiletries, a bottle of "Paco Rabanne Invictus" men's spray. He shaved, tried the Pacco, smelt good. So who else uses this little fuck pad? Eddie walked to the bed, she was fast-a-kip like an innocent little angel. He felt an urge to give her a cuddle, reached out but became self conscious, thinking "what the fuck" walked back to the bathroom and pocketed the Pacco. He caught the No 24 night bus home with a bunch of wasted clubbers.

Eddie gulped the pungent coffee. His head cleared, a parting of clouds on a stormy day. Fuck that tasted good and tried sorting out where things lay scattered in his life. He had a good thing going at the Moonlight, chances for more club work, plenty of ex-Mob lads wanting to earn some cash. Maybe Lofty could be promoted to 2.i.C (Second in Command), now he's in this Samurai mode thing. The Sir Omar gig was paying well; could be more wedge down the line. Was he into S&M sex nights now? Well, let's just go with the flow. The phone rang in the bedroom. Fuck, Rum ringing back.

'Hey Rum, you OK?'

'Sound rough my friend.'

'Yeah, had a session with a Sloane Ranger.'

'Well while you been riding four-by-four I been taking the young but much wiser Marlon home so he go church with Grandma and pray for his deliverance.'

'How was the little fucker?'

'Chastised. He's gonna report to me seven p.m. every night for a while.'

'Why?'

'Because he's too scared not to and I want to keep him fearful, do him good! Him in confessional mood this morning when he realise he gonna live.'

'Christ you a priest now?'

'That supposed to be funny Eddie? No, that not funny. Listen up, he was set on the deed by your good friend and neighbour mister fucking Jokevic.'

'Really that toe-rag thinks he can fuck with me does he?'

'Not think it Eddie, he doing it. What you gonna do?'

'I'll sit on it a while Rum, needs some strategic thinking and my brain is AWOL right now.'

'That Army for stupid, is it?'

'Means absent without official leave, Rum.'

'Is what I was saying, stupid. So he got your medals.'

'Fuck, he has.'

'Yo, laters - swing low sweet chariot.'

'Sure, copy that.' Eddie put the phone down. Well a few more complications; life getting hectic.

Chapter 30: A Ship Sails In

The huge ship slowed, entering the dock stacked high with containers bound for UK destinations. Seemed like the front came to a rest while the rear was still sidling up. Ninety percent of all the UK's goods come in from the sea.

The captain yawned. It had been a long and nervous voyage; his four passengers frightened the wits out of him, merciless men who threatened him and his family. He shivered and prayed to Allah that they would be gone by morning.

Deep in the ship's stack of sealed containers, four men were checking their weapons and packing bags. The leader Farouk sat on a bunk bed, smiling at his three companions. They had been with him many years, through the best years of Saddam's rule, he sighed, and the worst. When the American coalition had swept Saddam's army aside, Farouk had taken his elite strike force deep into the desert and ruthlessly taken over the small town that hid a huge underground store of Saddam's military treasures and he became rich on the spoils of post-Saddam Iraq.

Farouk stood up from the bunk. 'We leave at four a.m. Omar will have a car waiting for us at the end of the dock, best to sleep.' He stuffed some clothes from his bunk into a bag. 'And thank Allah we have arrived.'

Salim, thin lean and intense, was admiring the brand new handgun he held. 'Hey Farouk, we go clubbing tomorrow night yes? I want to get my hands on blonde English pussy, ha'.

Farouk shook his head and replied in a tired tone, 'don't worry Salim, plenty pussy for you in this town.'

Salim grinned like a hungry wolf, fantasizing about prey. He reached for his prick but dropped his handgun, the gun went off, the bullet zinged around the container ricocheting off the walls, the men diving under the bunks, hands over their heads.

Farouk swore at Salim in Egyptian, 'ya aars [*You wanker*], how many times? Concentrate on your weapon, not your prick!'

Salim picked up the pistol grinning. 'My prick is my

123

weapon.'

The other two climbed to their feet shaking their heads muttering "kos omak" [*mother-fucker*].

Salim pointed the gun at them 'Hey that was a dirty lie.'

Farouk in frustration threw his bag at Salim, 'Stop it you madman.' The bag bounced off Salim.

'Why?' Answered Salim.

Farouk put his hand over his face and balled his fists. 'Salim, we don't shoot our own people. How many times?' He turned away furious, thinking why he'd ended up with the psycho idiot of the family? The other two carefully hid their grins at another episode of the family feud between Farouk and his deranged nephew.

The car pulled up at the Waldorf. The doorman opened the car door and half bowed to Sir Omar, who got out, followed by four men, nervously chattering politely, 'How was the journey? You must be tired? Why don't you get some sleep?'

They trooped through the Waldorf lobby; Farouk striding purposefully while Salim and the other two sauntered behind, leering at the guests. The lift to the top floor was in strained silence, but once they entered the suite Farouk demanded his package. Sir Omar stood nervously fiddling with his hands, April stood behind him.

'Show me my package,' ordered Farouk. Salim grinned maliciously at April, the other two sat and lit cigarettes. Sir Omar stuttered, not able to get his words out, in the end, he settled for passing the buck.

'Ah, Miss Bentley-Forbes will eh ah . . . apprise you of the situation.' April gave Sir Omar a dirty look, turned to face Farouk and composed herself.

'Well sir, your diamonds are in the safe possession of Sir Omar's daughter and we are presently taking steps to retrieve them.'

'Your bitch took them?' Salim jumped up glaring at Sir Omar. 'A woman has our diamonds and this here,' he walked to April and prodded her like meat, 'is retrieving them? Do women do all your work, you pussy?' He pulled out his automatic.

'Shoot him now - then fuck this bitch.'

Farouk put a hand out pushing the pistol away. 'Shut up you stupid fuck.' The other two sniggered behind their hands. Farouk glared at Omar 'O.K, tell me Omar, what mess is this?'

Omar stuttering nervously explained his daughter had run off with an Englishman do-gooder with the diamonds. 'She thought you were dead but I have traced her, we know where she is.'

'Dead! Do I look dead?' Farouk roared at him.

'This man this aars,' Salim laughed, 'lets women run his life. He is not worthy, let me kill him slowly Farouk.' Farouk turned and slapped Salim across the face, his temper boiling over . . .

'Stupid, he handles our money.' He turned to April bubbling over with menace. 'So bitch, give me the address.' April took a frightened step back, trying to play it cool, these guys were animals off the leash.

'Gentlemen, in this country different rules apply . . .'

'Please don't hurt my daughter,' Omar butted in, tears rolling down his cheek. 'She is young and foolish. I know in this country the women have too much freedom.'

Salim got up, put his hands in Omar's face and pushed him sprawling to the floor, April winced. Farouk nodded.

Sir Omar tried to retrieve his dignity, rolled to his knees and pushed himself back up on his feet. He stood there on unsteady legs, face flushed, shaking with nerves.

'You're surrounded by degenerate femdoms, what happens?' Farouk said, putting his hands on Sir Omar's shoulders. 'Disaster.' Sir Omar mustered a last shred of dignity straightening his old school tie.

'Why do you allow your servants to behave in this manner?' Farouk brushed lint off Omar's shoulders. 'How long we do business ah? You make much money from merchandise we send you, but you forget where you from, I think. We are here to stay my friend,' he turned his head to sneer at April, 'and we bring our rules with us.' He turned back to Sir Omar, patted him, like he owned him, on his cheek.

Chapter 31: Lofty and Scotch

Lofty carried the tray over to Scotch John and squeezed into the window seat of the Italian coffee house on Greek Street, Soho. Lofty stirred his green tea, Scotch sniffed. 'What the fuck you drinking, seaweed?'

'Green tea Scotch how's your cappuccino?'

'Aye, lovely frothy with a wee sprinkle of choc on top, like a pudding so it is.'

They sipped and stared out the window at the late afternoon street bustle. Gay men on Old Compton Street greeting each other, in the weak sunshine, with big air kisses, hugs and animated chatting. Scotch nodded at a couple walking by hand in hand. He rolled his eyes. 'Why come here, we could go the boozer up the street?'

'That's your problem Scotch, the boozer.'

'Aye maybe but . . .' Scotch eyebrows did a foxtrot. He blew froth off his lip.

'You were a warrior Scotch, what happened? Lost your purpose in life?'

Scotch gave it some thought before he spoke. 'I left purpose when I demobbed out, now I manage a door, a wee fucking door so it is, aye!'

'You got to manage yourself, find your discipline again.'

'Aye, away with this Samurai shit laddie.'

'So, what you gonna do?' Lofty searched for patience. 'Drink yourself dead, is that it?'

'Aye, why not, fuck-all for us squaddies, look out there.' Scotch waved his hand, they gazed out the window, the corner of Old Compton and Greek Street was buzzing. 'Do I fit in that?'

'Rainbow City Scotch that's Civvy life, we all fit in somewhere.' Lofty cradled the tea in both hands. 'Basically, we protect this bit of the street, don't we?'

'Fuck away with you,' Scotch barked, 'I'm not looking after the shirt lifters.'

Lofty sighed, gathering his thoughts. 'That's what we're trained for, serve and protect.' Lofty pointed out the window,

'They aren't soldiers, we're the odd ones out here, a little bit of khaki in the rainbow.'

'Oh aye? Well it all sounds yellow brick road shit to me Lofty.'

'So, when you knock off, what you do, drink?'

'Aye, drink till I can sleep so I do, isn't that what we all doing?' Scotch stared, challenging Lofty

'OK, yes, I used to. But Scotch pull yourself together, man up, we're in Eddie's unit again. Way of the Warrior.'

'Aye, "way of the wankers" more like it.'

'Eddie already got that one Scotch.'

'Did he, ach I'll think of one so I will,' Scotch paused deep in thought. 'We were bloody good out there, but I dunno.' He stared at Lofty, 'I've used up all my bottle, dunno if I got any left, you know what I mean Lofty.'

'Come for a route march tomorrow.' Lofty suggested, sipping his tea,

'Ya fucking what laddie?'

Lofty smiled. 'See what you got left in the locker?'

'A three-legged race then is it,' barked Scotch.

'Just a march Scotch, just a simple route march, easy-peasy.'

Scotch cursed, thinking Lofty had trapped him with his challenge. 'This "way of the wasted" then?' Scotch's eyebrows did a tango.

'That all you can come up with, wasted?' Lofty shook his head. 'Well, it fits you right about now,' he smiled at Scotch, 'so it does.'

'Ah fuck away with you.'

Chapter 32: Payoff

'Hello Eddie, so good to see you again.' April smirked, cool as a cucumber in a little black dress and bolero jacket.

Eddie stared back wondering was that an invitational smirk, or just a dirty look. 'Saving me for a rainy day Showers?'

April smiled this time, but in a slightly disappointing way, indicating Eddie wasn't playing the game. She led the way, click-clacking high heels, swaying hips, like a boat in an ocean swell, through the Waldorf lobby.

Eddie wondered what was up now. Sir Omar had rung Eddie himself, my, my getting his hands dirty. "I'll have Miss Bentley-Forbes meet you at five p.m. in the Waldorf lobby. That's on the Strand old chap, we have a permanent suite there, don't you know."

'I know.' Eddie had confirmed, thinking Sir Omar sure does love the trappings of wealth and power.

Eddie and April stood in the crowded lift; April coolly stared at the ceiling, ignoring people getting in and out, on its way to the top.

Eddie was trying to work out the rules of engagement between him and April. Fuck the Ruperts, he thought; they never explain the rules of their games to outsiders.

Classical piano music twinkled in the background, just the two of them left in the lift now. April sniffed, 'Is that Paco Rabanne you have on?'

'Yeah Invictus, picked it up the other night, you like it?'

April smiled obviously enjoying the game. 'Did you now. Well, I always enjoy something classy on my men.'

The lift stopped at the top floor, they padded the deep carpet to the Astor suite. Eddie thinking, "on my men" what the hell does that mean? He felt the heat rise, his loins were letting him down, and he had sworn not to get involved with April again. Well, that won't last long she was too damn bossy.

'You certainly know how to enjoy yourself Showers.'

April gave him a sly look. 'And now you'll know, what to wear if you're in a classy situation again, won't you.'

'Don't worry Showers, I'll manage.'

They entered the suite. Sir Omar was sitting in the bay window, framed by the skyline of cranes. Eddie still thought of them as Pterodactyls perched on tall buildings, guarding their golden domain.

Sir Omar got up, crisp pinstripe charcoal suit, stiff blue shirt white collar and extended a cuff-linked hand. 'Ah, Mr Conway, so good of you to come. We use this suite to entertain our clients when they visit London. I think it says solid English conservative values, don't you think?'

'Yeah, I think.' Eddie wanted to pull his hand away, he was on the verge of laughing but felt it was some sort of test, he pretended to look around, struggling to keep a straight face, remembering the night with April, he was sure his eyebrows danced. He glanced at April, cat got the mouse look on her face and back to Sir Omar.

'Entertaining clients eh, I suppose that's important in your business is it?'

Sir Omar dropped Eddie's hand like a dirty cloth and stepped back. 'Quite so Mr Conway, quite so, I wanted to thank you for your efforts and reward you.' He curled his index finger at April. 'Now I know where my daughter is, a weight off my shoulders, don't you know.'

April stepped up and handed Eddie a brown manila envelope. 'I'm sure you prefer hard cash for all your,' she twitched a corner of the mouth smirk, 'hard work.' And looked him right in the eyes, enjoying the game. 'You earned it.'

Eddie took the envelope, fighting a blush while he weighed it in his hand. 'Nothing like a good wedge is there, Mr Agassi?'

Sir Omar looked put out again at Eddie omitting the 'Sir'. He waved Eddie to a chair by the coffee table; a knock at the door, April let in a waiter bearing a large tray, silver pot of tea and triangle sandwiches, and placed them on the coffee table. Eddie's mind drifted to the night the coffee table had lines of coke on it; he had to concentrate all over again at keeping a straight face.

'There is a signing off bonus in the envelope Mr Conway. I'm very happy with your work and I may need you from time to time, to perform other, how did we put it, "under the Radar", duties.' Eddie almost laughed out loud. Sir Omar oblivious to Eddies inner struggle paused. 'As to my daughter, I'm content to let her have some free rope and, ah, how shall we say, learn a few lessons of life, don't you think?'

'I still think, yeah.' Eddie cut Sir Omar off, thinking, this is a payoff but rather an ornate way to deal with a hired goon. Eddie wondered, this game was being played with rules and motives hidden below the surface.

Sir Omar waxed on about horse racing, asking Eddie if he ever had a flutter, that owning a racehorse was one of his greatest pleasures. Visiting the stables was his way of relaxing, the race a pure bonus of thrills to add to his passion for horses.

Eddie nodded along, hoping he could cut this formal chitchat nonsense short and get out. April was hovering behind Sir Omar running her eyes up and down Eddie as if she was preparing to saddle him.

Eddie started feeling sweaty and uncomfortable, he thought of opening the envelope, counting it in front of Sir fucking-jockey-club-Omar but that would just reinforce his own low social standing, he wasn't going to give them that pleasure. Anyway, if it was short he could always ring Showers and swear at her, she would like that.

Chapter 33: Break-in

They were good and they enjoyed what they did. They ripped the cushions, slashed the mattress, searched the toilet pipes, even emptied the u-bend under the sink, but no sign of the merchandise. They took their time and completely trashed the gaff, no worries about being disturbed or caught on the job; they knew they could handle anyone who might turn up.

Salim tapped numbers on his phone and held out a hand to quieten the others and whispered. 'No sign of merchandise, nothing.' The other two stopped and listened but not catching any distinct words from the muffled tones on the other end of the phone.

'We look every place,' Salim's voice rose in anger, 'what the fuck you think we do? It not here.' They could hear swearing coming over the phone now, one of the guys started to giggle, Salim ran his index finger across his throat. The giggler shut up, the other guy smirked at Giggler's discomfort.

'Yeah, we make like robbery.' Salim held the phone at arms-length staring at it and shouted, 'You think me stupid.' He hung up, glared at Giggler and Smirker, he picked up the ladies underwear from the bed, sniffing at it.

'OK, help yourselves to whatever valuable, I'm taking the bitch's underwear.'

Giggler stuffed a laptop in his sports bag.

Smirker held his hands out. 'Nothing worth anything.' Then he grinned. 'OK I shit on bed, that stop them fucking, ha.'

Chapter 34: Route March

'How far we marching?' asked a worried Scotch John.

Lofty was adjusting his prosthetic limb. 'We turn around at Kings Cross and back up.'

'Aye. You do this every day on one leg, Lofty?'

'When I can Scotch, I go all the way to Canary Wharf and back.'

'Fuck, that's a long way, aye.' Tring . . . tring . . . a shrill bicycle bell sounded behind them.

'Single file, Scotch.' Scotch dropped in behind Lofty and they moved over to the left of the canal towpath.

A cyclist nudged by 'Sorry. Thanks . . .'

They worked their way through Camden Lock, deviating off the tow path through the market section and back on to the canal past the dealers, winos and druggies who sat lazily dangling legs over the green scummy canal, puffing weed.

Scotch did a little skip so he was marching in time with Lofty. 'By the left march, eh Lofty! Fucking killing me so it is.'

'Left, ah left, ah left, and right . . . You stink like a brewery Scotch.'

'Aye, could do with a drink about now, so I could.'

'Hold up, you take the backpack now.' Lofty handed the pack to Scotch John.

'What's in here then, Lofty?'

'Boiled eggs, water, couple of Kagools, two folding chairs, sleeping bag, field stove, spare socks, usual stuff.'

'Fuck sake man, we on a wee exercise, aye?'

'You need it Scotch with your beer belly. A couple of miles and you're knackered. Not the form you had back in the Mob.'

'Aye. Good times in the Mob, but we not back in the Mob are we laddie?'

'No, we're Ronin?'

Three winos cheered at them as they marched out of a narrow towpath tunnel. One tried to get up to ape the marching but fell over, his mates hooting with laughter. Lofty cursed

'Bloody Ronin.'

'So really what's Ronin for fuck's sake?' wheezed a panting Scotch.

Lofty rolled his eyes wondering if Scotch would ever get it. 'When a samurai, that's a warrior, loses his commander, or his clan, that's his mob, mostly cos' they been defeated like, they're cast out wandering the land. No-one gives a shit about them, so either they find a new mission in life or end up like them.' Lofty pointed over his shoulder at the winos behind. 'They're Ronin.'

The towpath opened up a clear stretch down to Kings Cross; a duck waddled across their path. Scotch kicked it into the canal, the duck cartwheeled across the water, wings flapping, panic quacking.

'Don't take it out on ducks, Scotch.'

'Aye, feeling better, so I am.' He hooked his thumbs into the webbing of the pack and leaned into the pace with a ghost of a smile. 'Fuck aye, the pack sitting nice, back on patrol so we are.'

They marched in silence for a while. Nearer Kings Cross canal basin the new developments were going up, the gas towers were all gentrified, new blocks advertising two, three and four-bed town apartments and penthouses at very silly prices. 'How many Ruperts can there be in the world Lofty? Cos' there are a fuck of a lot moving in here, so they are.'

Lofty scanned the canal side. Pristine lawns were being laid, cinemas, clubs, coffee shops, deli's and gyms, all developed in a top class Lego build. All the Ruperts needed to sustain life in the inner city. Lofty led Scotch up the broad spanking brand-new steps, to what had previously been a sand and gravel warehouse area, now an artificial lake with fountains, more shops, offices and apartments. They sat on a plastic-wooden bench, opened the pack and shared out boiled eggs and sipped water.

Scotch, red-faced, out of breath but grinning. They tapped the eggs and rolled them on the seat, the shell flaked off.

'So, you taking this Ronin shit seriously then Lofty, aye?'

'Yeah, I decided in stir to make my own choices. When I didn't, other people made them and I ended up kipping rough on the streets and then, wham, bang! Prison. So now I make my own choices.' Lofty sighed, 'I needed to be back in the Mob.'

'How? We left the Mob years ago.'

'It's a mental thing Scotch, working for Eddie, like he's the soul of the Mob, so I feel I'm back in. What about you?'

Scotch thought hard, the march had rekindled that army feeling of belonging, being on manoeuvres, being part of a unit again. Yet there was still that lick of terror deep under the surface, in a place Scotch was a feared to go, deep inside, lest it reveal a truth about himself. Sitting by the canal looking at the young people gathered on the bank smiling and enjoying themselves, he knew deep down he should confront that sense of dismay, the horror. Maybe Lofty was right. Better to die fighting than slowly crumble to nothing.

'Ah fuck it, what else we good at? Eh, Lofty.' The sun peeked out from the clouds, the canal water sparkled, the marching had released endorphins. Scotch felt high. 'I was next to him you know Lofty and then he copped it. Should have been me, not Dinger, should have been me.' Both men sat in memory of a fallen soldier. Then Scotch broke the mood. 'Sun came out Lofty.'

Lofty looked up at the patch of blue sky. 'Makes life worth living, eh Scotch.'

Scotch was shocked to realise he was enjoying just sitting, sipping water, eating boiled eggs and nodded in agreement.

Chapter 35: The Mural

The guy wearing a floppy beanie hat dumped his heavy sports bag against the dirty concrete wall and walked its length checking out the fading graffiti. His mate, shaved head, big earrings, pulled spray cans out of a holdall. 'We'll give it an undercoat then, Benzi?'

'Ya Spider, cover shit graffiti, ya, spray a base coat, jungle green gonna work.'

Eddie watched with Jassi. 'So these guys are gonna paint something with spray cans?'

'Ask Fitz, he organised it.' Jassi pointed across the space between the three brick tenement blocks. Fitz and Rainya were nervously making their way across the dog-fouled grass. 'They're staying with me, their place got burgled, bit of a mess.'

Fitz and Rainya stepped up she was hugging his arm.

'Sorry about your gaff, I had mine done recently, not nice is it?' said Eddie.

Fitz took his glasses off wiping them. 'They didn't get much, just made a nasty mess.'

Rainya let go of his arm. 'They didn't find what they were looking for you mean,' Fitz tried to shush her, 'no might as well face it, my father's behind it I'm sure.'

'What?' blurted Eddie, 'Your Dad has robbed your gaff?'

Rainya turned to Jassi and held her arms. 'I might need a lawyer, Jassi. My father is a rather unscrupulous man and I have something of his.'

Eddie was going mental joining up the dots.

Benzi wandered over scratching under his beanie-hat, breaking the moment.

'Hey Fitz, ya man nice wall, good place to work eh?'

Fitz changed the subject. 'I been getting them walls at squats but this is the first time we got permission from a proper place.'

Benzi smiled at Eddie and waved at the balconies overlooking the area. 'Yeah, it's good.' The wall stood at the end of a three-sided valley of housing blocks.

Eddie smiled. 'Well I'm working on an old army saying, it's better to be forgiven than forbidden.'

Benzi turned to Fitz who looked at Eddie anxiously. 'What does that mean?'

Eddie smiled calmly, 'It means I'll get the permission after they've done the painting.'

'But . . . ' sputtered Fitz.

'Don't worry mate its paint innit,' said Eddie pointing at the wall, 'can always paint it over and that wall was so shitty, can't get any worse.'

Benzi laughed. 'I like this attitude. I give you something good for the people here, ya.' He walked back to his collection of spray paint cans, pulling his beanie hat over his locks.

Jassi gave Eddie a big warm smile. Eddie shrugged.

Valdrin and the two stooges sauntered over, the dogs sniffing the ground. Fuck, thought Eddie, no chance getting this done on the QT.

'What the hombres doing Eddie?'

'Well Valdrin we making an outdoor art gallery, know what I mean.' Valdrin paused, index finger on lips, like he was middle-aged art critic now.

'Yeah, Ricardo here good man on the spray can, ain't you?' The tall Ethiopian kid cracked a big smile at Eddie, the other kid nodded, like he was from the BBC.

'Ricardo, that your name cute boy?' laughed a surprised Eddie.

'Yo, man's name no laughing ting, innit.'

Rainya was helping Spider sort through the spray cans, Benzi was sketching an outline in grey on the wall.

Eddie introduced the holy trinity. 'This is the estate patrol, they gonna look after your mural.'

Valdrin hailed the spray-can jockeys. 'Yo Bro, where you from?'

'Rio, Brazil but staying in Bristol,' Benzi indicated his helper, 'with Spider.'

Spider stood proudly in the middle of all the spray cans. 'We came up by train today.'

Three Amigos cooed in unison. 'COOL!'

Benzi and Spider, locked into their work, total concentration on the wall. Benzi shouted to Fitz. 'Need a ladder, I wanna do the whole wall.'

Fitz turned to Eddie, who nodded, pulled his phone out and dialled. 'Ashok, yeah, I know I'm with them now, listen need a ladder, ask Larry to bring one from the container.'

Rainya excitedly started blurting. 'When we get the funding, we, we are going to set up a proper office with storage and equipment and a van, and buy a warehouse and . . .'

Fitz cut her off. 'Rainya shut up.'

Rainya looked hurt and guilty. 'Sorry, just, but well, money makes all the difference.'

Benzi was working very quickly, outlines and shapes appeared, Spider handed spray cans to him. Garish strong colours sprayed from the centre outward with assured touches.

Eddie looked around. A little crowd was forming, excited kids running between adult's legs.

Katy stood next to Eddie, grey anorak matching her long grey hair with the lined grey face of a heavy smoker. 'This you're doing then Eddie? Like it, know what I mean, bit of colour.' A couple of little mixed-race kids were tugging at her jacket.

'Who the kids Katy?'

'My youngest Sue, her kids, you remember Sue, don't ya?'

'Sue . . . The little kid who used to strop about with a fag in her mouth?'

'Yeah, you remember Eddie; she lives up Malden Road now. I get the kids when she's working at Tesco. You know what, I'll get Joan our councillor down to see this. Labour'll support this, you think Eddie?'

Eddie shrugged. 'Well they sent me to a bloody war, so what harm can this do'.

Katy nudged him in the ribs, 'Oh you . . . '

The wall was turning into a jungle, a riot of reds, yellow, purple and green. Fantastical birds with huge wings, a mosaic of plumage spread across the wall. A big-eyed toucan with two opposing beaks dominated the centre.

'Oi there, mate.' shouted Katy to Benzi. 'Why this then?' Waving her fag at the wall.

Benzi paused surprised at the little posse gathered around. 'It's jungle, they killing my jungle back home, so I paint my jungle where I go, it nice protest eh?'

Katy smiled and shouted at her grandchildren. 'Oi you two, this the Amazon jungle right in our yard innit?' Katy turned back to Benzi and Spider. 'Would you two like a cup of tea? It's no bother, I only live over there.' She hooked a thumb behind her.

'English tea, we like very much,' Benzi laughed.

Larry walked his slow caretaker waltz passed the children's play area, ladder balanced over his shoulder. 'This what you want?'

The spray-can jockeys took it. Benzi grinned amazed at all the help he was getting, 'Ya mate, just what we need.' He leaned the ladder against the wall.

Larry walked over to Eddie sitting on the bench rolling a smoke. 'It won't last you know, kids will spray all over it and muggings here be lumbered with painting it out.'

'Fuck me, Larry, you're mister negative. Look around mate, it's going down well.' Larry shrugged and sat next to Eddie and borrowed papers and tobacco; the artists were having a cup of tea and chatting to Katy. Rainya was playing with Katy's grandchildren. Valdrin and his posse sitting on the swings in the children's play area, rolling spliff's. Fitz was in a heated discussion with Jassi.

Larry lit his roll-up. 'Heard about your run in with Djokevic, Eddie.' He blew a smoke circle and watched it waft away. 'He's a wrong un', you know, loan sharking, drugs, got lots of people round here in poke to him.'

Eddie smiled. 'Not over yet.'

'Well they ain't gonna stick their noses out.' Larry indicated the people gathering around the wall. 'You ain't got the army behind you anymore, Eddie.'

Eddie chuckled. 'What's that film, Larry? Oh yeah "High Noon".'

Eddie stood up. Shania had arrived. Fuck me, thought

Eddie, what is it, a bloody festival now. Shania smiled a big warm embracing smile, gave Jassi a big tweety hug and a peck on the face and walked over to Eddie, who shook his hand. Shania laughed at his formal attitude in public.

'So this Dodge City Eddie, looks bad styli.'

Larry shook his head, 'Like a different language ain't it?'

Eddie nodded. 'Yeah, well these graffiti guys have changed up the atmosphere.'

Rainya ran over bubbling with joy at being in the middle of social housing.   'What people need Eddie, is change. Shania, really glad you came over, great isn't it. Fitz is very happy with the day.'

Eddie looked at the unhappy Fitz struggling with his temper. Shania and Rainya big-hugged each other.

Eddie introduced them to Larry who stood up and bowed. 'Welcome ladies.' He paused, 'And gents,' he said and settled back on the bench for a good old sit down, smoke and chat.

Shania smiled and sat next to him. Larry took a breath and launched into a story, 'When I was a young un' round here . . .'

'You look good to me,' giggled Shania.

Larry spluttered, 'There was no LGT lot then, I can tell you.'

Shania laughed, put his hand on Larry's shoulder. 'No its Lesbian, Gay, Bi-sexual and Transgender, LGBT.

Larry lit another roll-up. 'Oh yeah, well bi, that's just being greedy.' He put on a smug look as if he'd scored a point.

'You want to try, never too late you know,' replied Shania.

Larry flinched backwards as if he'd been hit. 'Bloody hell.' Took a big drag on his roll-up and started to smile. 'Bugger me, at my age I should take that as a compliment then.'

Shania burst out laughing, Larry protested. 'What I say?' He looked briefly puzzled and then joined in the laughter with Shania.

Eddie found himself standing close to Jassi. He nodded

at Larry and Shania. 'They're getting on.'

Jassi linked her arm through his, she wore a black parka, fur hood, tight jeans and hiking boots.

It all looked cute to Eddie, who was desperately thinking, what do I say? What the hell, this is silly. I'll just bugger off home. Maybe I should say something about the mural?

But Jassi pulled him close. 'Little things make a difference and then before you know it all adds up to something bigger and better.' Jassi looked up at Eddie, a thoughtful expression on her face.

Eddie thought, I don't know what she's talking about, maybe I should try a smile, he tried one, didn't really come off ended up gurning instead.

Jassi chuckled, a warm warbling bubbling, a log fire lights down low sound.

Eddie blew out his cheeks wishing he knew what it all meant.

On the fifth-floor walkway of the far block, Djokevic walked out of his door with his lumps in tow and stared down at the wall painting. He swore at his lumps and stalked back indoors.

Chapter 36: Curry & Rum

'Eddie good to see you and this your friend?'

'Rumpunch, Faisal.'

'Good to meet you, my friend, so what you having Eddie, usual?'

'Yeah Bhindi bhaji, Chicken Dhansak and sweet Peshwari Nan.'

'And you Mr Rumpunch.'

'No. It's Mr Preston, Rumpunch is a school nickname.'

The rotund owner of Curry-Love, a front room curry house, loved stories. 'How so, my friend?'

'I'll tell you, Faisal,' Eddie said as he squeezed into one of the three booths running down the side of the front room café. 'When he was a fifteen-year-old school-kid, he knocked out this older kid who was calling him a nigger; one punch, one "rum-punch" we called it. Teacher took him straight to Tavistock boxing club, isn't that right Rum.'

Rum settled into the seat opposite Eddie. 'As he says, as he says.'

'OK, for you I make special, you like lamb or chicken, Mr Rum?'

Rum gave up on his name. 'Lamb would be good.'

'OK, Eddie, you both have drink on house tonight, OK.'

'We got our own bottles,' said Eddie, holding up a carrier bag.

'That's why people like my place eh, bring their own drink, two glasses on the house then.' Faisal bustled away laughing at his own joke.

Eddie poured two ciders. 'So, let me get this right. Marlon coughs up that Djokevic set him to rob my flat.'

Rum sipped the cider and nodded in appreciation. 'Telling ya. Says this Joke geezer has fifty percent of the take. Means Jokevic must have someone spotting your gaff.'

'Fuck, don't like this Rum, he's got informers on the estate, who knew about my Mum?'

'Narrows it down don't it.'

Hot steaming food arrived on wooden platters. Eddie licked his slips. 'Fuck knows. I hardly came home a lot when I had leave.'

'So, talk to her mates.' Rumpunch spooned the curry. 'This is good. Hey.' He called out to Faisal behind the counter of the open plan kitchen. 'What's this called?'

'You like it?'

Rum nodded, working on a mouthful of food.

'OK.' Faisal beamed. 'Just ask for Rumpunch Lamb Special when ever you come in.'

Rum sat up pleased. 'You gonna name it after me?'

'Well only when you're here, otherwise it's just Lamb Special.'

Eddie grinned at Rum tucking into the curry with relish. 'Yeah, brasses always know what's going on, innit Rum.'

'That's why they're called working girls Ed's, you get me.'

'Not something I'm keen on doing Rum, you know, me talking to me Mum's old working mates.'

'Got to be done, Eddie. What you call it in the Army? Recce? This Joke fella coming at you.'

'Yeah, I'll go recce! Talk to Marigold, been meaning to anyway.' Eddie took a long pull of cider. 'Fact one, his moves show his nature, he's a sneaky fucker, hanging in shadows, coming from the side, no fronting up.'

'Yo, I know, no neat meet on the battlefield like English gents, eh?' Rum spoke through a mouthful of curry and licked sauce of his top lip.

Faisal sidled up to the two men, smiling, rubbing his hands. 'So Mr Rum what's your game now, no more boxing?'

'Boxing got me noticed but that was short term, so I took a strategic view on life and plumped for an executive career.'

'In what?' asked Faisal, eyes dancing with merriment.

'The only place in this society that talent, ambition and bottle rises to the top.'

'Ah, in the self-employed sector of supply and demand eh.' Faisal nodded to Rum.

Rum nodded back, they were on the same page, 'You

need anything, and maybe I can arrange a supply.'

Faisal smiled. 'OK Mr Rum,' and walked back to the kitchen.

'Try this, it's got coconut in it mate, lovely.' Eddie broke off a chunk of the Nan bread and offered it to Rumpunch,

'Why, cos' me Caribbean?'

'I like it.'

'Oh yeah, you saying I'm a coconut?'

'What's that supposed to mean?' Eddie looked puzzled.

'Means black on the outside, white on the inside.'

'A coconut is brown and hairy on the outside.' Eddie put his fork down.

'It's a fucking metaphor, Eddie, means we sold out our brothers to be English. Or some shit.'

'No, it's a coconut.'

'Whatever Eddie, any way you got to expect more moves, you know it.'

'Like sneak attacks, dob me to DHS, that sort of thing.'

'Yeah Eddie. Keep your guard up; get a metal door on the outside of your gaff.'

Eddie sat back, sipped his cider thoughtfully. 'I'll keep an eye on his motor; when he stops parking on the estate I'll know he's making a move. Meanwhile, yeah, I'll chicken wire the balcony and roof and metal up the front door.'

'You white boys all go heavy metal in the end.'

'Better than ending up a coconut, Rum.'

Chapter 37: Tantrum

'Have you an appointment Sir?'

'Oh I got one of them alright.' Eddie was back at the Alexandrian Private Members Club. He'd rung earlier and asked for Sir Omar but apparently, he was busy in a meeting and April was not answering her phone.

He barged past the flunky mannequin at reception and the door goon standing at ease in the foyer, they followed in his wake. He stopped and squared up to them both. 'Really, you want some?' They made their minds up really quick and returned to their posts. Eddie stomped through the deep shag-pile carpeted club.

Sir Omar jumped up in alarm as Eddie burst in. 'Mr Conway how unexpected, didn't your bonus satisfy you?' April looked excited at the prospect of violence.

'You,' he pointed at Sir Omar, 'set me up and robbed your own daughter's gaff.'

Sir Omar walked around the coffee table and placed his hand on Eddie's arm. 'Mr Conway my daughter stole something very valuable from me, a package, one I was keeping safe for certain clients, so you see, I had to keep it very private.'

'Yeah under the radar, you used me eh, well I don't fucking like being used.' April's eyes were shining now she was getting revved up. 'What did your daughter take from you that is so important?' asked Eddie.

'Sorry Mr Conway, that's private information. Mrs Bentley-Forbes could you sort this situation out.' April stepped up and squeezed his arm. Eddie suddenly realised he was going off the scale and had to dial it back down, he let April lead him to a small room by the entrance.

'Goodness Eddie, you were quite the berserker back there.' She pressed herself up against him, whispering in his ear, 'very primitive behaviour.' April nibbled on his earlobe. Eddie shook his head away.

'Fuck me, Showers, you love the hard stuff, eh?'

'Harder the better Eddie.'

'Look I was out of order,' Eddie replied, shrugging her off, 'but Sir bloody Omar Agassi thought he could play me like a flunky and that makes me rear up, OK.'

'Oh, I get it, Eddie, you're rearing up,' she giggled high on adrenalin.

Eddie tore himself away, he knew he'd lost it and walked to the entrance, fuming; the front desk mannequin raised his eyebrows mockingly. Eddie swept his arm across the desk knocking everything off, the big leather appointments book flopped to the floor facing upwards, pages turning over. Eddie barked a sharp laugh, daring the door goon to step in. Door goon hesitated and then stepped back. Eddie barged out the big main doors shouting.

'Fucking Ruperts!'

The desk flunky turned to door goon. 'Ruperts?' He asked confused, the Lump shrugged.

April watched him storm down the street, her eyes still shining, slightly out of breath.

Chapter 38: Cooking Jassi

Fifth floor, seventy-five steps, counted Eddie. Old Peabody Estate in Covent Garden, no lift. He'd come via Covent Garden Tube, two hundred and thirty-four steps spiralling up from the depths of London underground. So that'd make it three hundred and nine, total, he mused, must be keeping me fit, need another run over the Heath, soon as.

He was typical army, being early, so he hung around the landing, looking down out the big windows. On one side Drury Lane, theatreland, very trendy bars, lots of gaping tourists and theatre crowd milling around. On the other side the big courtyard of the Peabody Estate, part car park, part garden club, large sunflowers in big tubs next to a greenhouse.

The door to the flat opened. 'I can see you, Eddie, why you hanging around outside my flat?' Jassi in tight pants, fluffy boots, tailored shirt, hair thick and loose. Eddie was slowly realising how fit she was; a regular gym bunny.

'Got here early love, army habit, arrive early, parade on time.' Eddie entered the flat, the warm smell of a hot bath with perfumed crystals, reminded him of a sober Mum, overlaid with cooking aromas. The memory stopped him in his tracks.

Jassi's place was a tiny bedsit, bathroom opposite the front door, combined living space and bedroom to the left, with kitchen alcove at the far end. Jassi observed Eddie checking out her place, 'It's cosy,' she said and held out her hand. Eddie tried to shake hands. 'No silly, the wine,' she laughed, a red-faced Eddie handed the bottle over and struggled out of his coat.

They sat on the futon couch, facing a small dining table nestling in the bay window three feet away. Well, it's not going to be a snort, slap and shag night is it, Eddie thought.

Jassi handed Eddie a glass of wine, leaned in and stroked his upper arm affectionately. 'So, my lovely man, what have you been up to?'

'What?' Eddie shifted uneasily on the futon.

Jassi smiled at him over the rim of her glass. 'Yes, Eddie everyone has a story, so part one while we wait for dinner to cook, it's a Savoy stew, lots of meat for you big macho types.'

'Oh right, yeah.' So, she wasn't clairvoyant. 'Uh, not much to tell, been out the army a while now.'

'How long did you serve?'

'Long enough, I got glandular fever and then pneumonia after my first month of training; was hospitalised for three weeks.'

'You know I'm interested why young men join the army, is it adventure?'

'Maybe, that's part of it but more like something to belong to. My Mum wasn't the mothering kind. She went missing a lot when I was a kid, I got passed around a bit.'

'Missing?' Jassi topped up his glass.

'Yeah, high on drugs, pissed up on some bender, at work for days.'

'Goodness me, what did she do?'

'She was a Brass.'

'Sorry. A what?'

'A working girl, in a house, she would take me with her when I was little. My Dad had fucked off. Sorry, he moved back to Wales.' Eddie paused, sniffed, fuck's sake, bit emotional or what. Why am I telling her all this crap? She's got the voodoo on me.

Jassi leaned over and rubbed his arm again, her eyes were large dark pools. Eddie sensed deep waters. Jassi walked to the kitchenette and brought pots of food to the living room. Eddie got up and sat at the table, Jassi ladled a big portion of food on to his plate. They ate dinner slowly, sipping wine and chatting easily.

'So, what's it like now you're out the army?'

Eddie paused in thought, Jassi kept quiet, giving him room to speak. 'You know it's like falling off an ocean-going liner,' he replied, looking into her eyes. Feeling safe, he opened up. 'You're all at sea, drowning. So, you grab onto anything that will keep your head above water, but too often the lads grab booze, drugs, any adrenalin high's. But deep down you know we're all falling soldiers.' Jassi poured more wine and kept silent, a trick she'd developed when interviewing her legal clients.

Eddie took a big gulp of wine and filled the silence. 'It's like Peter Pan losing his wings.' He wiped his lips. 'We become the lost boys. Lost but getting older. And nobody gives a shit, sorry, cares.' Eddie stared into his glass, lost in thought. Jassi kept quiet, Eddie looked up. 'Sorry,' he wiped his damp eyes and coughed, embarrassed.

'So now you're one of the lost boys?' Jassi smiled, emoting sympathy, thinking how very complex this man was, from a world of war she could not even imagine. '

'Yeah, man overboard trying to swim home.' Eddie laughed breaking the tension.

Nevertheless, Jassi sensed the deep well of vulnerability and wondered if she should unlock it, could be dangerous, could get hurt. God that surprised her, she was relaxed, enjoying the intimacy of two people and something was clicking. He'd be nice to curl with in bed, strong arms, she thought. 'I don't think wars solve anything Eddie. Violence is a downwards spiral, I mean what did you achieve over there?'

'Achieve,' he barked. Eddie was caught off-guard. 'Well soldiers don't get much say in the matter, but Afghan ...?' He took a long drink finishing the wine and stared into his empty glass, lost in thought. He spoke slowly. 'We stirred up a hornet's nest and unleashed Jihadi,' he continued, in a bitter tone. 'Guys died but we up-graded our soldiering skills and invented the Invictus games.' He looked up out the window but only saw sad memories and fell silent.

Jassi opened another bottle of wine and refilled their glasses. Eddie was clearly embarrassed by his out pouring.

Jassi tried lifting the mood by telling him funny stories of being a posh Indian at an all-girls' school, falling in and out of love with older girls. Eddie raised an eyebrow.

'It's a pre-teenage girl thing,' she laughed.

Eddie shrugged off his dour mood trying to work out Jassi's age, probably early thirties, more or less same age as himself, same era, same music, the same fads and fashions but very different lives.

Jassi was tipsy now. 'But men, Eddie, are such bloody useless creatures.' Eddie smiled hearing the Indian accent coming out and liking the lilting rhythms. 'Oh, they get bloody lost searching for their own masculinity. But you Eddie? I think your experience has taken you beyond the modern male crisis.'

Eddie was not sure where this line of chat was going, flirting was OK, but this was a bit deep and personal, like talking to the Regimental Chaplin. Eddie helped Jassi clear up the plates, they walked them into the kitchen nook and stacked the dishwasher, and he found it strangely intimate.

'My father is a very modern Sikh. He wanted me to be a lawyer but also a good Sikh girl, marry a nice Sikh boy have kids and cook meals when he visits the grandchildren.' Jassi sighed as she turned the dishwasher on.

Eddie not sure what to do went and sat down on the futon couch. 'So, are you kinda cast out then?'

'Oh no Eddie I have insurance.' Jassi bubbled with laughter.

'What do you mean?' Eddie was confused.

Jassi raised her hands to her hair. 'I cut my hair and I drink booze but luckily I have two sisters who are good Sikhs, so my father is content with two out of three and you know I think he is secretly pleased with his rebel lawyer daughter. My mother on the other hand . . .' Jassi stopped, looked at the wall clock. 'Is that the time?'

Eddie shuffled on the futon, thinking is it time to go, not sure what the next move was. Civvy Street was complicated and again a woman had taken the initiative.

'Well Eddie that was a lovely evening but it's getting late, don't want you thinking I'm a pushover.' Jassi walked to the door. 'And it is my time of the month.'

Eddie shot up, plainly embarrassed and fumbled for his coat, turning around to say good night. Jassi reached up tucked his collar in and kissed him full on the mouth and hugged him tightly, she drew back, looked right into his eyes and stroked his face, tenderly. Eddie felt another tearful moment, breathed in, and recovered well. 'So, I'll ring you, uh? Do something soon, I mean . . .'

'Relax Eddie, we're doing really well.'

'Huh! Are we, what at?'

'I'll come over to your place, you cook a meal, one of your army meals even.' Jassi did the low bubbling laughter thing again. 'I'd really like that. I'm curious to see your place, bet it's a regular man-cave isn't it?'

The burbling cascade of warm laughter notes floated in Eddie's head, he was hardly aware of leaving. Suddenly he was out in the Peabody estate courtyard, the cool breeze woke him up and Eddie tried to figure out what the hell was Jassi Singh doing to him.

Chapter 39: Acid

Seventy-eight steps, only twenty-three to go, Eddie head down, just concentrating on jogging up the steps. He was blowing now, feeling the pace. It had been a long night on his feet checking between clubs. Jabba had opened another venue off Carnaby Street, which had been packed out, a huge disco cellar, a ground floor bar, lots of trade, drinking, noise, and the rave crowd.

He had taken Scotch with him and another ex-Mob lost boy, Darkie Sullivan, to work the door. Darkie had very solemnly stated that they couldn't call him Darkie in Civvy Street. It was Jessekiah now. 'Fuck that,' said Scotch, 'if we can't call him Darkie after all these years, you can't, call me Scotch.'

'It's not the same,' said Eddie. Scotch shrugged.

'No, I don't know why. Look just shut the fuck up, both of you.' Eddie tried again. 'Darkie's Jezzer now. It's a coconut thing OK,' he added, looking at Jezzer for confirmation. Jezzer rolled his eyes, muttering, 'coco-fucking-nut.' Eddie nodded.

'See, and you're still fucking Scotch, Scotch.'

'Aye all right, that'll do well enough,' said Scotch.

'Fucking Jezzer,' Darkie laughed, 'I bet it will be Jez before the end of the week.'

Eddie chuckled at the memory and looked up. Fuck, no lights on the sixth-floor landing. Typical, last sixteen steps in the dark. Eddie slowed, just in case he stepped on a coke can or something. He lifted his head to soak up any light filtering from the walkway at the top of the steps, just in time to see the flash of the bottle thrust towards him. Instincts kicked in, from long tense patrols in the dark shadowlands of bandit country. He dropped below the arc of the incoming liquid as it spilt out over his head, hitting the stairwell wall behind him, but some splashed on his back as he dived. The sizzle and stink of acid fumes reeked up the stairwell. Eddie's mind cleared instantly; working out his next moves, he had to take the high ground. Pumping his knees, he drove up off the steps at his assailant; head butting the attacker's midriff, arms up warding away any weapon. The bottle exploded out his assailant's hand and over the top of Eddie skittering down the stairwell. They slammed back against the rubbish chute outside Eddie's front door. He felt the bite of stinging pain on his lower back, some acid had burned through his coat.

Eddie drove his fists into the guy's balls, grabbed and twisted. The attacker shrieked and another shadow stepped forward. Fuck, two of them thought Eddie as he heaved the guy, one hand gripping his balls, the other holding him around his neck. Into the shadows they fell, sprawling along the walkway, another bottle spilt acid, catching the guy Eddie had thrown. He screamed while the other one attempted to throw the bottle at Eddie.

Eddie dived back down the stairwell, hit the middle steps painfully and rolled down to the lower landing, slid, picked himself up and jumped down to the next landing, crashing in a heap. Acid trickled slowly down the steps above, dripping from one to the next and on an empty coke tin, fumes rising in a hissing stink.

Eddie crouched back under the lower level stairwell, switched on in full fighting mode, adrenalin and rage coursing through his system, heart pounding. He looked around for a weapon. Leaning against a door was a piece of shelving. Eddie picked it up and in full stealth mode crept up the dark stairs placing his feet carefully to avoid any acid.

At the top of the stairs under the dull night-light glow of London, an empty walkway, the acid container spinning, the assailants gone. Eddie dashed along the walkway determined to catch and hurt the bastards. Fucking acid he thought, cowardly cunts. 'I'll fucking hurt you bad, make you cunts scream!' He raged.

He shivered as he realised how close he'd come to being blinded, dimly aware of pain in his lower back and bruising along his side where he had tumbled down the steps.

He cleared every level on his way down, at the bottom he burst out through the entry door, ran into the middle of the children's' play area and looked around. Not a sign, empty, just rows of amber-lit walkways glaring back down at him. Eddie walked to the bin area, opened the big metal doors to the bin shed, turned on the water hose at the back and sluiced off any surplus acid. He chucked the shelving into the nearest bin and rooted around, pulling out a computer desk leg. He hefted it, felt like it could do damage and decided to patrol the estate. Eddie wanted to lay down his marker, pissing on his lamppost. Wherever those two fuckers were hiding or anyone else associated with the attack, someone would be watching. Let the fuckers see who the top dog was on this patch. Eddie circled the estate noticing Djokevic's car was missing. Fuck, he should have checked that on his way on to the estate.

Back in his flat Eddie sat in the kitchen with the Afghan hash in his hands, pondering the sit-rep. 'OK, so war is declared, game on then you sneaky fucker,' he muttered to himself and went out to the rubbish chute on the landing and binned the hash, no more off-duty. He was on active service now, Eddie smiled, the buzz was back.

Chapter 40: Marigold

'Take ya coat off and give me a hug.'

'Ouch.'

'What matter wid you buoy.'

'Nothing, just a pulled muscle.'

'So ya see me now, now you is coming see me? How much I tell ya come see me, eh'

Eddie replied sheepishly, 'yeah I know Marigold. Giving me a guilt trip OK. The meals you brought over when me Mum died, really appreciated, thanks.'

'Was ya Mama's friend, Lord save her, more than she friend to herself, tell you. Sit down Eddie. I'll make tea.'

Eddie sat in the large old leather armchair in the open plan kitchen and living room, one side big table farmhouse style, the other half front parlour, lots of photos in a glass cabinet and African carvings on the wall. With Marigold, you were never far from a teapot and kettle.

'Yeah, it's been a bit mad, to tell the truth. Coming out the army is weird and me Mum passing. Didn't know what I was doing first few months.'

'Well, you look good to me now.' The kettle boiled a crazy banshee wail. Marigold flipped the whistle on the spout, lifted the kettle from the gas stove and poured into a large teapot covered in a hand knitted tea cosy, green, yellow and red. She wheeled a tea trolley between them settled into her comfy chair and poured the tea.

'So, I tell you how I met your Mama? Was in dis city six months looking for that no good runaway husband. I got me a room in Catford with old Jamaican lady, me speaking Gambian French and Pidgin English. By six months gone I was talking like Jamaican, good thing too; you don't mess wid Jamaicans in this country. I think to myself, yes this the place for me, no going back to Paris be treated like some bush African, patois French-speaking servant girl, grovelling at de great French civilisation.'

'Marigold you told me this story loads of times, when I was a kid.'

'Yes, that right and I tell you again so you don't forget where come from. Your Mother talk about you all time, my little buoy, him dis, him dat.'

Eddie cut in, 'somebody stole her jewellery.'

'What you say?' Marigold opened her mouth in shock.

'Broke into the flat and nicked it. No worries, I got it back. But I'm wondering who she talked to, who would know she had jewellery?'

'Eddie buoy, she talked bout that all de time, my buoy bought me dis my buoy bought me dat. She wore the jewellery whenever she could, even working at de house. No secret you bought her jewellery. Your mother big you up, all time.'

'I should have come home more the last few years but I got fed up.' Eddie nodded a sad smile and sniffed, 'Mum's shouting and crying, picking arguments over nothing, ranting about my Dad, crying about her life.'

'Your mother a troubled soul, she wired up de wrong way. Eddie. I must tell you, she'd go off and get high in a crack house up Malden Road, be there couple of days arguing, shouting, what a carrying on. Then, next few days she in bed, won't get up. I did what I could for her, go around clean her up, feed her.'

'Jesus Marigold I didn't know she was doing crack. I thought it was just booze, maybe a bit of coke now and again. Malden Road you say?'

'I say she with Jesus now.' Marigold rolled her eyes, 'Lord save her she wired up wrong. I think passing on was almost a blessing for her.' They sat drinking tea. Marigold fussing over Eddie like an old aunt, poured another mug and kept offering him the old biscuit tin, full of coconut macaroons.

'You me buoy; now ya mother gone upstairs. My son up there with her Lord bless em.' Marigold got up and reached for the top of the glass cabinet and clutched a framed painting of her son Imobi, done from a school photo. 'Been fifteen years now, coming home from school.' She dabbed her eyes. 'He was coming home from school not running in no gang, I had educational dreams for him, so I worked in the house.'

'Why on the game, Mum and you must have had a

choice?' Eddie shifted uncomfortably.

'Choice you say, maybe had choice but not many, we had child and no man doing his bit.'

'I remember I was little,' Eddie took a bite of coconut macaroon. It was stale. 'Mum took me down the house, you lot would fuss over me, then I grew up, realised it was a knocking shop and pretended I never knew.' He placed the macaroon on the side of the saucer and sipped tea, rolling it around his mouth trying to dislodge the gritty bits of coconut stuck to his gums.

'Ha, let me tell you it was a laugh Eddie. We girls looked out for each other, and we making money from sad lonely men, some not so sad, some just lonely.' Marigold paused, lost in thought, hugging the painting to her. 'Imobi, him had dreams, him go university. You know that Eddie, you know that why I worked. We both a bit broken, got bits missing, son wid no mother, mother wid no son.' She kissed the painting and tears ran down her cheeks.

'OK.' Eddie got up and hugged Marigold, she sniffled, and patted Eddie.

'Me fine, me OK, every so often have a little cry over him, does me good to remember.'

'I know Marigold, never forget, me, Rumpunch, Imobi and Charlie Green heading to the park to play football. Then they ran past us, slashing knives, then Imobi's on the pavement.'

'You all got hurt, my lovely boy died. Him bleed to death on de ground and nobody caught.' Marigold placed the painting back on the glass shelf, shook herself, sat down and poured more tea from the never-ending teapot. 'So how you little business going running doors?'

'Picking up.' Eddie sat down, relieved to change the subject. 'I got two doors an' looking like I'll pick up another club who want use my boys. Lofty training lads from the Mob to be Prince Charming door guys. People like it but it's getting complicated.'

Marigold chatted on how running the house was just like running the doors, odd shifts, odd people and dodgy accounts. By the time Marigold had made another pot of tea, Eddie carried away by emotion, had agreed to let Marigold run the books.

'Don't worry I make sure business is well looked after. You in the black economy, you need black business person, ha, ha.' The rain rattled the windows, driving in from the north.

'I got to go Marigold.' Eddie stood. Marigold brought him his coat, Eddie shrugged it on carefully and Marigold took his hand and patted it.

'You need a woman?'

'What, Jesus, Marigold you still on the game?'

'Me? No just saying you need boom-boom, me know many independent girls, from days I ran the house.'

'No, no, I'm OK.'

'OK, now listen, when you bring new guy on crew, they come by me for assessment and cup o' tea. Me not just the booker, me is the HR department as well. After me years I can spot a bad un! You concentrate on big picture, I'll sort jigsaw pieces.'

Chapter 41: Eddie v Therapy

'You run up all the stairs again, you crazy.' The fat receptionist rolled her eyes at Eddie. Then realizing she had just called a Veterans Mental Health Clinic patient crazy, she tried to recover, 'I mean you mad running up steps, not mad cos' you were in the army and all, I mean . . . '

'No worries darling,' Eddie laughed, 'you're right, what the hell am I running up all those flights of stairs for, eh?' The receptionist, slightly flushed, smiled apologetically at him.

'Ninety-four.' Eddie said proudly.

'Uh, sorry.' Receptionist really confused now.

'I counted them. Ninety-four steps, love.'

'Ah OK,' she said, revising her opinion back to crazy. 'The new therapist, Melissa, is on her way, take a seat.' Eddie sat down gingerly, the acid burn still stung. He had washed the puckered skin on his back carefully this morning and applied lots of ointment and a bandage.

The connecting double doors opened, Eddie looked up at a stick thin intense woman, jeans, trainers and roll neck sweater. She beckoned Eddie to follow and walked ahead of him hugging herself. Eddie binned the big tits nurse uniform image he'd been holding on to.

'They put me in an office at the end of the corridor, very small I'm afraid, hope you don't mind. Want a coffee? She ushered Eddie into the tight office, two plain armchairs faced each other next to a low coffee table squeezed next to a work desk, plastic beakers, bottle of water, box of tissues, and small brown lavender sniffing bottles.

'No worries, love.' She frowned at the last word. Oops mustn't call a Feminist love. 'Sorry,' said a worried Eddie but she smiled, forgiving him. 'Water is fine, ma'am, so what we doing?' Eddie sat straight and idly picked up a sea-canoeing magazine that lay open on the table. 'You do this?' He waved the middle page spread picture of a canoeist battling through choppy sea.

'Oh, you noticed that!'

Eddie thinking well it was laid out open on the desk for

me to see.

'Call me Mel. I'm training to canoe around Scotland in the summer.' Mel beamed with pride.

'Fuck sake, girl, that's serious, good on you!' Eddie reappraised her, seeing no longer a neurotically thin female but a whipcord fit young athlete sitting opposite him. OK, she wants to impress me, interesting.

'So, I read your file. May I call you Eddie?' Eddie nodded. 'But I didn't get a whole picture, do you mind if we get to know each other in this session?'

'Yeah, OK, that works for me.' Eddie sat back feeling the initiative was all his. 'So who are you?' he asked.

They talked about her traditional military family, which again surprised Eddie, a Rupert's daughter, who actually likes soldiers. He began to relax, chat sports enjoying her company. Eventually Mel cut to the chase.

'So how has your week been Eddie?' she demanded.

'Yeah well - bit up and down, got into a bit bother.' Mel's head jerked up.

'And how are you feeling about that?'

Interesting thought Eddie, doesn't jump in wanting all the murky details, his respect notched up another level. They talked for a good hour, it came easy and then unexpectedly Eddie confessed to her that the women entering his life confused him.

'Tell me about it. What do they want from us, eh?' Mel folded her arms.

'What?' Eddie was confused.

'My girlfriend doesn't understand my ultra-canoeing, wants me to go to the theatre all the time.' Mel laughed, rolled her eyes, 'I mean really.'

Eddie laughed covering his confusion, thinking, she's a lesbian? 'I haven't been asked to go the theatre yet,' said Eddie awkwardly and then started laughing, Mel joined in the laughter.

'OK, just women problems?' Inquired Mel, smiling conspiratorially.

Eddie felt a connection. She was OK. 'Not sure, to tell you the truth, I haven't had much experience, you know in the army, bit of a lads world, all lads together.' Eddie wobbled his hand side to side.

'Oh,' said Mel, 'how old were you when you joined?'

'Seventeen,' said Eddie.

'Often confusing at that age.'

'Bloody right it is.' Eddie blew out his cheeks, 'Me Mum put me off women.'   'How so, Eddie?' asked a very sympathetic Mel, leaning in very close.

'She was revved up all the time, everything a crisis, a drama and hitting the bottle but . . .' Eddie pulled back from more details of his youth, 'put me right off.' Mel looked so understanding that Eddie blurted out, 'few months after I came out, the army . . .' Eddie leaned over staring at his feet and mumbled, 'I felt like topping out.' Melissa looked confused.

'Killing myself.' As soon as Eddie said it, he felt the warm swell of emotion threaten to breach the dam he had built. He was surprised at his admission and the intense sadness he was feeling, which had come out of nowhere.

Mel handed him a tissue, Eddie took it hesitantly and then realized he had tears running down his cheek. 'Excuse me,' Eddie got up and lurched to the door. 'Need a toilet break,' he muttered as he yanked on the door handle. Melissa, concern writ large across her face, carefully watched him go out the door.

Eddie swore to himself as he quickly darted down the corridor and into the toilet. He sat on the toilet seat shaking. 'Christ what's the matter with me,' he rolled his neck and rubbed at his face, his hands came away wet with tears. 'Fuck, come on!' He shook himself and got control over the shakes and mentally pulled himself together, took a few deep breaths, walked out of the cubicle, washed his face and hands, dried off with a paper towel. He looked at himself in the mirror, sniffed, 'Fucking wus.'

Melissa was writing furiously in her note pad when Eddie entered the cramped Office. 'Sorry about that,' he muttered and sat down. Melissa put the pad down as if she had been caught cheating at an exam. She searched his face, worried expression.

'You OK? We don't have to carry on if you don't want to.'

'I'm fine, took me by surprise that's all.' Eddie shrugged.

'What did Eddie?'

'Oh, you know, talking about topping out, anyway that was before! But not now.'

'Oh,' replied Mel, 'what's changed?'

'I think I needed an enemy, a fight, a mission.'

'You want to explain? It's confidential off course.'

Eddie studied her and thought maybe I do, tough Lesbian therapist girl. Yeah, you're all right. 'I got a few battles lined up.' He leaned in confessing, 'looking forward to it,' and explained the bare bones, skating over the details. Melissa tried nodding in a very sympathetic way but her eyes twitched with alarm at every revelation. For Eddie on the other hand, the talking brought clarification, I got a mission, he thought.

Chapter 42: Crack House

'Well, they're not answering the door, how many times you gonna knock?'

'Let me have a go.' Lofty planted his size thirteen prosthetic boot on the lock with the force of a pile driver, the door banged open. Eddie barged in followed by Rumpunch, shapes screamed and scurried away in the shadows; the pungent smell of stale sweat and sour crack hung like a damp fog.

'Lofty take upstairs, clear all rooms, herd everyone down here.' Lofty hefted his baseball bat and took the stairs two at a time, crump, crump.

'Rum, with me.' They barged into the large open plan ground floor. Dirty blankets hung over the windows, but enough streetlight seeped in to reveal torn sleeping bags scattered on mattresses, an old couch leaning drunkenly on busted legs beneath the window. Two stoned youths, boy and girl, looked up blearily at the guys.

'Hey!' shouted the girl, strong northern accent, 'You can't come in here, fuck off!'

'Shut it,' replied Rum twirling his baseball bat. 'So, what's your play Eddie,' he grinned, 'this white on white thing?'

There was a crashing sound upstairs followed by a cry of pain. Rumpunch cocked his head at Eddie. Eddie raised his eyebrows. 'He's got big feet.'

Lofty herded two guys and a scruffy skinny crack-head woman struggling to pull a coat around her naked shoulders. The guys looked very similar, floppy hair, bad acne, dirty clothes, one of them bleeding from the mouth. The woman had tangled dirty long hair and missing teeth. 'Found these two hiding in the toilet and this,' he pointed at crack woman, 'half-naked off her skull on a mattress.' Eddie stepped up and looked closely at bleeding mouth.

'You! You fucker!' Eddie nutted him on the bridge of the nose, bleeding-mouth went down crying in pain. 'One of the acid fuckers.' Eddie kicked him, the acid guy grunted in pain.

'There were two of 'em right Boss? 'Lofty kicked the legs out from under the other one; he flopped in a heap next to his partner.

'Yeah, didn't get a good look at the other fucker, check his arms for acid burns.' Lofty stooped and tore the guy's sleeves up, fresh puckered skin on the back of hand and wrists. 'Him all right.'

'All right, usual drill,' snarled Eddie.

Crack woman was unsuccessfully trying to light a ciggie but her fingers were shaking so much she dropped it.

Lofty barked at the junkies in his most threatening parade ground voice. 'OK you fuckers, where is the house stash?' Prodding them with the baseball bat until they stood facing the dirty blank wall.

The girl and boy were sobbing now, scared shitless, snot dripping down their faces, looking over their shoulders in wide-eyed terror. 'It's a locked container in the back. We done nowt, please . . .' the boy pleaded in a northern accent.

'Lofty check it out, I'll talk to the acid brothers.' Lofty stomped off.

'You wanna do them, bet I could crack his head open?' Rumpunch played his bat over the faces of the acid brothers. 'Like a coconut eh Eddie?' Large crashing sound from the back, bloody mouth started mewling in fear while acid hands fainted.

'I would fucking love to crack both of them like coconuts!' barked Eddie. Rum laughed.

'Load of stuff from the lock-up.' Lofty stomped back in carrying a large holdall.

'Ok fuck'rees, turn round.' Rumpunch pulled his phone out. He photoed each of them in turn then bent down and snapped the prone acid brothers.

Lofty hauled bloody mouth to his knees, Rum measured his head against the baseball bat and took a few practise swings. Bloody mouth cracked and started begging for his life, 'No, mister please,' he began to cry, wailing pitifully, 'I don't wanna die.'

Rum flicked the baseball bat without any real force behind it to the side of bloody mouth's head, who shit himself and went down like a sack of spuds, rejoining his partner. He rolled on to his back staring up at Rumpunch in terror.

'They said we was to do it or they'd do us, promised us loads of gear,' he rambled on traumatised.

'Who?' Eddie leaned over him.

'We had to, honest, or he'll do us . . .' bleeding-mouth sobbed.

Eddie in a fury stamped on bleeding mouth's hand, the sound of breaking fingers started the youths crying again, the northern boy pissed himself. Bloody-mouth's screams changed key to gasps of soprano pain, he cradled his throbbing broken hand.

'You can't do this, this my place you know! I got rights!' Crack woman started screaming at Eddie.

'Not anymore, you been cuckooed love. Running a crack house gives you fuck-all rights.'

'He's my boyfriend, him,' she said pointing at bleeding-mouth, with a certain air of disappointment. 'It's him and that evil fucking foreign fella.'

'OK Lofty lash 'em up.' Eddie tossed his rucksack to Lofty, who pulled out plastic ties and gaffer tape.

'Rich tapestry of life Eddie.' Rumpunch snorted out a laugh.

'How do people end up like this?' Eddie shook his head.

'They lost, got nothing to believe in.' Lofty grabbed the woman sat her next to the acid brothers and herded the couple over. They were shaking with nerves, the fear butting up against their high, which was now a nightmare ride. He carried on efficiently lashing them all together.

'Don't fucking tell me they Ronin Lofty,' muttered Eddie angrily.

'That'll keep em.' Lofty said standing back looking at his work.

The junkies, acid brothers and crack woman were lashed together back to back in a sitting position, legs splayed out in the middle of the room, mouths gaffer-taped, staring wild-eyed and pleading at Eddie and Rum, the stash laid out before him.

'My suggestion - burn this place down with these guys in it.' Rumpunch tapped his baseball bat in the palm of his hand. Muffled wailing from the bunch. 'OK maybe that'd be cruel to

171

dumb life. I'll whack them first, knock em out, be humane.'

'OK we got photos of your faces.' Eddie shook his head and stared hard at the junkies. 'We got your ID. So, if you don't want to get burned, my assistant here,' he indicated Lofty, 'will be taking confessions.'

Lofty pulled a mobile out of bleeding-mouths pocket, then ripped the gaffer tape off his mouth, bleeding-mouth whimpered. Lofty flicked the phone to record and then slapped bleeding-mouth in the face with his other hand. 'OK, tell me all about your crack house business . . .'

'Well done, Lofty.' The three of them stood outside on the street. 'Confessions nicely recorded.' Eddie held the acid brothers' phone up.

'No worries Boss, what now?' Eddie dialled a number. It rang, he gave the address and listed the drugs, then phone still connected, he taped it to the letterbox. 'Let Plod sort it.'

The three of them took off blue plastic gloves and handed them to Lofty who stuck them in a rucksack.

'That's it then.' Eddie looked at Rumpunch. 'I got to take the fucker out.' Lofty nodded.

'We back on active service then, Sarge?' Eddie nodded, noting he was Sarge again, Rumpunch held up his hands.

'OK. But hold up. First I set up a meet with the Malones.'

'They still run the action.'

'Yeah Eddie and Boss Malone's son Mickey is the head honcho now.'

'I thought he went to Uni.'

'He did but dropped out, but don't underestimate him, he's a Malone all right, a real nutter.'

Chapter 43: Spratt

Spratt took his cam-pants off the ironing board, inspected the creases, tight neat and perfect, his rucksack was packed but he emptied it again and re-checked the contents: camera, blanket, gloves, water bottle, and field dressing. He barked a bitter laugh. 'Won't need that.' And stashed the field dressing back in his bedside locker. Pistol army issue, loaded, he flipped out the magazine, checked the rounds, cleaned and oiled, snapped the magazine back in the pistol. He looked around his room, faded John Wayne film poster, a large framed photo, army Land Rover in the foreground, Spratt standing in the back on the machine gun swivel, Mosque tower in the hazy distance.

He pulled his pants on, snapped the Regimental belt tight round his waist, put his anorak on and studied himself in the mirror. OK, not bad, receding hairline and a bit of a waistline but neat and tidy, ready for checkout.

Spratt savoured the end of pain, end of crippling anxiety attacks, no more visits by ghosts in his nightmares, days spent hold up in the woods. The last few weeks he'd chatted with the lads and laughed and joked. Nobody suspected a thing. He felt peaceful, the end of it all at last.

He shouldered his rucksack, took one last look around the room, everything very neat, he nodded. 'Job done, dismissed,' he told himself, 'proceed to check-out.' He breathed out slowly, feeling a final deep relief. His Mum and sister were at work, the house was quiet, he locked the front door, pushed his house keys through the letter box, stood to attention, snapped a salute to the house and marched away.

Chapter 44: Tail End Charlie

Lofty was switched on, he sipped his Guinness slowly so nobody would suspect and checked the camera he'd got from Spiky Harris, ex-Mob. From the window of the Newman Arms, he could see the alleyway connecting Percy Passage to Newman Passage, a narrow foot tunnel that cut through into a cobblestone courtyard and the old coaching entrance to Newman Street, north of Oxford Street. When Eddie had told Lofty that he was sure someone was tailing him, Lofty felt the click of the switch, drew a deep breath, and snapped into hyper-alertness, his world came into focus, mission on, he was tail end Charlie.

They came up with a plan to pick up the tail. Eddie would leave the Estate pulling a wheelie suitcase and head downtown on a pre-planned route. Lofty would set up a Forward Observation Post (FOP). Lofty had picked the Newman Arms as an ideal FOP. He took another sip of his Guinness; it tasted sharp. He felt as if he'd come alive after a long hibernation. He automatically scanned the pub, working out who he'd clobber first if it kicked off and then which exit to make a dash for. Daft, he knew, but switched on was switched on, alert to every potential danger around every corner. He smiled, he was on active service, on a different plane to all around him, but scowled in irritation as the phantom itch below his knee kicked off, he scratched his prosthetic leg, it seemed to work. His phone beeped, Eddie signalling his position. Lofty walked out of the pub down the tunnel, cut left into Newman Passage courtyard and stepped back into the shadows and waited.

The sound of a wheelie suitcase bumping down the cobblestones, Eddie emerged from the tunnel casually, as if deep in thought. He paused in the courtyard and then walked to the right. Sure enough, Lofty spotted a tail hanging back in the foot tunnel watching Eddie. Unseen, Lofty snapped photos, the tail slunk across the courtyard, following Eddie up through the entrance to Newman Street.

Lofty checked the pictures on the camera, he knew Eddie's route so he was in no hurry. Eddie would meander around to Oxford Street and take the alleyway steps down to

Ramillies Street. It was all about working out where the choke points were to spot surveillance.

Just as Lofty was going to emerge from the shadows another tail came into view, then a third hurrying through the tunnel to catch up. They had a quick chat and changed positions so the last one took point duty now, they were following Eddie's tail. Lofty felt a surge of joy, real threats not imagined, this wasn't paranoia, this was bliss, a real mission to live and die for, he was back on duty. So, he thought, Eddie's tail has two tails, what was that about a tale of two cities, a city with two tails. Or, three tails now. Lofty had to pause, he'd confused himself, he shook his head and wobbled up the cobbles.

He texted Eddie, "Take long way to Ramillies Steps – others in the game." Ramillies was a narrow squeeze of steps leading down from Oxford Street, into a narrow dogleg lane that ran around the back of department stores into Soho. It was another perfect choke point. Lofty scuttled down Newman Street crossed Oxford Street, down Ramillies Steps, turned left into the dogleg and sat in the back doorway of the department store, in his once familiar homeless person posture. All I need is that bloody dog on a string, it could wag its tail, and then they'd be four tails, one city. Lofty chuckled at his stupid thoughts; he was switched on happy. He stuffed the camera in his shoulder bag and waited, still trying to unscramble his tail metaphor. A text alerted him, Eddie was on top of the steps. Then Eddie passed him, then the first tail, then the other two, leapfrogging each other. They had taken their coats off, very pro of them. Lofty texted again, "Go slow." Lofty wanted to beat them to Moonlight, he felt the joy of serving a mission, his life mattered again.

Eddie rocked up at Moonlight. Scotch was on the door.

'Lofty said hang out here with me for a couple of minutes. He's in the upstairs window, wants to take photos so he does. What the fuck is going on, eh?'

'Lofty and his Samurai shit "way of the watcher" innit,' replied Eddie.

'Aye that's a good one.' Scotch chuckled. 'And he told me you beat me to "way of the wankers".'

'Come on Scotch, not like you not to have a good slag off.'

'Ach man, I'm working on it, so I am.'

In the basement kitchen at Moonlight, Eddie, Scotch and Lofty looked at the photos on an iPad. Eddie didn't know any of them. Lofty reckoned the first tail was a junky but the other two looked military-trained, Special Branch surveillance maybe.

'So, who the fuck are they?' demanded Scotch. Eddie thought back through the specialist training back in the Mob.

'No idea. Lofty, show the other lads the photos and let's see if they pop up again.' Lofty beamed and nodded to Eddie, he felt serene and almost bowed, he was on a missi0n, no more a Ronin.

Chapter 45: Funeral

Eddie stared at the rafters high up above, in the ceiling of the old Norman church. It looked like the inside of a Viking longship. He imagined he was one of Odin's ravens flying above Viking raiders battling across the North Sea to sack the monasteries on the East coast of England. What were their names, oh yeah, Huginn and Muninn . . . the Norse god's spies . . . the service washed over him.

"At the going down of the sun and in the morning,
We will remember them..."

'Will he fuck - he's just gabbing on about fucking Jesus,' a voice behind him whispered loudly.

'Shusssh for Christ's sake . . .!' Eddie turned his head, annoyed.

'That's funny,' another voice whispering, as if on night patrol.

"They mingle not with their laughing comrades again;
They sit no more at familiar tables of home..."

More mumbling from behind. 'Shut up you idiots,' whispered Eddie in the same sharp command tone he had used on night patrols with this same bunch of idiots. Decent turn out from the old mob he thought, no Ruperts just us Toms for the funeral, although he suspected it was the chance for a piss-up with old comrades for most of them. The Vicar droned on and on, the guys were getting fidgety; church parades had never been a big hit back in the Mob.

At last the service finished and they all lined up to shuffle past Spratt's family, shake hands and murmur a few words. First up Spiky muttering, "He was a good soldier" to the mother and sister Jenny, which wasn't even true. Eddie had to keep a sharp eye on Spratt most of the time. Eddie shuffled forward, found himself holding the mother's outstretched hand, he snapped back into the present. This is all the family Spratt had; his Dad had been a farm labourer, killed in a tractor accident when the mob was out in Iraq. Spratt had taken that bad.

'He was a good soldier.' Now I'm the liar thought Eddie.

The mother just nodded, red-eyed and worn out, Spratt's sister Jenny, leaning in, hugging her Mum's arm, supporting her, being strong.

The lads all gathered in the churchyard, some in ill-fitting suits, the rest in jeans and jackets, apart from Lofty in odd matching tweed pants and jacket. Their hair was longer but Eddie could spot soldiers in Civvy clothes a mile away.

'You'll all come to the house then. It's good of you boys . . .' the mother broke off, crying silently. Jenny hugged her and spoke quietly, 'Me an Mum would like you all to come over to our house, after. Have tea and a bite to eat like . . .' She bit her lip, pleading with her eyes.

'OK lads it's over to Spratt's Mum's after the burial.' Eddie ordered as he turned around facing the lineup. Lofty, take a whip round and get some drink for the house.' He turned back to Mum and sister Jenny. 'We'll give Spratt a proper send off.' Mum sniffled and forced a smile, Jenny reached out and touched Eddie's arm.

'Thanks, Eddie.'

They buried Spratt next to his Dad, and a lad from the local T.A. blew "Last Post" on a bugle, the lads shuffling to attention. The family house was a few minutes away on the edge of Spratton village; hence Spratt's nickname, a council house crescent, fifteen grey houses, gardens front and back. They ambled slowly through the village; the sun was out, the day warming up. Lofty and Spiky peeled off to the village post office shop to get the carryout.

A couple of the lads had to carry Gillespie in his wheelchair through the narrow kitchen to the back garden. They gathered around, rolled smokes and got some banter on the go, while Spratt's Mum started brewing tea. Sister Jenny made cheese and tuna sandwiches.

Lofty and Spiky arrived with two carrier bags full of beers, a bottle of vodka and bottle of gin, setting them down by the garden bench. The lads grabbed beers, Jenny moved among them with a tray of food. Spiky made a big chivalrous play of taking the tray from her. He had been the Mob's signals guy and on account of everybody reckoning he was the best-looking lad in the Mob, he felt it was his duty to chat up every woman he came across. Marty 'Twitchy' Doyle was there, getting changed into his running gear, worried he'd miss a day's training. He was doing an Iron Man next month. These days Twitchy was a keep-fit fanatic.

You use what you can, thought Eddie, at least he'd got his paranoia under control. Twitchy Doyle was convinced special agents were following him, so he'd taken up running to make the supposed surveillance team work harder. Eddie leaned against the fence as the lads jeered Twitchy Doyle off on his run and rolled a smoke, watching his mob getting into story time and laughing it up.

'Hey Sarge, what was the name of that officer, you know the one with the golden retriever?'

It never took long for Legal Evans, the barrack room lawyer, to spout up. Some of the lads stood around him sipping beer with expectant grins ready for his punch line.

'Collins!' Eddie shouted back.

'Cheers Sarge. That's right, Collins was his name, anyway, the silly fucker had the map orientated west instead of north and he says to me, "Corporal that mountain shouldn't be there", an' I says well sir, some fucker has moved it then, maybe it was Mohammed.' The lads burst out laughing. 'You know let the mountain come to Mohammed.' Another round of laughter, daft Rupert tales always went down well.

'Light Sarge,' Spiky nudged Eddie on the arm. Eddie flicked his Zippo, Spiky cupped his hand over the Zippo, puffed and drew in a lungful.

'Heard you avin' a bit of bother back home then Sarge.'

'Oh yeah, what are you G.C.H., fucking Q. then,' replied Eddie, annoyed that the mob was gassing his business. 'Lofty!' he bawled. Lofty leaned out the kitchen door, cheese butty in his mouth holding his hands out shrugging his shoulders.

'Sorry Sarge, don't mean nothing but you know the lads chat like.' Spiky shuffled nervously.

'Yeah, all right then Spiky, I was out of order there. So, what you up to?'

'Me Sarge, I'm in audio-visual business now innit.

Set up with Jacko from REME. We even supply shops, with small unobtrusive recording cameras. That's a great word unobtrusive, sound like an intelligent way of saying hidden. Yeah, shopkeepers like that.'

'You and Jacko, eh, well done Spiky.'

Legal Evans started up again, 'Oh Sarge, you got Lofty an Scotch John working doors, which one opens the door and who shuts it then?' Muted laughter.

Lofty stepped out the kitchen doorway in his mismatched tweed suit. 'I can still shut your fucking door, Evans.' Laughter rippled around the garden, banter had officially broken out but Spratt's Mum started wailing.

'Why, why the fuck did he do it.' She sat down sobbing on a garden bench. Jenny rushed over and hugged her. The lads went sheepish and quietened down to muted chat. Jenny looked up at the lads not sure what to say.

'He used to go bird watching,' she said and looked around at the lads confused.

'What!' sputtered Evans, 'Spratt bird watching, you mean ones with feathers.'

'Yeah,' replied Jenny, 'he'd get all dressed in his army cams and off he go with sleeping bag and camera,' she shook her head to herself, 'up the woods and hills for days.' The lads looked surprised.

'What were his photos like?' Fat Phil butted in.

'I never saw any,' replied Jenny.

'You know love,' Mum rubbed her eyes, 'I don't think he ever took a photo, he just hid up in the hills. That's what he was doing.'

'Got a point innit Sarge,' Fat Phil sidled over, whispering to Eddie, 'I feel like hiding away lots of times, an him by his self up in the woods, an he puts a gun in his mouth and pulls the fucking trigger.' Fat Phil shivered all over. 'Horrible way to go.'

'So, how about you these days Fat Phil?'

'Putting on bloody weight Sarge. When I was the skinniest guy in the Mob the nickname "Fats" was cool, like Fats Domino innit, cos' he played a piano.' Eddie shook his head at the logic. 'But since I got out its become a bit prophetic like.

That's fucking driving trucks for you.'

Eddie chuckled. Robbie Williams' Angel started playing on the sound system.

'Come on lads,' shouted Spiky and started singing the lads all joining in. It was one of the anthems of the tour. They gathered in the garden, arms around each other's shoulders, singing about loving mothers. Spratt's Mum had cried herself out, she sat on the garden bench sniffing and smiling sadly, as a bunch of soldiers sang their version to her.

Eddie thought it summed up the contradictory nature of the Mob, a bunch of sentimental ex-Toms marching out of step with the world.

When I'm sick and fucked / On my arse in a busy Civvy street
I Don't ask for help
Everyone joined in the end chorus,
Army life wont break me / orders must be obeyed
My mates will stand by me / With my Mob on parade.

Mum got up and walked around hugging the lads, they wore soft smiles.

'Com'n Sarge your turn . . .'

'Yeah, Yellow Rupert Sarge.'

Eddie smiled, he couldn't sing a note but everybody did a turn on tour, long boring nights stuck in camps. Eddie stood on the kitchen steps.

'There's a one-eyed yellow Rupert to the north of Kathmandu . . .'

The lads cheered, the Mob together again.

'There's a little marble cross below the town;
There's a broken-hearted woman,
tends the grave of an N.C.O,'

The lads all joined in,

'And the jealous Ruperts forever gazes down.'

Eddie got into his stride; knees bent arms outstretched, pointing at the lads . . .

'He was known a 'Mad ranker'
By Ruperts in officers mess,
But was better than they felt inclined to tell,

But, for all his foolish pranks,
He was worshipped by the ranks,
Eddie held his arms out.
And the C.O.'s daughter smiled on him as well....'
The lads cheered.

Shadows lengthened across the back lawn, Evans hauled out the Vodka. It had to happen thought Eddie, our time is passing and we're surplus to requirements, were becoming long shadows.

Mum had stuttered to dry heaving; she sat in the middle of the garden, drinking Gin and sharing her grief with the lads, who took it as a sign to quieten down. Soldiers can talk all day in a whisper if they have to.

Spiky brought Eddie a beer, they sat at the end of the garden on an old rotting log seat, next to tall weeds.

'Makes you think, you know Sarge; any one of us could do it. It's when you been out a while it hits you. I dunno, kind of alone just marking time is a dull existence, almost wish some fucker was shooting at me again.'

Spiky was just saying what all the lads were feeling, thought Eddie, he sipped his beer and thought of Jassi, 'you know Spiky leaving the Mob is like falling overboard from an ocean liner, you're all alone in a big sea, you just grab anything to hang on to, so as not to drown.'

'Bleeding spot on Sarge.'

'What was Spratt hanging on to?'

'Spratt. He was doing lots of drugs you know, prescriptions like, for depression and anxiety,' Spikey blew out his breath. 'He would ring me middle of the night ranting on in circles about some conspiracy theory or other, just like Twitchy.' Spiky took a swallow. 'Fuck me Sarge, he should have talked to Twitchy Doyle. Anyway I stopped answering the phone, an' he kills himself.' Spiky paused. 'Was I his lifebelt?'

'No Spiky, there are no lifebelts, booze and drugs don't keep you afloat. Got to hang on to yourself mate, give your self a mission. It was drummed into us for combat, that shit sticks, use it.'

'Lofty says he's going Samurai. Silly sod. What's your

mission then Sarge?'

'Funny Spiky, just hit me. Maybe I been grabbing any mission that comes along just to stop me drowning out there.'

Spiky went and sat on the grass and put his arm around Jenny. Mum had three of the lads around her, telling funny stories about Spratt. She was laughing tears now. Eddie strolled over to Gillespie who was rolling a joint, bottle of cider in his wheelchair drinks holder.

'Good send off, isn't Sarge,' he offered the joint to Eddie.

'No thanks Gilly, been drinking, mustn't mix it.'

'I got medicinal dispen-fucking-sation.' Gilly drew in a lungful and blew a smokestack.

'So, when you getting the prosthetics then.'

'Won't give 'em me till I pass psyche test, Sarge. They say I got extreme P.T.S.D, got me in a residential mental home run by a charity. I tell 'em yeah I got bad dreams, wake up screaming Sarge, you know, I.E.D. an' all. I tell 'em I lost me fucking legs, not me head.' He took another long draw. 'Funny all I remember is the flash, can't remember the bang.'

'Well we all remember the bang Gilly, it was a big loud bang. I get the same dream but it's me that loses the legs not you, fucking shame mate.'

'Is what it is Sarge. Anyhow I'll be a freaking blade-runner soon, wanna get a grant to train for the Para Olympics, be on T.V.' Eddie laughed.

'Fancy a gold medal, do ya Gilly.'

'Oh yeah, Invictus Games, tea with royalty. – You know it's funny but I got more'n these guys to look forward to,' he waved his joint at the garden, 'I'm in the system, what these lads got?'

'Funny; leave the mob an' all we got is bad dreams.' Eddie took a swig. They both went deep in thought. Fat Phil shouted to Jezzer Sullivan.

'Oi Darkie give us Green, Green Grass of Home.'

Jezzer looked very annoyed, Scotch put a hand on Fat Phil's arm.

'He's wee Jezzer now you ken, we don't call him Darkie any more.' Fat Phil looked confused, 'Nobody told me. How we supposed to know?'

'Aye well you have a point there so you do.' Scotch scratched his head.

'But not Jez, I'll take Jezzer but not Jez.' Jezzer jumped up on the weed-cracked patio, bottle in hand, 'OK then Green, Green Grass, lads.' They all cheered, Gilly nudging Eddie.

'His version is bang on, innit Sarge.'

Jezzer took a swig wiped his mouth and sang in a clear, sad tenor

The old airfield looks the same as they land the plane,
The families in the chapel to meet me.

The lads formed a circle arms around each other, knees bent stamping out the beat with their right foot and with a tribal "Hooh!" they belted out the chorus.

The old barracks still standing, tho' my comrades are
long gone,
  and there's that parade ground I used to march on.

Jezzer was note perfect, the lads were connected to that tribal feeling they had when the Mob was in bandit country . . .

For there's a guard of Honour and a mad old padre -
arms at port they'll stand to attention.
"Hooh".
And carry a' coffin to final destination.
"Hooh".
Yes, they'll all salute me in a military graveyard
So young to lie, six foot beneath the ground.

Jezzer finished singing and the silence rang out. Nobody wanted to break the spell, the lads stood still, arms around each other, their heads bowed. Lofty stepped up in his odd mismatched tweed outfit. Marched to the centre of the garden, stamped his right foot down bringing him to attention, it somehow looked right. He shouted in his best parade ground corporal voice

"Ahhhh-ten...shun."

The lads snapped to it.

Lofty looked them over and coughed once,

'And In the going down, we will remember him.'

'We will remember him.' The Lads answered in harmony.

Lofty saluted, the lads paused in silence and then loudly,

'Rest in peace.'

'Spratt!' All of them shouted together,

Eddie had a tear in his eye, but he hoped nobody noticed. Maybe it wasn't just bad dreams we're left with. We got this though; he looked over the lads, standing in a council house back garden getting drunk. Work out whatever this is . . . Doctor Fuck-me-Boots Vaughan.

Chapter 46: Mental

'They call him Mental Mickey Malone but not to his face, just so you understand the situation.' Rum flicked his indicator and turned into the north London pub car park. 'This is where he holds court, and I'm not joking.' He parked the Range Rover and looked through the windscreen at three suited lumps standing in the Pub entrance. 'In there he is King, with the power of life or death,' Rum tapped a rhythm on the steering wheel and pronounced his words slowly on the beat, 'people, can, disappear, Eddie.'

They got out, Eddie fully switched on, followed Rum to the entrance, the lumps frisked them and ushered them through. Inside brass hangings, shiny mirrors, dark wood and forest green walls, lined with pictures of boxers and celebs posing with the Malone family, the Celebs looking scared. Mental Mickey Malone was sitting in the far corner, back to the wall, a scattering of Malone troops hung around. They all wore suits. Mickey stood up, pinstripe suit, hard bony face, floppy Brian Ferry hairstyle.

'This 'im then, fucking war hero is he. What you aving, ave a lager, go on, its Belgian, brewed by fucking Monks, can you believe that?' asked Mickey.

'Prefer an Ale if you got one,' replied Eddie. Mickey gestured to the seat facing him.

'Don't ya like me Lager, then?'

'Thought you said it was Belgian Monks.' Eddie sat, well aware that his back was to the rest of the Pub and Mickey's troops.

'Hear that, that's funny,' Mickey cracked up. 'He's a funny cunt.' The retinue chuckled. He shouted to the barman, 'Get 'im an effing Morris-Dancing mucky fucky Ale!'

'Straight glass mate!' barked Eddie, the barman switched glasses and started pulling the pump.

'Now according to Rum here,' Mickey nodded to Rum who was standing by the bar, arms folded, flanked by a couple of moody family members. 'He says you done your wartime but you ave stepped on some fucker's toes in your own yard. That right?' Eddie turned to look around, only one exit route and way too many lumps to even think about surviving a rear up.

'Yeah, I seemed to have upset a fella called Djokovic; he parked in the children's play area.'

'Did he now? Oi, you fuckers move back,' Mickey waved his boys back; they had all leaned in to listen. 'Uncle Delaney come sit here and you too Rum.' Rum moved from the bar, followed by a thickset grey haired broken nose big guy with a comfortable belly.

'This is me Uncle Delaney.' Mickey patted Uncle Delaney on the knee. 'He keeps me in line see, I got a mental condition, did you know?'

'Isn't it confidential between you and your doctor then?' Eddie sat back expecting a blow out. Mickey and Uncle Delaney burst out laughing, Uncle Delaney farted loudly.

'Me uncle's got a medical condition too, only its prostate cancer he's got, he's medically approved for farting, he got to let the effing wind out.' Delaney farted again followed by a low growl.

'I'm fucking good at it,' Delaney winked at Eddie.

Mickey waved his finger. 'So you run a couple of doors in Soho, who you got working them?'

'Ex-Forces lads, they're used to checkpoint work. Nobody else is looking out for them.' Mickey nodded in thought.

'What you think uncle Delaney, army lads.'

Delaney leaned forward growling like gravel slipping off a tipper. 'It's a fucking shame, the way they're treated. Put themselves in harm's way for pocket money Mickey, but let's get to the Serbian.'

'How's your ale, enjoying it are ya, it's four pound fifty a pint here,' Mickey cackled, 'but I own the fucking pub.' He paused. 'So you can have it at wholesale cost.' He burst out laughing, slapped his knees, and pointed at Eddie. 'See his fucking face, got 'im, good innit?' Uncle Delaney smiled like he'd heard it before, a joke wearing thin.

Mickey stopped giggling and pulled himself together. 'Yeah, anyway the Serbian joker has a beef about you, wants you sorted see, wants' you to disappear.' Mickey waved his hands in the air. 'What's your fucking version?' he glared at Eddie. Eddie glanced at Rum, who gave him a slight nod.

'Well he's upsetting the neighbourhood, he parks his Merc in the children's' play area, he treats our citizens like shit and the fucker robbed me gaff, me Mum's jewellery and . . . ' Eddie paused looked over his shoulder, 'my medals.' The lumps all shook their heads.

'That's out of order,' said one of the crew. Eddie nodded to them and turned back to Mental.

'And then he sent a couple of junky fuckers to acid me, so he's declared war and I'll finish it.' Eddie half raised up from his seat, 'Unless you want to do the magic act on me.' Eddie sat back, 'Abracadabra,' he waved his hands in the air, imitating Mickey. 'Poof,' Eddie took a few deep breaths to calm down; his voice had raised an octave.

Mickey and Delaney laughed. 'Magic trick, fucking remember that one eh uncle Delaney? We gonna use that one all right. Hey geezers what's a magic trick?' His retinue looked puzzled. 'When you make the fucker disappear!' They responded with smiles and chuckles. Mickey turned to Eddie and flung his arms out, 'Abracadabra. Fuck me! It don't work on soldier boys then, ha, ha, ha.' He pointed at Eddie, 'So Eddie you good at magic tricks?'

Uncle Delaney leaned in and poured more gravel out. 'What my nephew means is, can you handle the Serb?'

Mickey, eyes gleaming, 'Cos I hate the cunt.' He peered at Eddie. 'He won't drink me lager.'

'Nice pint.' Eddie held the beer up, adding, 'And yeah I can look after myself if it comes to a tear-up, but what's the repercussions, it's your Manor.'

'What suits us? Eh Uncle?' Mickey looked at Delaney who leaned in again, started to speak, cleared his throat, swallowed, coughed and farted loudly.

'Fucking prostrate! Don't get cancer it's a fucking nightmare.' He pressed a big fist down on the table and straightened his back. 'Ah that feels better. A tear-up's no good, we'll have to step in and sort shit out, but if you do a magic trick . . . '

'Cos that suit us,' Mickey butted in, 'Inde-fucking-pendent action, nothing comes back to us. Private beef settled, 'cos he upset our boys back from the war,' Mickey dabbed at his lips with a napkin and lowered his voice, 'wasn't our business, so no repercussions with the other firms, neat solution. London families will swallow that.'

'I brought my friend Eddie here for clarification,' Rumpunch spoke up. 'The Serb's under your license aint he?'

'My fucking license and he thinks he's fucking cock of the yard, doing business behind my back with his fellow fucking ex-warlord cunts.' Spittle-flecked at the corner of Mickey's mouth, 'So fucking Abracadabra to him,' he turned to Eddie, 'Right soldier?'

Eddie didn't look to Rum this time. 'So, you get a free pass, while I sort out your problem?'

'You know I'm getting to like you, aren't we Uncle Delaney. Let me taste your fucking Ale then,' Mickey reached across and raised Eddie's beer to his lips. 'Tastes like shit, musty rotten mushroom and nuts. How the fuck can you drink this Morris Dancing clog wearing shit.' He wiped his lips and spat. 'Aarrrgghh anyway, you get that drink free. Oh, and no interference, no repercussions.'

'Be good P.R., go down well with the other families,' growled bear-in-the-woods Uncle Delaney. Eddie wondered what P.R?

'Yeah, we looking after our boys,' added Mickey, 'and if Djokovic can't handle a few squaddies in his manor, well then, he's not a fit and proper person to run things.'

Rumpunch raised an eyebrow that told Eddie he'd got a lucky break.

'Now have a glass of the fucking Belgian monk's lager and tell me a war story for fuck's sake.' Mickey chuckled. Uncle Delaney farted; the barman pulled.

Chapter 47: Dream Walker

Lofty lowered himself into an uncomfortable chair, facing Gilly in his wheelchair, dressed in a thin hospital gown and surfer shorts. They were in the day room. It was quiet.

'So, what's your beef on the Bushido virtues then?' Lofty asked.

'Yeah, with the fifth one, compassion particularly; the other six are OK, kind of near to the Mob values anyway.'

'Yeah, know what you mean Gilly, although we never talked about virtues in the Mob, we kinda understood what a warrior was.'

'The stuff you sent me talks about respect, courage, honour, righteousness, loyalty and honesty.' Gilly wheeled in closer and spoke in hushed tones, 'OK, I get all that, but the crap on compassion comes over all social worker bullshit.'

'Maybe we take the other six and put number five on hold for special occasions.' Lofty rubbed his chin, a habit he picked up from studying the hero actor Toshiro Mifune in Kurosawa samurai films. He thought it gave him gravitas.

'Well we ain't Japanese samurai are we,' said Gilly, giving it some thought, he nodded at his missing legs, 'and anyway they didn't entertain cripples did they?'

'Never thought about it, Gilly.' Lofty mentally re-ran clips from the films. 'I guess we shape the Bushido template to fit our situation.' They sat for a while in silence.

'I've been doing the Zen meditating thing and even been practising some fighting moves in my mind.' Gilly looked at his legless torso. Lofty followed his gaze to the stumps, surfer shorts tied off at the ends.

'Do they still itch?'

'Yeah my toes, like it's fucking crazy, innit Lofty.'

'It's all in the mind mate, does meditation help?'

'Toes still fucking itch, Lofty.'

'Yeah, know what you mean, I still feel the leg but Bushido got me out of a hole.'

'Ex-Toms like us Lofty,' Gilly pointed at Lofty's

prosthetic, 'we're the way of the wasted, are we kidding ourselves?'

'Up to you. You either get on mission, or crash out.'

'OK, OK I'm buying it Lofty,' said an anxious Gilly, 'need something to keep me going in here.'

'What are they doing with you?'

'Won't sign off on me new legs until I stop being a nutter. My head is fragged mate, wake up middle of the night screaming, trying to run in the bed then I hoist myself in the wheelchair and try to break out, don't get far.'

'No forward planning then? I'm sure Bushido virtues mention planning.'

'Huh. Yeah, bang on mate, but like I'm in other peoples' bad dreams.'

'Well,' Lofty rubbed at his chin, not sure how to respond and came up with, 'disturbing development.'

'Oh yeah, really weird and these buggers . . .' Gilly pointed back into the ward to emphasize his point. 'They're all having really bad nightmares.' Gilly wheeled himself around. 'Come on, let's go have a smoke on the balcony.' Lofty followed the wheelchair through the big double doors leading out to a balcony of the old mansion, it was covered in wire mesh.

'Looks like an aviary,' said Lofty.

'Stops us loony birds flying away.'

'Very secure,' said Lofty. Gilly rolled a spliff while Lofty felt the wiring, 'Just like the grenade barriers we had on that OP on the crossroads.'

'Yeah, and I'm still at the bloody crossroads.' Gilly lit up, took a big drag and exhaled a plume of smoke, 'Lofty get me out of here mate, I got to force some action on me legs, can't do nothing cooped up in here. The nightmares are freaking me out, know what I mean.'

'The dreams, you know, is it the dope?' he nodded at Gilly's spliff. Lofty had decided to adopt a, considering the situation look, and stroked his chin again, thinking he must watch the film again to see what else Mifune did.

'No mate, this is the only thing that blocks it all out.' Gilly took another drag.' Lofty nodded, understanding.

'OK, so in your dreams, can you do anything?'

'Dunno,' said Gilly obviously surprised Lofty was taking him seriously. 'Maybe, think so; I run in 'em, run the fuck away from what's coming after me.'

'OK. Listen Gilly, Bushido means we find a way to take the initiative back.'

'Bugger me!' Gilly looked up at Lofty in astonishment. 'Why didn't I think of that, fighting back then, eh Lofty?'

'Mate you're frag-mental-legless in a nuthouse, you're on drugs, so, how you supposed to think?'

'No brains and only one leg between us.' Gilly laughed and spluttered spliff smoke out his nostrils. 'So yeah my dream innit, and I got legs in me dreams, so bollox to em!'

Lofty and Gilly laughed just this side of crazy. Finally, they subsided and drew breath. Gilly wiped at the happy tears rolling down his cheeks.

'Always pick your ground, arigatou gozaimasu Gilly minna-san.' Lofty spoke slowly, attempting a man of wisdom pose, and bowed to Gilly.

'What's that mean Lofty?' Gilly bowed back from his wheelchair.

'It's like, thanks to you for these moments, but I'm not sure, may have mispronounced it.'

Gilly laughed again.

Chapter 48: Lunch with Rum

Rumpunch drove to the North Circ, hung a left and headed west. The traffic was the usual snarl-up.

'He's a sarnie short of a picnic Rum, fucking Mental Mickey, that was right on the edge mate,' said Eddie.

'Eddie, he's a five-course-slap-up-dinner crafty department but behind the nut job, Machiavelli.' Rum flicked his indicator and muscled into the outside lane passing a huge slow moving truck. 'When the old man died, his cousins, two very nasty twisted brothers, even for that family, thought they should be in charge.'

'So what happened?' Eddie turned in his seat.

'Well they had it over Mickey on the physical but Mickey played them and took them down.'

'How so?'

'He showed a ruthless hand that impressed everyone. He used his Uncle, the very terrifying Delaney as his muscle.'

'You mean!' Eddie rocked back, 'against his own sons?'

'Oh yeah, that's right, so don't underestimate Mental Mickey, a very clever and ruthless fucker, if you're in a deal with him, you stick to the deal, no cutting short.'

'So, you working for him then Rum?'

'No. The Malones run North London. I pay them tax and they provides services and connections. The Malones are one of London's big five. You're in now, like it or not.'

'Not sure I like that Rum.'

'It's the way it is on the dark side of the street Eds. London's been organised for centuries. Knew a brother, coke dealer, thought he was king of the hill, wouldn't take advice. I found him in the boot of his own car, hands and feet missing.

'What, the Malones had him done?'

'No, his competition was a Triad running coke out of China-town. What I'm saying is, he weren't connected, no career counselling, no insurance, no cover, know what I mean.'

Eddie watched as a Bentley convertible pulled past, he recognised the driver, a young football star flashing the bling.

He looked over to Rum, who rolled his eyes, envy and disdain echoed in one brief glance between them.

'When they say London's organised crime, the emphasis should be on the organised bit, O.K.?' Rum changed down gears and nipped into the outside lane, smiling as he tailgated the Bentley. 'You should know what chaos brings, you lot stuck your heads in a wasp's nest out there, didn't you?'

They fell silent, the road opened up past the Finchley turn off under the overpass. Rum hung a left, wriggled through a posh housing estate and sneaked onto the A1, did a right up Winnington Ave, even bigger posh houses, to the Spaniards Inn, top of Hampstead Heath.

Eddie stared out the window at the city appearing below them through the gaps in the trees. Deep in thought, mulling over the Malones, wasn't until Rum dropped down past Primrose Hill into Camden Parkway that he spoke.

'So, if I expand the doors operation, the Malones tax me?'

'Yeah, you're in the West End, so one of the families is going to come calling, if you're with Mickey you get fringe benefits. He's clever like that, in his interest to makes sure you prosper. He did economics at university.'

They pulled up in Parkway, a one-way street, shops both sides leading down to Camden tube.

'Pass me the folder in the glove box will ya?' asked Rum. Eddie popped the glove box and handed a leather folder to Rum. He flipped through the divides and pulled out a parking permit, Camden Highways Officer, and placed it on top of the dashboard. 'See, fringe benefits.' He showed Eddie the inside of the folder, layers of official looking permits. 'Covers all London, part of the Malone service, like Rotary Club, you get me. Come on let's 'ave an English fry up.' They walked into the Good Fayre Café on Parkway, gingham tablecloths, dark wood tables.

'Ah, Rum, you wanna the back seat?' said a Portuguese waiter, hurrying over, greeting Rum with respect.

'Yeah Donato, this is my friend Eddie,' Donato did a little bow and smiled. 'How you Eddie, hungry?'

'Yeah cheers,' Eddie replied as they both sat in the back

booth, Eddie back to the wall, so he could see the street. Donato put two menus on the gingham tablecloth. Rum waved the menu away and asked for the Breakfast Royal for two with a pot of tea.

'Ah, nothing like a cuppa before a fry-up,' said Rum, pouring two cups and adding milk. He took a sip. Eddie stirred his own tea vigorously.

'So, I'm tied into the Malone's now?'

'You're in their territory and availing yourself of the local underworld service scheme, carve out your niche my man.' Rum said, smiling as breakfast arrived, big plates of "Full English", steam rising off the baked beans. Donato returned with a large wooden pepper mill.

'You want pepper?' asked Donato, Eddie nodded and Donato twisted a shower of crushed peppercorn on his plate.

'Got any HP?' asked Eddie.

'Sure, we're a classy establishment, aren't we Rum.'

Rum nodded. 'You are that Donato and thank god you're still here, not some fancy latte coffee house.'

'Ha Rum, its family business, nothing as important as family, eh.' Donato walked off waving his hands at what looked like his daughter inspecting her red fingernails behind the coffee counter.

'So, Eddie, how you gonna play this joker, fella?'

'Well, I'm not rushing in Rum. Take time - recce the lay of the land.'

Rum forked a big mouthful of bacon egg and beans but didn't stop talking, 'Meanwhile Eddie, he be taking more pops at you, thinking he's covered by the Malones.' Eddie spread thick dollops of HP sauce over his bacon, Rum watched. 'How the fuck can you eat with that sauce all over the food.'

'Army grub mate, used to keep a bottle of this or Tabasco in my webbing.'

'Jerked up your food eh, respect.' Rum laughed.

'So, I've just gone from one mob into another,' demanded Eddie. Rum glugged a mouthful of tea and wiped his chin.

'What you expect Eds, anarchy?'

'Yeah I get you Rum,' said Eddie thoughtfully. 'Civvy life is full of unwritten rules.'

'Oh yes my man, sometime war breaks out but that's why we have the families, they talk to each other.'

'Like the fucking U.N. is it?'

'No Eddie, our shit works.'

Eddie soaked the yolk up with his fried bread and spread more H.P. on top. He stuffed his mouth savouring the taste.

'Know what never in all my years I sat down with any General and discussed strategy, maybe you're right. There's no gap between flash to bang in your world is there Rum.'

Chapter 49: Dial and Deliver

Eddie had a headache Civvy Street was complicated. Mental Mickey's deranged style had almost made him feel nostalgic for Ruperts running the show. Rum dropped him off at the Estate and he walked though the lock-up shed area, screwing his eyes against the pain, thinking, there was too much to think about, too many of the old mob depending on him, time just seemed to slip by. He was, he realised, top of the chain of command, no more pushing HR stuff upwards anymore he was top dog in this show he'd created, and it was giving him a fucking headache.

'Yo, Eddie, what you think,' Valdrin held his arm out, 'of my fleet?' The three Amigos were working on a couple of clapped out mopeds, lashing Deliveroo boxes on the back.

'What the fuck?' Eddie's head was splitting. 'Did you knock off Deliveroo for pizzas?' Eddie said, annoyed for no reason, and pointed at the logo on the box.

Valdrin felt defensive. 'It's a big moment Eddie. Innit bros! We in the "Dial and Deliver" business now. Yo get this, run out of weed, thinking be nice to light a fat one up, bell us. We Dial 'n Deliver - be there soon, you get me!'

Eddie noticed a bandage on the side of Valdrin's neck. 'What happened love bites?'

Valdrin touched his neck. 'Got stabbed innit, over Primrose Hill. Gang of kids run over and stabbed me.'

Eddie jerked in surprise, headache forgotten. 'You know them?' he asked. Valdrin smiled viciously.

'If I knew them they wouldn't trouble me. Bunch of Somali kids trying to prove they tough, innit.'

The quiet one piped up, 'they ain't integrated yet and we is independent operators, we'll take care of it, you know me!' He said with pride.

Eddie was thinking they live in a parallel universe. He looked the mopeds over. 'You know guys, you just might be on to something.' He tapped the delivery box, 'and if you got the munchies why here's some cold pizza to go with your score. Valdrin, that might be brilliant.'

'We independent thinkers, you know that!' chipped in the quiet one again.

'Valdrin, I may be asking you for a job in your business empire soon.'

'No worries Eddie, so we talked to your friend.'

'Friend,' said Eddie alarmed, 'what friend?'

'Tall thin guy, wide shoulders and a limp.'

'Ah Lofty, he's got one leg.'

'Yeah!' Valdrin snorted, thinking Eddie was joking. 'Anyway, the guy lives in Dunkerque Block.'

Eddie screwed his eyes against the headache. 'Sorry lads you got me there, who we talking about?'

'Your guy, he showed us photos innit,' said the quiet one.

Valdrin took over. 'We know the waster, English junky boy live with junky sister, he one of the Joke's run-arounds.'

'OK, now I get you,' Eddie replied joining the dots, the headache receded. 'Cheers lads, appreciate the local cooperation.'

'Yeah Eddie.' Valdrin nodded at his two compadres in a yes I'm going to ask him. 'So, we wondering, you and the Joke, going to rumble?'

'Rumble in the Jungle eh, you guys boxing fans?' Eddie was warming up for a nostalgic chat about Ali.

'Whats the jungle got to do with it? Why you ask that?' said the quiet one, busily rolling a joint on top of the Deliveroo box, looking over his shoulder checking no one was around.

'Never mind lads,' Eddie was slightly disappointed and reflecting that these kids didn't know, who Ali was. 'Before your time, might be I have to sort him out soon.'

'OK, Eddie, me and my spars here are betting on you, just to let ya know.'

'Valdrin, that right good of you, bet is duly noted.'

'It's OK Eddie, good for our business.' Eddie nodded, the headache rushed back in and he walked away, massaging his temple.

Chapter 50: Lofty v Snitch

Lofty knocked a soft rat tat tat, the door opened, a woman, tight jeans, long dirty pullover, rat face, rotten teeth.

'Yeah?' She had a cigarette on the go, held high in her right hand, elbow resting on her bony hip. Took a long look at Lofty, noted the mismatched Tweed suit and umbrella and pulled a big drag.

'This man I believe is co-habituating with you.' Lofty said, flashing the photo of Eddie's tail at her.

'You housing snoopers or what?'

Lofty bent over so he had eye level. 'No, now you may invite me very nicely to come in and interview this person.' Ratface took another drag and blew smoke at Lofty, he gave her a disapproving look. 'Or I'll kick the fucking door off its hinges with my bionic leg,' he pulled his pants up to the knee showing the artificial leg, 'and without a door how you gonna keep the jackals out?'

Ratface looked at the leg in wonder. 'Terry, it's for you!' she shouted over her shoulder and walked down a threadbare corridor into the front room. Lofty padded behind.

Terry the snitch was laying on the couch in a dirty scruffy tracksuit, watching "Home in the Sun" on TV. Another guy, same hoodies uniform, was slumped in an armchair, baseball bat across his lap. The place reeked of sweet and sour crack, syringes lay scattered on the floor. Ratface sat by Terry's feet end of the couch, she pushed a skinny cat on to the floor. Lofty shut the door.

'Fucking cyborg geezer wants talk to you.' Ratface indicated Lofty with a wave of her fag hand. Terry looked away from the TV with dazed eyes, as Lofty leaned over him.

'So, Terry pay attention we're having a nice chat.' Lofty showed him the photos of him tailing Eddie. 'That my friend is serious.' Terry gazed at Lofty not processing what was going on.

'I don't know you,' he grunted.

'You were asked to follow a person, now you tell me the who and the why.'

'Does Djokovic know you're here?' Terry struggled to sit up rubbing his face, like he was having a bad dream. 'He'll 'ave you mullah'ed mate, so fuck off.'

Lofty sighed and slapped Terry hard across the mouth. His lip split and started bleeding, he wailed in shock. His sister just watched with dead eyes, she'd seen it all before. Terry slumped back on the couch.

'Fucking sort you out, you lanky fucker!' screamed the other guy, jumping out of his seat, high on crack and roaring at Lofty. He picked up the baseball bat and swung. Lofty leaned back as the arc of the bat flew passed his face. He flipped the umbrella, hooking the handle around the bat and pulled in the direction of the arc and stuck his artificial leg out. The big guy toppled off balance, fell over Lofty's leg and crashed to the floor. Lofty unhooked the brolly, jabbed the handle into his face and repeated the blow three times in quick succession. It was a big handle, but Lofty snapped a kick to his belly just to be sure.

'Friend of yours was he?' Lofty grabbed Terry, hauled him up and sat him facing backwards in a chair, pulled gaffer tape out of his pocket and lashed Terry's hands to the back of the chair. Terry looked wide-eyed, he was in a nightmare, one he'd seen in a film, which didn't end well.

'Now I break your hands or you work your mouth.' Lofty rapped Terry across his hands with the brolly. Terry poured it out like a leaking tap. Djokovic had them in hock, they needed drugs to sell and Djokovic was the main wholesale geezer. He'd earned a stash for following Eddie and please don't hurt me.

'It might be your lucky day. D'you know what a double agent is?' As Lofty spoke, he rapped Terry across the hands again, his victim let out a little boy scream. '
He and his sister, gave Lofty their full attention now and shook their heads, the cat ignored him. 'It means you're both on double pay, so tell me all about Mr. Djokovic.'

'You'll pay us for that?' piped up the sister, 'we can do that mister, he's a nasty cunt.'

'Yes sir. Yes sir, he bloody well is.' Slow-witted Terry finally caught up with his rapidly changing world.

Chapter 51: Jassi Rings

It was Goth night on Chalk Farm Road. The Roundhouse Theatre had a big-time Goth band, the Assembly Rooms were hosting a heavy metal bash, even the Brazilian bar on the corner of Ferdinand Street had a sign out proclaiming "Metal Samba Night".

The streets were full of kids in black, dyed black hair, long black coats hanging over black metal studded boots. They covered the pavements, like an oil slick of grunge Metallica. Eddie weaved his way through the dark tide outside the Roundhouse to the tube station. His phone rang.

'Hello. Jassi . . .' he answered, 'how are you? - What, say again . . . sure in twenty minutes.' He pocketed the phone, 'Fuck.' He muttered and descended the stairs to the southern platform of the Northern Line.

Lofty was stoically doing his duty, as efficiently as possible, in the new uniform of tweed jacket, cravat and tweed shorts, showing off his shiny prosthetic leg. Guys jostled in the doorway, skinny pants, canvas trainers, half pissed, high on the release of bottled up nine-to-five energy. It would be a drunken, crass, nihilist, Sodom and Gomorrah, flash-the–card-out-of-your-mind-fuck-tomorrow-party-night.

His phone pinged, a Whats-App message. "Hold the fort, be there soon, honest, Scotch John." It pinged again, Eddie this time. "On an errand, laters at Oasis." Another Ping, Marigold, "Jezzer doing Carnaby Street club tonight." Lofty grinned, Mob back in business.

Eddie rapped the opening bars to "Ride of the Valkyries" on Jassi's door, it opened mid-tune, a very tense Jassi scanned the landing and pulled him in. Rainya sat on the futon sniffling, staring at the floor. 'OK, looks a bit serious, what's up?' asked Eddie.

'I'm afraid we have a serious situation.' Jassi folded her arms in a protective way and cocked her head at Rainya. 'Her father, or people her father knows have kidnapped Fitz.'

'What the fuck!' exclaimed Eddie.

'It's true, it's all my fault,' wailed Rainya, 'I was stupid taking them, but I thought it would do some good.'

'OK,' Eddie said, 'get the kettle on, let's have a brew and take it from the top.'

They were on the second cuppa by the time a tearful Rainya had sobbed out the whole story. Eddie stood up and paced.

'So recap, your Dad deals in valuable items for middle-eastern gangs, converting them into legal assets, and you, or I should say your Dad, thought they had recently become deceased but they haven't. Now they're here and you've got their swag.'

'And they have Fitz,' Rainya cried. 'He warned me not to take the diamonds.' She broke down, sobbing again, Jassi put an arm around her and looked to Eddie.   'They want an exchange, it's way out of my line, you're the only one I could think of, said Jassi.'

'Yeah, cheers for that, and we were getting on so well.' He turned to Rainya, 'Look, if they're from that part of the world, they won't stop. Best to hand it over. Who's arranging the exchange? Your Dad?'

'Yes, well no, not him, his PA, Mrs Bentley-Forbes.'

'Showers!'

'What's that mean Eddie?' Jassi and Rainya looked confused. Eddie ignored them.

'So, that's what the break-in was about?'

'Yes,' Rainya said, sitting up, 'but I didn't keep them at the flat I put them in a safety deposit box, obviously, at Coutts Bank, you see.'

'Oh yeah, I see.' Eddie laughed. You couldn't make this shit up.

'It's not a laughing matter Eddie,' said a disapproving Jassi.

'Oh Jassi, in the mob bad news is always funny, only way to deal with it, so when's the exchange?'

'She told me to get the diamonds,' said Rainya, blowing her nose and wiping her eyes. 'She'll ring tonight and give me instructions.'

'OK, give me your phone. You don't talk to her. I'll handle this. Get the diamonds out of the bank tomorrow. I'll have Lofty and Scotch go with you. Who knows you're staying with Jassi?'

'Nobody, I don't think, Fitz wouldn't tell them.'

'Yeah right!' Eddie paused, not wanting to worry her even more about the state her boyfriend could be in right now.

'I can look after her,' Jassi stood and looked Eddie in the eye, 'no one would dare come here.'

'Jassi you're traceable as the E.R.M lawyer, so my lads will look after you.' Eddie searched for the right words, not wanting to mention torture in front of Rainya. 'I'll have Lofty come here now.' Jassi exhaled and lowered her shoulders releasing the built-up tension. Eddie pulled his mobile out and rang.

'Lofty who's on the door with you? Scotch, good, right you're needed for guard duty tonight, damsels in distress, texting the address, come now!'

'You're a good, good man, Eddie Conway.' Jassi hugged Eddie. 'I'm sorry I got you involved in this situation . . . I . . .'

'Don't mention it, no worries,' Eddie was plainly embarrassed. Jassi added a bit of humour.

'You're a rough diamond though,' she smiled at her lame joke. Eddie looked guilty but it came over as sheepish.

'Yeah, well I feel responsible,' Eddie said in a clumsy attempt to hide the truth, thinking what was it with this woman, making him feel awkward.

'He's so desperate to be English, since mother passed away.' Rainya started talking about her Dad. She looked up at both of them. 'I thought of all the good the money could do. Fitz is so passionate . . .' she choked thinking of her lover, ' . . . about the cause, I, we, can help people but . . . ' She paused wringing her hands. 'Will they hurt him?'

'Course not,' lied Eddie.

Loud knocking on the door, opening bars of the Valkyries again, Eddie motioned to Jassi to back away. He opened the door, letting Lofty in.

'Arigatou Boss,' Lofty said with a little bow.

'Lofty, these ladies are under your protection. This lady is Jassi,' Lofty bowed to Jassi, 'and this lady is Rainya. Stick like shit on a stick to them, until further notice. Scotch will join you after his shift, find a safe place.'

Lofty drew himself up, squared his shoulders. 'Ladies no harm will come to you while I have life left in my body.' He looked serene. Eddie cocked his head.

'Lofty here is Bushido.'

Lofty bowed. 'Watashi', the women looked confused. Eddie walked to the door, Jassi followed him to the door, she pulled Eddie back and clung to him.

'What a mess, it will be alright won't it?'

'Yeah sure, be fine,' he lied, rolling his eyes. Mind working overtime, the fragments of jigsaw pieces fitting together and his own guilt fuelled his rage, 'Laters,' he marched out the door.

Lofty asked them to pack for a few days. Jassi glad of a set of tasks to occupy her mind, got organised, sorted out spare clothing and toiletries for her and Rainya, stuffing them into a holdall.

Lofty led them downstairs, clearing each landing as he went, in full Mob mode. Outside on the street he hailed a black cab and bustled them in, another mission, he was ecstatic, truly alive again.

Chapter: 52 Mob Calls

'Yo Rum.'

'Yo? You Yo'ing me? What, you think you're Yardy now?'

'Who doesn't in London, need transport, non-traceable.'

'What you planning, trip to the seaside?'

'A people carrier and a van.'

'OK, you making your move?'

'Soon.'

'I'll swing round'

'Swing low.'

Eddie tapped out another number.

'Gilly, still got access to the web?'

'Hi Sarge, yeah, sweet here, got brill broadband innit, got the lot, we spend all day on the net. What's the gen?'

'OK, Good lad, I want you set up secure comms for the lads.'

'Fucking well copy that boss, bit of action is it?'

'Yeah, night ops in bandit country, so get on it, I want it running by twenty-one hundred hours. Give the lads call signs.'

'On it, I can encrypt one tap dial-in circuit...'

Eddie cut him short, 'Yeah. Whatever, Roger that Gilly.' Another number:

'Spiky listen up.'

'Yeah, Sarge.'

'I need some of your gear, night-time cameras, directional microphones, laser pointers, that sort of thing.'

'Shit Sarge, we back on active service.'

'Yeah night time covert ops, a handover and I want the area covered, sniper style.'

'Oh fuck me sideways, yeah Sarge, you're on. Send me G.P.S., I'll crack on, get a box o' tricks sorted.'

'OK, we go live on comms from twenty-one hundred hours, Gilly will run it.'

'Fucking sweet. Copy that Sarge.'

Eddie switched his phone off and stood staring at the

wall. A lick of fear curled in his belly. What the fuck he thought, beats wearing a green dress and trying to top out. He laughed out aloud, the fear spiked an adrenalin surge, oh yes, better to die fighting than dropping from a balcony feeling sorry for yourself. What say you Dr Vaughn?

Chapter 53 The Demands

'Ah hello, Rainya, so this is where we shall meet . . . '

'I'm not Rainya . . . '

'Whom am I talking to?' said a very worried April.

'My name is Clifford, from the E.R.M. We are handling this for our sister Rainya . . . ' Eddie gave the thumbs up to Rum, the phone was sitting between them, loudspeaker on. 'Who is too upset and very worried, as you have her partner Fitz?'

'Do you have the items?'

'Err, no. Not yet, it will take some time to retrieve them, but we will have the package tomorrow . . . '

'That's not convenient for us, we want to exchange tonight.'

'Well I'm terrible afraid that's just not possible,' Rum was doing his best middle-class voice and smiling his head off. 'Rainya was taken quite ill with the news, she actually fainted you know, and is in a bad way ...' Rum was on a roll. Eddie gave him more thumbs up. 'But we can retrieve the package tomorrow.'

Sounds of shouting came from the phone and then April's voice again.

'Excuse me a minute will you, I'll just need to confer with . . . ' another voice came on, guttural English. 'We have your Fitz you pussies, give trouble we will send you bits of him.'

'And to whom am I talking to . . .?' Replied Rum

'You're talking to bad news, you fuckees - you don't deliver and Mr Clifford Englishman get his infidel head cut off . . . '

'That's rather gruesome, lets keep this as pleasant as possible shall we.' Rum gave the phone; he's a Wanker sign with his hand. 'I'll text where we will be tomorrow evening at 7.30pm.'

'Or we cut a little bit off this Fitz eh, his little small dick.' Laughter could be heard in the background. 'Make it happen Mr English.' High pitch giggling and the phone went dead.

'Rum, what the fuck, Clifford?'

'He's a Q.C. I know, got me off a tricky charge. He's an Oxford Dread, a posh brother you get me. So what now?'

'Well they're off balance and April is off the case now that Rainya's not in the game.' Eddie pulled his tobacco and cigarette papers out of his pocket, the ritual of rolling had always helped him think through strategy back in the mob. He gave the paper a final lick and held the rolled cigarette between his fingers. Rum reached for the lighter.

'No thanks Rum, I'm trying to give up.' Rum rolled his eyes.

'So, the way I see it Rum, hopefully the fuckers think they're dealing with a bunch of wally middle class hippies. They'll seriously underestimate us, and we've got,' he looked at his wrist watch, 'twenty-Two hours.'

'What you mean, we?' Rum gave Eddie that look.

'I mean my Mob.' Eddie gently tapped the end of the roll-up on the table. 'We're trained for this, got the experience of dealing with these characters.'

'So what? You going to shoot these fuckrees!' Eddie playing with the roll-up was irritating Rum.

'No Rum, not that,' Eddie laughed. 'I wouldn't mind taking them out permanently but Geneva Convention, and playing at home and all that. No can do.'

'Yeah bringing the war home not cool, even if you get the Malones to cover your arse.' Rum held his arms up.

'Yeah, OK Rum,' Eddie played with the roll-up a while, thinking. 'I'll stand-down artillery and plan a low-vis op.'

'What's that mean, in civvy speak?'

'We do the handover at night, without fire-arms and seize the advantage.'

'Oh yeah, of course you do.' Rum shook his head.

'Yep the Mob be back in business my friend.' Eddie tapped numbers on his phone. 'Old soldiers never die mate; they just hang around waiting for a mission. Hello Gilly, yeah you got it done? Any problems your end? . . No, OK . . . good, yeah . . . Google earth, everybody plugged in when I send. Yeah, Darkie Sullivan is Jezzer. Sunray out.'

Rumpunch stood up and straightened his shoulders. 'I

didn't understand a lot of that but did you just call a brother Darkie? You got to be kidding me right?'

'I tell you Rum in the mob it kinda made sense, but you're right in Civvy Street, sounds really bad,' admitted Eddie.

Chapter 54 Refuge Marigold

'Eddie my buoy, will sort it. Don't worry darling.' Marigold made another pot of tea. Rainya red-eyed, finally all cried out, sat next to Jassi.

'It's very good of you to put up with us,' said Jassi.

'No trouble me darling; I looked after plenty of girls in a spot of bother. Lofty come have more tea and biscuits, this is more company than I had for long time.'

Lofty was picking bits of coconut maroon from his teeth. He glanced back into the room from the window where he was standing guard. 'Scotch John coming up to the door now.'

A loud rat ta tats, Dambuster style on the front door. Lofty walked over, baseball bat in hand and let Scotch in. 'It's Ride of the Valkyries, not Dambusters, you idiot.'

'Ach man, I'm tone deaf so I am, aye, reporting for escort duty.' Scotch looked at the women carefully. 'And it be my pleasure, how do you do ladies.' He shook hands with limp, red-eyed Rainya, a quick nod and shake with Jassi and slowed right down when he came to Marigold, feasting his eyes on her plump rump.

'Taking a good look,' laughed Marigold.

'So that's a no, right off then, eh lady, ha, ha.' Scotch let go of her hand. Marigold pushed him in the chest

'Me never said that, me big problem not saying no enough time.'

Lofty coughed loudly, interrupting the flirting. 'OK Scotch, listen in, I'm escorting the Miss here.' He pointed at Rainya. 'To Coutts bank, you're staying put, looking after the ladies.'

'Och aye, that's me all right, so it is.' Scotch sat at the table. Marigold patted Scotch on the shoulder.

'Cup o' tea me darling?' Marigold asked.

Scotch beamed. 'Whatever you give me, is just fine, aye.'

Marigold passed Scotch the biscuit tin, he fished out a coconut maroon and took a greedy bite. Lofty smiled to himself.

Chapter 55 Exchange & Mart

Jezzer ordered three pints of London Pride at the bar. The Mob had enough shit lagers; in shit combat bases, real ale on a rainy day, in an old English pub, was a fantasy that had grown with every combat tour. It was a slow day at the Spaniards Inn, the swayed walls and low ceiling were warped with age; history creaked in the dark floorboards. Out of the window he spotted the van pulling up in the car park. Fat Phil and Spiky got out, walked into the beer garden, and sat in one of the wicker shelters. Jezzer took the pints outside.

'What did you get us?' asked Spiky.

'London Pride, it's a Fullers ale, try it, it cost enough,' replied Jezzer. They raised their straight glasses, Jezzer had made sure to get straight glasses and took a gulp.

'Not bad Darkie,' muttered Fat Phil as he wiped his lips. Spiky rolled his eyes. 'What?' said Fat Phil.

'It's Jezzer you idiot, how many times?' warned Spiky. Fat Phil shrugged and pulled rolling tobacco out of his pocket.

'I'm taxing ya for political incorrectness,' said Jezzer and took a Rizzla and a pinch of baccy from him and out the corner of his mouth muttered, 'you getting fat, d'you know that, Fat Phil?'

'Bollox,' Fat Phil replied, but held his hand out, palm up in apology. 'Scrounge one of me smokes, why don't you,' he paused and shrugged, 'Jezzer.'

'Cheers mate,' replied Jezzer accepting the apology wrapped in banter, they sipped their beer.

'Who's on eyeball duty Spiky?' asked Jezzer.

Spiky pulled out the briefing notes, a Google earth map covering the target area. He pointed at arrows marked delta 2, 3 and 4.

'Lofty and Scotch went in hours ago. They're dug in here.' Spiky pointed at the map. 'A clear line of sight down to Wildwood Road, and across the clearing, top of the slope, here. You'll cover any bandits on the left, here.' He tapped the map. 'The cam net is stashed in this tree and I put go-pros in place last night. If its a snafu (Situation Normal All Fucked Up), improvise but keep to Ops priority, neutralise the bandits.' He handed out laser pointers to the lads. Fat Phil held the pointer up and flicked it on. A red dot appeared on a tree way down the bottom of the beer garden.

'Fucking Star Wars?' He said mockingly.

'So, you volunteered to be back on Ops then?' Spiky rolled his eyes at Fat Phil

'Aye, why, are you in on this?' asked Jezzer.

'Remember that village?' Fat Phil took a long pull on his beer, put the glass down and looked at each of them as he spoke.

'Jesus, I try not to think of it mate.' Spiky looked into his pint.

'Fucking women and kids, not right was it,' agreed Jezzer.

'Well,' continued Fat Phil, 'the fuckers who massacred the village were holed up in the next Valley, but the Yanks had done a deal, we were ordered to deliver ordinance to them, I drove over, with this fucking Yank Rupert from HQ.'

'Who were they?' the two whispered, leaning in.

'A bunch of very fucking evil ex-Saddam army mob, they boasted to the Yank of how many jihadis they killed mate. They had the village women chained up. The Yank was laughing with them, pretending to buy a woman.' Phil suddenly looked up. 'Maybe he did, fuckers . . .'

'Fuck me mate, right out of order.' Spiky shook his head.

'I thought these fuckers needed slotting mate, now Sarge is up against a bunch of 'em.' The lads sipped slowly, re-living the village massacre scenes, a shared Mob nightmare. Three blips came over the security radio on Spiky's collar, he listened.

'Roger that Sunray.' Spiky whispered. 'OK, knock it back,' he said to Phil and Jezzer, 'time to move in to positions, before dusk.' He downed his pint; they picked up their rucksacks, walked out of the beer garden, following the trail into the woods.

Lofty had dug in earlier in the day, manning an OP (Observation Post) above the exchange area. He wore tweed anorak and green cargo pants, the side pockets stuffed with boiled eggs and fruitcake, and a plastic bottle of cold green tea.

He laid up, rock still but full of adrenalin; all systems go, like the old days. He'd watched dog walkers go by, lovers holding hands and mid-afternoon, a gang of teenagers with mopeds, trying to jump Evel Knievel style over a fallen tree. But they'd crashed the mopeds and sat on the fallen tree, rolling spliff's. He'd reported in to Gilly, the answer came back. "Sunray says clear the area by 1600." Lofty emerged from the undergrowth like Robinson Crusoe.

'Ok boys piss off, or I do you for possession.'

'Oi, Mr, you're not a Cop?' The teenage gang leader stood up, smirking at his mates.

OK, thought Lofty, young kids playing street gangsta. 'I'm a "Friend of the Heath" so I'm asking nicely.' He grabbed the leader by his collar and effortlessly raised him a foot off the ground. 'But when I count to ten, I'll break your arm.'

'We were going anyway.' Teenage leader nodded vigarously.

Lofty let go; the leader slumped to his knees and scrambled away from Lofty.

'Come on dudes let's leave.' They hurried off, pushing the battered mopeds, but just before they disappeared, they turned and gave Lofty the finger. Lofty chuckled at the memory.

He caught a movement to his right, in his peripheral vision, slowly swivelling his head, no sudden movement to betray his position. It was the lads taking cover in the undergrowth. Lofty texted "Check in," on the group-net comms. Confirmation came back from Gilly, "All checked in Delta 1." Lofty tried breathing in through his left nostril and out through the other. The You Tube guru recommended it. He was back on a mission, with the mob, contentment wrapped round him like a security blanket, adrenalin ticked slow deep inside him. Waiting.

Eddie did a quick area recon'. All the lads were in position up on the high ground, with Spiky in a dell to the left controlling the kit. Eddie had picked a strategic place he knew well from his runs, off the beaten track, between two roads that bisected Hampstead Heath extension. Heavily wooded, no houses nearby and at this time in the evening fairly deserted.

The exchange point was fifty yards up from the lower Wildwood Road, Eddie had made sure of a line of retreat, a running trail, with good cover through the trees, two hundred yards up to Spaniards Inn car park. A drizzle had started again, the ground muddy underfoot, sprinkled with damp fallen leaves. Dressed in black, balaclava perched on back of his head, he leaned against a tree, rolled a smoke, watching the light fade and waited.

Lofty emerged, scrambling up the slope he called to Eddie. 'Everything Green-on Sunray.'

'Ok Delta one,' answered Eddie. He enjoyed using the old call signs; it snapped them back into being the Mob again. Lofty pointed his torch uphill, he had gaffer-taped it so only a thin beam escaped the lens. He flashed three times and got the answering tight two flashes from the trees above.

'So this is Hampstead Heath, where all the Ruperts walk their dogs?'

'They even dress the dogs Lofty,' replied Eddie. His phone buzzed, he looked at the screen. "1 Car 4 Bandits."

Four figures appeared below on the Wildwood Road, looking lost. Eddie flashed a lamp twice. The figures made their way up through the shadowy woods, one of them stumbling, three holding automatics.

'You ERM fuckees? Salim shouted, 'Hey what's with the masks?' He was thinking this is easy, hippies playing at being bad guys, idiots.

'You don't know us, we don't want to know you,' replied Eddie, trying to sound nervous and scared, he wanted to keep the bandits off balance.

'Fucking pussies, we got your business card,' snarled Salim. He tugged the rope round Fitz's neck who, slipped in the mud, and stumbled forward, looking much worse for wear.

Lofty stepped down and ran his hands over the terrified Fitz. 'Nothing broken,' he said, and stepped back up besides Eddie.

Eddie shrugged. 'So, you know us. Who are you guys?'

Salim laughed. 'We're the fuckers that chop heads off, infidel.' The other two giggled, they all sounded high on something.

'You telling me you ISIS or some bullshit.'

'We're your ISIS head chopping nightmares pussy man, and we're walking your street.' Salim yanked on the rope pulling Fitz to him, kicked him behind the knees and slapped his head as he fell to the ground. 'Give the fucking merchandise over, or idiot here gets the chop.' Salim slung the automatic over his shoulder, and pulled a large knife from his belt and held it above Fitz's head.

'OK, OK. Take it easy now.' Eddie raised his voice an octave, playing the nervous wally, confident these guys had totally misunderstood who they were dealing with. 'We got the diamonds here.' He nodded to Lofty, who reached up in the low branches above him and pulled a carrier bag down. He handed it to Eddie. 'Now you let go of Fitz.' Salim kicked Fitz who moaned loudly.

'Let me see the stones first,' Salim said and swaggered across, waving his knife in the air enjoying the show, he grabbed the bag and bumped Eddie aside. Eddie smiled under the balaclava and stood back hands in the air. Salim sheathed his knife, groped in the plastic bag for the diamonds, pulled out a small leather pouch, and shone his torch on the diamonds; they sparkled, he nodded across to the other two. 'Look pretty, eh.' He poured the diamonds back into the small leather purse, tucked it in his top pocket, pulled his knife out and waved it at Eddie. 'So now we have diamonds and your leader, you fuckees deserve to be chopped, why should we let you fuckees go, eh?'

Eddie stepped back a few more yards and gestured for Salim to look at his chest, a red laser light dot appeared. Salim stared down at his chest, the dot moved up to his face and settled on the end of his nose.

Salim went cross-eyed. 'What the fucks this?'

'We've employed former army snipers,' said Eddie, smiling at him. 'You want a hole in your head?' Two more laser dots appeared on the other men, they looked round terrified, trying to spot the snipers. 'One false move and your fucked. Now drop the weapons.' Cursing, but clearly worried, they dropped the automatics.

'You fuckees in trouble now, we know who your are.'

Salim glared at Eddie. '

Scotch and Jezzer came out from the bushes and spread apart, holding a cam net between them. They dashed either side of the gunmen and covered them with the cam net, then they pulled baseball bats out of their webbing; a couple of whacks from a smiling Scotch John.

'Ach, ye wee beastie.' He put the gunmen down.

Eddie took a look around. 'OK Delta three, take Fitz to H.Q.'

Jezzer hauled a stunned Fitz up, cut the rope and hustled him away up trail. In that moment Salim noticed the laser pointers, hanging from lanyards around Scotch's neck, comprehension slowly dawned on him.

'You fuckee hippy shits!' screamed Salim, diving for his weapon.

Eddie cursed and leapt at Salim They slammed together, through the bushes, and crashed down slope, rolling head over heels down the slippery leaf strewn steep bank.

Salim struggled to bring his automatic up. Eddie lashed out, blocking Salim's arm, the gun spiralled out of his grasp. Salim fell backwards but clawed his knife out. 'Cut   your fucking head off,' he spat.

Eddie rolled on to the balls of his feet and crouched fists out. 'Fuck you Pussy boy,' he mocked.

Salim lost it, screamed in rage and charged. Eddie slid feet first on the leafy ground under the knife arm, took Salim's legs out, flipping him in the air, and rolled back onto his feet. Salim covered in mud desperately scrambled to his knees. Eddie gave him no time to recover and charged in laughing, high on combat adrenalin.

Salim flinched, still trying to deal with the shock and surprise at the turn of events, now this crazy hippy fucker was laughing.

Eddie blocked the clumsy knife thrust with his left, punched Salim in the balls, but the knife arm hooked across Eddie's head, cutting his ear. Eddie curled his hand around Salim's wrist, and twisted as he fell on Salim. The knife went into something soft, with a sucking noise. Eddie let go and rolled away.

Salim screamed, lying on his side, the knife stuck in his arse, blood pumping from the wound, he tried reaching behind him but couldn't get a grip on the slippery bloody surface.

Eddie stood breathing heavily. 'OK, lash them fuckwits in the cam net up. Delta one check this fucker isn't dying.'

Lofty strode over, bent over Salim and slapped the back of his head. 'Got something sticking in yer arse ave you?' He yanked the knife out with a vicious twist. Salim screamed and slumped on the leaves.

'Now, lads what do we do with these fuckers, Geneva Convention?' Eddie calmly brushed himself down.

'I've never been there,' laughed Scotch, 'but been to Glasgow, different rules there, so they are, aye Sunray?' He tapped the baseball bat in the palm of his hand, glaring at the two cowering in the cam net.

Suddenly Police sirens split the air. Two cars and a wagon screamed up an access path twenty metres away. Searchlights flashed, a megaphone squawked. 'Stay where you are, on your knees hands in the air, we have Police marksmen on duty.' Lights lanced up towards the mob. Eddie calmly held his hands up, adjusting to events swiftly, blood dripping from his ear, out of the side of his mouth he whispered into his collar mic.

'Those under cover scatter,' he whispered, 'they ain't seen all of you yet.'

A squad of Police started climbing up through the woods.

'We got no weapons, we're not moving.' Eddie shouted and sank to his knees, hands up in the air. Lofty and Scotch joined him.

Chapter 56: Nicked

The cell door opened, Eddie stood up, two coppers entered.

'Come on you, teatime.' They smirked. A fuming Eddie was escorted down the corridor, into an interview room. They shut the door behind him. He sat down, after the designated minutes of the "make you nervous" waiting period, two people entered, a woman in a comfy cardigan, hair swept back in a bun carrying a folder, and a smartly dressed pinstripe suited man.

'Sergeant Conway, you are in a spot of difficulty.' Eddie's eyes narrowed.

'Captain fucking Henley-Rees,' the anger spilled out of Eddie, 'last seen at a briefing up-country.'

'Colonel now, if you please.' Henley-Rees sat down opposite Eddie. 'Yes, sergeant and you bolloxed up that mission as well.'

'One of us lost his legs.'

'Touching, but soldiers?' Henley-Rees held his hands out. 'To do and die etcetera, etcetera . . . '

'But not you fucking Intel Ruperts,' snarled Eddie.

'Mind your language, ladies present.' Colonel Henley-Rees crossed his legs, smiled and adjusted the crease in his pants. 'And this is Director Dame Carter.' The woman raised her eyebrows at Henley-Rees, placed a phone on the table and pressed record.

'Caused us a lot of bother sergeant,' she spoke softly almost maternally.

'It's mister now,' said Eddie defiantly.

'Mister! Bloody hell Conway!' Henley-Rees bristled. 'You have interfered with a complex security operation, and bloody well bolloxed it up.'

Eddie smiled, and answered calmly, enjoying a chance to slag off this smug Rupert. 'Oh have I, we quit then, cos you fucked up ours.'

'Will you two stop these childish exchanges,' Director Carter butted in. OK, thought Eddie, that's interesting, she's the Boss, and maybe doesn't think that highly of Henley-Rees.

'Conway, it's a little matter of national security,' she continued, 'we have spent valuable resources, diligently weaving a web, around a certain gentleman trading in Middle-Eastern valuables, and we were hoping to snare something more valuable than yourself.' Carter smiled at him. 'If you don't mind me saying so.'

Eddie looked at her closely. Slightly amused, intelligent eyes stared back at him.

'You tell us all.' Henley-Rees banged his fist on the table. 'Or we will throw the bloody key away.'

'Like when you gave us a bullshit Sit-Rep and sent us on a fucked-up mission.' Eddie's eyes blazed with anger.

'Now, now boys.' Director Carter switched on her full maternal mode. 'OK Conway, maybe web was the wrong analogy, more a honeypot, thus we may uncover lots of sticky-fingered enemies of the State.'

Eddie cocked his head. 'Who the hell are you, Winnie-the-Pooh?'

'Well we did catch you in the woods Conway,' Carter said, enjoying the banter. 'But you remember signing the Official Secrets Act, in the army, so you're not in any position to bargain are you Conway.'

'Under the Prevention of Terrorism Act,' said Henley-Rees, full of smug self-satisfaction and jumped in again, 'you'll rot in prison.'

'We were set up!' protested Eddie, holding out his hands.

'Yes, quite, so yet again your country calls on you, to do your duty.' Carter steepled her immaculately manicured hands, rolled her eyes at Henley-Rees. 'Oh, by the way, we have your associates tucked up nice and tight.'

'Always the same, Ruperts click their fingers expecting us to do the heavy lifting.' Eddie leaned back in his seat, crossed his arms staring at Henley-Rees and Carter. Carter gave him a worn out but polite smile.

'So, do start lifting Conway.'

Eddie laughed at them. 'Haven't had me cup of tea yet Ma'am.' Eddie refused to talk until his tea arrived. Henley-Rees rolled his eyes at Eddie's obvious flirting with Director Carter.

Minutes of strained silence passed before the tea arrived.

'Bloody parched Ma'am, cheers.' Eddie stirred his brew, thinking, they must have an informer or be keeping close tabs on this terror gang, certainly explains the tails who followed me. 'So how did you know about the exchange?' He asked. Henley-Rees just laughed.

'We saved your bloody bacon, Conway.'

'Like hell you did,' replied Eddie, 'we had 'em wrapped up nicely.'

Director Carter opened her folder. 'Colonel Farouk Hakimi commanded an elite Iraqi force, a very nasty guy. Saddam would send him in, to pacify a town he thought might be disloyal.'

Eddie nodded. 'So, now he's ISIS? Now you got him, what's the problem?' Dame Carter flipped a page of the folder as she answered.

'No, we have not got him, only a few of his troops blundered into the honeypot.'

'And thanks to you Conway, he now knows we have eyes on him.' Henley-Rees placed both hands on the table, leaned back, smug with satisfaction at dressing down Eddie. Dame Carter calmly flicked more pages of the folder.

'He's smart, ruthless and looks like he's extending his operations here, in the UK,' said Dame Carter.

Eddie ran a mental thumb over his reasoning, Carter was the Boss and Henley-Rees had eyes on the ground in the Middle East, but was in hot water for the mess Eddie had caused. So how the fuck did I walk into this shit storm?

'So you spooks are all over Sir golden-cuffs Omar and when I popped up, you thought hello, ex-Mob?' Eddie said. He was joining the dots, they must have turned someone on the inside. Showers maybe?

Henley-Rees stood up pacing the interview room and leaned over Eddie.

'What other work are you doing for Sir Omar, Conway?'

OK, Eddie thought, their Intel wasn't that good, or were they protecting Showers by pretending to grill him on the job description. He answered, 'wanted me to fly under the radar,

227

find his daughter, a bullshit story about her running off with some lover.'

'Our knight of the realm, Sir Omar, is fronting a money washing exercise for Middle-Eastern antiquity looters, and probably people traffickers.' Director Carter smiled. 'The money trails may lead to terror cells in the UK, which you, Conway, have just buggered up.'

Eddie played the dumb NCO a role that always fooled arrogant Ruperts, but maybe not Carter.

'They kidnapped a British citizen and we sorted out an evac.'

'You lot of washed up Toms are for the high jump Conway.' Henley-Rees in his bad cop role steamed in.

'It's Mister you jumped up twat.' Eddie felt himself go cold and held onto the chair. 'You got nothing on me, or the lads, no weapons, no evidence, no nothing mate.' Director Carter snapped the folder shut.

'Split infinities but erudite just the same.' She tapped her fingers on the desk, as if playing the piano. 'In the game of shifting Jihadi sands, from Iraq to Afghanistan, I'm wondering, if you're a piece we can play?'

'Play him?' Henley-Rees spluttered. 'Play this fucking oik. He's totally unreliable.' He rubbed his face, exasperated. 'And rude, and ignorant.'

Eddie glugged back more tea, calming himself and winked at Carter. 'He's got his knickers in a right twist.'

'If you don't mind,' said, Carter, as if talking to a naughty boy and just about kept a straight face as she looked at Henley-Rees, then turned back to Eddie. 'There's only one way you are getting out of this situation.'

'My Mob done their time being pieces on the game board, we're off the board now.' Eddie sat up feeling angry again. Carter gave him a patronising smile.

'Mister Conway, I'm afraid you have blundered back onto the board, and right now I'm considering my next move, are you an expendable piece?' Carter looked like a cat that got the mouse.

Eddie thinking, hang on, has she just promoted me to Mr?

Chapter 57: Cat

Clifford A. Thompson arrived in the UK from Guyana, with a scholarship to Oxford. He was an Oxford cricket and rowing blue, a double first in law and ethics, and had studiously learnt the demeanour of the upper-class English, but still carried the threat of dreadlocks. His aide, a very smart black woman in courtroom suit, opened an expensive leather briefcase, pulled out cream parchment papers and handed them to the Savile Row suited Dread QC.

'I represent certain individuals you are holding, have you charged them?' Clifford took out his mobile phone. 'I'm ringing the Press now.' The phone rang on loudspeaker.

'Hold on a minute Sir I'll check.' The front desk Plod panicked and phoned upstairs, within minutes a smooth operative from C.I.D. came through the security doors and offered to shake hands. Clifford shook his head.

'Oh no, we ain't got a deal yet young man, I got certain news outlets on speed dial.' He handed the phone to his assistant, who held the phone in one hand, briefcase in the other, like the sword and shield of justice.

'Ah yes. Mister Thompson Q.C. indeed,' sniffed the smooth operative, 'this way if you please, Sir, Miss.' He led them inside.

Eddie was ushered out of his cell, only one cop this time. He joined Lofty and Scotch in the corridor.

'Arigatou Boss,' said Scotch.

Eddie laughed. 'So, that's what you lads been doing, "way of the waiting" eh?'

Scotch grinned at Lofty. 'Oh Boss, that's rubbish, so it is.'

They marched down the corridor, as if on C.O.'s orders, a big-bellied cop opened the door. They stamped in, bristling with aggression, to be greeted by Clifford A Thompson.

'Ah gentlemen, any complaints about brutality, I'll sue their arses.'

Eddie did a double take on the situation, Scotch's eyebrows danced.

'We was strip searched,' he snarled, 'fucking arse searched by the fuckers, so I was.' Lofty looked surprised, Scotch winked at him and continued his banter, 'I want compen-fucking-sation, so I do.'

'How do you do, I'm Clifford A Thompson QC.' Eddie looked the pinstripe suit up and down and smiled.

'Rum?'

'Indeed so, we're old boys,' he whispered to Eddie in patios, 'London Caribbean cricket team. He my spar, you get me.' He shook hands with Scotch and Lofty, who stared at him, as if he was ET.

'Now gentlemen, I suggest you say nothing, the walls here are probably electronic. So you were illegally strip-searched were you?'

'Aye, me human rights abused, so they were.' Scotch drew himself up in a dignified but hurt pose. Eddie spotted the duty cop, raising a pair of eyebrows to rival Scotch John's.

'And they took my boiled eggs and nuts.' Lofty joined in the banter. Clifford A Thompson QC hid a laugh with a cough.

'I've arranged for your release gentleman, say nothing more here, we're gone.' He and his smart assistant led the way out of Paddington nick.

The large BMW 4x4, headed west over Paddington flyover, Eddie, Lofty and Scotch scrunched in the back seat. Miss Smart Assistant at the wheel. Clifford A Thompson QC held his phone in the air, so the guys in the back could hear.

'Yo, my man Cat, do your ting innit, respects me, man. So Eddie - everything cool?' They could hear Rum chuckling over the phone.

'He got us out of the glasshouse, I thought we were proper fucked mate,' said Eddie. Clifford smiled and turned to Eddie.

'Ah yes, well Mister Conway, it seems that when I mentioned the press and an open court hearing, they suddenly found legal reasons to drop any charges and thus, forced to release you.'

'OK, I get it,' Eddie nodded understanding. 'But they'll be at me again Rum, nothing looks like what it is.'

'Well you in good hands with the Cat.' Rum's voice echoed from the phone,

'Cat?' replied Eddie.

'Yeah Clifford A Thompson, C-A-T, Cat get it? Best wicket keeper we ever had.' Rum chuckled.

'Laters,' said Clifford and switched off the phone. 'It seems, we may have some civil liberties leverage Mister Conway.'

The BMW swished into the entrance of Grays Inn, parking attendant lifted the barrier and they trundled through a cobblestone entrance into the private square, a world never glimpsed by the soldiers. Cat and his assistant got out and ushered them in to chambers, past busy clerks, up broad carpeted stairs to Cat's office.

'OK Miss Evans will take your particulars and I'll have some forms for you to sign, making it all very legal.'

Eddie examined the office, mahogany tables and ornate chairs, overflowing with documents and files stacked against the walls on the thick carpet. He gave Clifford a through looking over, trying to recognise a type and gave up. It was Scotch who broke in with the obvious but stupid question.

'So you a real lawyer then, are you?'

'When you look at me, are you seeing a black man, or a pinstriped suited member of the bar?' Cat fixed Scotch with a sad stare. 'When you listen to me, are listening to well-spoken public school educated officer class person, or a "You get me dread"?' Scotch looked totally confused.

'I operate in the margins between confusion and stereotypes, I come at you from both ends.' Cat laughed. Lofty had been listening intently and nudged Scotch in the ribs.

'You have to look below the surface Scotch.'

'Yes my friend,' agreed Cat, 'and you do not look like a soldier boy, anymore.' Scotch felt a glimmer of understanding. Eddie reached over and offered Cat a hand. They shook.

'Thanks,' said Eddie, 'we are still coming to terms with the confusing world of Civvy Street.'

'Well my man,' Cat grinned warmly at Eddie. 'That is the first step, recognising the confusion. Now sign up.' Miss Evans pursed her lips, and handed the form to Eddie. Eddie turned to Lofty and Scotch.

'You two get down to Midnight Oasis, make sure the doors are covered tonight.'

'Arigoto Boss,' replied Lofty, he and Scotch bowed to Miss Evans, 'Arigoto Onna-musha.' They trooped out, Miss Evans smiled, slightly confused. Clifford Thomas watched, thoughtful, as the door close behind them.

'They're becoming samurai,' explained Eddie.

'They're what?' Clifford snorted, and sat behind his large desk. 'So, you commanded those guys in the army?'

'I did,' Eddie leaned his head to one side. 'They were top soldiers.'

'You know that is an important asset in this town, having a squad of trained soldiers.' Clifford shuffled some papers, as he was thinking.

'Oh,' said Eddie looking up from the form he was signing, curious. 'How so?'

'That document you're signing means I'm your lawyer, the Malones may retain me but now you signed, I'm your lawyer. Client privilege I take seriously. I may work in the margins of society but I have my own moral compass.'

'Seems like you're a Rupert to me.' Eddie looked the ornate Victorian chambers over. Cat shuffled the forms into a folder and handed them to Miss Evans, who shook Eddies hand firmly and left.

'To be effective in a combat zone, as a soldier, you need effective weapons, wouldn't you agree?'

'Sure but . . . '

'Hear me out.' Cat held out a hand. 'This,' he waved his hand around the office and then pointed at himself, 'my mode of dress, my speech, are my weapons allowing me to operate effectively within the law, but I am a black man, an immigrant who had to struggle against the odds to get here, but in court? The odds favour me, because I'm the smartest badass barrister in front of the Judge and we're all playing the same game, same rules. The legal game my friend, is like being in the boxing ring, there are rules referees and judges. So, I use them to win.'

Eddie walked to the window and looked down at Grays Inn, which screamed Rupert privilege at him. Cat joined him; they took in the cloisters, archways, stained-glass windows, cobble stone yards and neat green cut grass.

'So if I have you as my brief, I get all this as back-up?' said Eddie.

'Preciously so my friend.'

'What's the catch?' asked Eddie.

'There is no catch my friend.' Cat put his hand on Eddie's shoulder. 'It's an alliance, between me as councillor, and you as commander in the field. Out there Eddie, it's a combat zone in the richest city in the world.'

'If we shake that's a contract between you and me.' Eddie offered his hand to Cat. 'But I do it my way, my own moral compass.'

'Exactly so, Eddie, and I will do it my way, think of it as team work.'

Eddie took a moment to ponder, 'Lets just say it's a work in progress for now.'

They shook, taking the measure of each other.

'And I'll keep you in the loop,' said Eddie.

'And I'll keep you advised of legal cover in the loop,' replied Cat

Chapter 58: Club Mental

Lofty stood at ease, in the doorway of Moonlight Oasis, he was king of the doors, wearing tweed and most importantly, not in nick. An old-fashioned Rolls, coasted to halt in front of him, the Mental Mickey entourage disembarked.

'Oi, where is that cunt Conway?'

'You talking about my boss.' Lofty stood legs apart, flexing in his tweed pants. 'I think some respect is due in the verbal department.'

'Fucking love it,' Mickey paused mid-stride and turned to Uncle Delaney. 'Hear that Uncle, fucking loyalty with a touch of class. That's what you get with soldier boys, they will effing die for their comrades.'

Lofty bowed and spoke in a more conciliatory tone, 'ah, you must be Mental Mickey.' Delaney winced and shut one eye expecting the explosion to blast them all, but Mickey clapped.

'That's fucking front line shit Uncle, we got to get some soldier boys.' Mickey quipped.

Jabba came rushing to the door, shitting himself that Mental Mickey was getting a roasting from his weird doorman.

'Oh Mr. Malone, come, come. The VIP area, drinks on the house.'

'Shut the fuck up Jabba, you fat cunt,' Jabba's belly wobbled like a tsunami hitting the shore; the outgoing tide drained the blood from his face.

'Ha got ya, see his fucking face head south, course I'll have a drink, won't we Uncle.' Mickey marched in, arm around the wobbling Jabba, 'Got any religious lagers?'

'Word to the wise, I do have people done in, for front like you dished out.', he whispered to Lofty, as he passed him.

'Daramatsu Daimyo,' said Lofty as he bowed again

'Fucking class act, sweet,' Mickey barked to Uncle Delaney and the Mickey flotilla cruised through the front door creating human bow waves, people parted.

Eddie was hanging loose by the top bar, keeping an eye on a bunch of reality stars that were giving it large and loud sloshing Champers. He caught a whisper in his earpiece,

'Mental incoming.' It was Lofty and then Mental Mickey bounded up the stairs.

'Abracadabra, heard you've been in the house of Plod?' He took a drink off the tray, held by a nervous thin blonde balancing a boob job bigger than suited her.

'This is Ivanka, another of our little stunners,' said Jabba, in a desperate attempt to distract Mickey. It fell flat; he resorted to rubbing his hands in supplication.

'Fucking bet she is. Looks like a blow-up doll.'
Ivanka, leaning like the tower of Pizza, tottered off down the bar. Mickey, big shark smile, swaggered towards Eddie. Jabba slid away on a trail of his own sweat. Mickey was like the chainsaw massacre dressed in a smart suit, a full-on crazy charismatic ticking time bomb.

'So what's up, Mr Malone?' inquired Eddie, keeping his voice nice and steady.

'Oi, you Morris dancing drinking fucker, I'm getting mixed signals. Why was you pulled by Plod? Who you think forks out for the QC?'

'Much appreciated Mr Malone. It's spook stuff, a gang from ISIS world are in town.'

'You trying to re-start your effing war again?'

'No, it never stopped, now its come over here Mr. Malone.'

'Be a right fucking tear up, if they're messing in our manor.' Mickey knocked back a shot and grimaced. 'Prefer lager meself.

'Yeah, so consider that we ran deterrence on them, on your patch.' Eddie leaned in and whispered to Mickey. 'Nipped it in the bud.'

'We got our own Home Guard Uncle.' Mickey laughed and gave Uncle Delaney a don't-you-fart look. Eddie looked at them both, he couldn't work out if it was an elaborate act or were they really like this. He started explaining.

'They got a posh Arab running their banking and buying up properties . . .'
A shriek from the reality celeb table, a tall blonde in a tight

dress, throwing a glass of champers all over a smooth looking, pretty boy. He jumps up and slaps her in the face; she falls back on the leather couch shrieking like a stuck pig, kicking her feet out. The table goes over and the group scatters outwards. The blonde struggles up, grabs a bottle by the neck and smashes the end.

'I'll fucking slash you a smile, you cunt,' she shrieks.

Eddie darts over, twists the bottle out of her hand, she backs away panting, ready to unsheathe her claws.

'OK, time to pay your bill and leave.' He motions to pretty boy and rest of the reality stars.

'Cunt, cunting fucking bastard.' The blonde starts shouting like an Essex fishwife.

'She should go, not us, we're the "Kings of Kensington" show.' Pretty boy leered at Eddie.

'She is going mate, after you pay up.'

'I think you have this rather mixed up, my friend.' A big gym muscled type, butted in on pretty boy's side and the reality show boys squared up, flexing their Celeb star entitlement. Eddie stepped forward. Uncle Delaney backing him and Mental Mickey grinning like a loon came alongside.

'I fucking hate that show, bunch of posh twats, how about we cancel it,' Mickey spoke softly with an ice calm. The reality show boy's world stopped turning as they stared at this alternative harsh reality confronting them.

'So I strongly suggest you "Kings of Kensington" just leave peacefully,' Eddie spoke pleasantly, 'without getting into any bother and enjoy the rest of your night elsewhere.' Eddie stepped back and indicated the stairs behind him. Mickey and Uncle Delaney stepped to the side, offering a route between them to the stairs.

'It's just a shiny pleb place after all,' said pretty boy attempting to save face, 'and she's just a dressed up slag.'

'You isn't getting any of this.' The blonde still panting in anger snapped back. She stuck her chest out, flashing cleavage.

Eddie eyed the 'D' list Celeb's and cocked his head at the stairs. The reality show boys shuffled nervously between Eddie, Mickey and Uncle Delaney, avoiding eye contact, they headed downstairs. Eddie turned to the blonde.

'You want a coffee, got any friends with you?'

'Yeah, coffee be good.' She smiled cautiously at Eddie. 'Fuckers think they bought me for a glass of champers, he was sticking his hands up me dress.'

'Live and learn girl.' Eddie gestured down the stairs. 'Tell Ivanka at the bar, you got coffee on me, OK.' The blonde headed for the stairs and turned back.

'Which one's she?'

'The one with the massive tit job.' Eddie laughed.

'Oh, that one.' The Blonde giggled.

'Nothing like a rumble eh Uncle?' Mickey sat back down and indicated Eddie should join him. 'So, Eddie, these fuckers from the war zone?'

'Evil bastards, warlord types,' Eddie kept his voice low, 'all they know is guns, violence and intimidation,'

'So we got to play smart?' Mickey nodded to his Uncle.

'What do you think soldier?' Uncle Delaney farted and looked at Eddie for an answer.

'I'd say that's about right, it's a tactical situation, Mr Delaney, Mr Malone.'

'A war ain't good for business,' snarled Mickey.

'Listen, the top brass will be happy, if it stays in your yard,' replied Eddie, 'they call it containment.'

'What's that mean?'

'Keep in a tight box,' said Eddie, shaping a box with his hands.

'I know what fucking containment means, you ale loving Morris Dancing cowboy,' scowled Mickey.

'I was just giving you context,' Eddie shrugged off the insults. He was used to the Malone banter now. 'Means they'd be happy for us to kill each other off. Solves lots of problems for them.'

'But ya sorted the fuckers, right Eddie?'

'For now, but maybe they'll be more on the way Mr Malone, lots of 'em and they'll keep coming if they have a bridgehead here.'

'You hear that Uncle, an effing bridgehead, these cunts

think they can invade our manor. Well, looks like we need a Home Guard, ain't that right soldier boy.'

Eddie wondered if he would need that advice from Cat Thompson sooner than he thought?

Chapter 59: Marigolds Safe Harbour

Eddie walked in.

'You want I make tea Eddie,' asked Marigold.
The Mob were crowded into Marigolds knock-thru downstairs space. Eddie nodded a yes.

'You did a good job Spiky, download a snippet of the handover footage, and get Gilly to send it to Col Henley-Rees and Dame Carter at Paddington nick. Should keep the fuckers up for nights.'

'Henley-Rees? Not the dobbin who dropped us in it up country?' Spiky pulled a laptop from his haversack.

'Roger that, the same clown.' Eddie walked over to Jassi, who was sitting with Rainya on the couch, surrounded by the Mob, cans of beer and mugs of tea. 'How's Fitz?' asked Eddie.

'He's gone to stay with his parents in Wiltshire.' Rainya paused, and in a slightly disappointed tone continued, 'says he needs some space. Oh I hate my father, and now we haven't got any thing, for all the trouble you have been through.'

'Come on, let's leave the boys to their macho re-union.' Jassi gave Eddie a kiss. 'We still got a date, you and I.' The lads jeered, Eddie looked embarrassed. 'Yeah, no worries,' he said quietly, the lads smirked, lots of elbow nudging.
Jassi got Rainya's coat.

'I'm no pushover, you know,' announced Jassi, looking at them behaving like school kids, she laughed. The lads pulled serious faces and nodded back at her.

'Don't do anything silly,' said Jassi and gripped Eddie's hand for a second, then let go. 'I know, silly thing to say.' Jassi walked Rainya out the door.

'Looks like she want some boom, boom, eh Eddie,' Marigold chortled and handed the kettle to Scotch, who was now her loyal little helper.

'Aye, the lass is right enough, pity they got all the swag, eh Eddie. We get the shit end of the stick, as usual, so we do.'

'Spiky ask Gilly to send the photo's as well to Paddington Nick. The ones Lofty took of the spooks that followed me, keep em off balance.' Eddie looked at his Mob feeling that familiar post-operations satisfaction. 'OK Lofty lets have it.'

'Scotch you wanna reach into my back trouser pocket?' Lofty said as he stood up.

'But no one pulled a card yet.' Scotch looked confused. He moved behind Lofty, reached into his back pocket and pulled out a small faded calfskin ring bag. He opened the bag and spilt small diamonds on the table. 'Fuck my old boots,' exclaimed Scotch. 'That's real fucking magic so it is. Where did you hide it, when the cops pulled us?'

'Where they wouldn't look,' Lofty broke into a wide conspiratorial smile, 'with out trampling on my civil rights, so I did, eh Scotch.'

Scotch walked to the sink and washed his hands mumbling at Lofty.

Eddie held a sparkle in his hands. 'Rum will know how to deal with these. Usual divvy on swag lads?'

The lads all nodded, trusting in the old agreement.

'Good, that's settled. Now, I've got some unfinished business, back at my yard.'

'You mean we have Boss. Arigatou Daimyo san,' said Lofty in his most referential manner.

'Fuck me,' laughed Scotch, "way of the witless." The lads joined in the laughter.

'Not bad Scotch, good one in fact,' admitted Lofty.

Eddie took a mug of tea from Marigold, and looked at his comrades with pride. 'OK Mob back on duty, forty-eight hours count down.'

Chapter 60: Take a Ride

'Ok, Amigos, how long has he been back in his gaff?'

'He back in his crib a few hours now Eddie.' Valdrin twitched his head in the direction of the housing blocks on the far side of the lock-up sheds.

'Looking big time pissed off when he came,' the quiet one butted in.

'Slamming his car door, no way to treat a Merc, know what I'm saying,' the Ethiopian kid joined in,

'Yeah, I hear you lads, you did a good job, respect.'

'Was easy Eddie,' smiled Valdrin. 'Real easy, we been out here on Dial and Delivery reception innit, him seen me out here most nights, no big ting yeh.'

'It's the doing of a request, not the "ting" itself that sets up respect,' replied Eddie as he looked over the three.

'Oh, I get you, deep bro. Deep.' Valdrin raised an eyebrow. A van and a Range Rover rolled up, the Mob lads got out, dressed in workmen boiler suits, sports bags in hand. The Range Rover window rolled down.

'On observer duty,' said Rumpunch leaning out.

Eddie checked his lads over. He looked at each of them in turn, they were up for it, no doubt. So it had come to this he thought, visions of combat flickered across his mind. Now I'm on home turf. So this is what fighting for home means, and this lot just want to fight, for what? Me? Or maybe the same reasons I'm fighting, makes me feel like I matter. The lads stared back waiting for Eddie to say something.

'Were ready Boss.' Lofty stamped his prosthetic.

'OK Sit Rep, target in place,' announced Eddie in his old familiar briefing style, 'five hours to sun-up, you know the score, done it enough times. Same way, same result, in fast, round 'em up.' The lads were all beaming with anticipation of action.

'Now make sure your balaclavas are down and tattoos covered, I don't want any recognition.' Eddie could see they were purring at the chance to be on active duty again. It was like a drug you got hooked on as a teenage soldier and secretly craved for in Civvy Street. They responded to his old Mob authority, he was switching them on. 'Use your call signs, OK?'

Scotch tugged a mask out of his boiler suit pocket and put it on, a "V for Vengeance" mask.

'Scotch what the fuck is that?' asked Eddie.

'Laughing Cavalier, so it is.' Scotch said, pushing the mask up.

'That's "V for Vengeance", Jezzer cracked up, 'its what all the anti-capitalist protesters wear.'

'The Cavaliers lost, didn't they?' Eddie shook his head in despair.

'Did they?' Scotch said, in shock. 'Aye all right then its V for fucking Vengeance, so it is.' He pulled the mask down.

The lads split up, heading for the Djokovic place from different directions.

'I got our calling card.' Lofty yanked the back door of the van open and pulled junky boy Terry out and frog-marched him behind Eddie.

Lofty knocked on Djokovic's door, he held junky boy by the scruff of his neck, thrusting him up against the spy hole.

'I got to talk to the boss urgent,' Junky boy pleaded, 'it's about the fucking soldier, he's on his way with a mob.'

The door rattled and opened a notch. Lofty kicked, his size thirteen-boot slammed the door wide open, the lump went down.

'We're early,' said Lofty and stepped in, the rest of the mob steamed out of the staircases, bats in one hand, bin lids, held like shields in the other. Junky boy scuttled away heading for a fix.

Eddie followed in behind, a drill they had perfected in the line of duty. Lofty was on point, he bounced off the toilet door facing the entry, careered left, treading on the downed lump as he charged. The first bedroom door was padlocked from the outside. Lofty ignored it, swung right and galloped down the corridor, bin-lid shield up, his target was the end main bedroom on the right. Halfway there a lump, leant out of the kitchen doorway, gun in hand. Lofty swung the bin lid, the edge took the lump straight under the chin, he went down with a strangled yodel.

The lads fanned out behind and took rooms in pairs. Cries of alarm were raised. They caught two lumps sleeping in the middle bedroom, and banged them out. They had practised in Eddie's flat, the layout almost the same; they knew the drill.

Lofty smashed the end bedroom door in with a mighty kick and piled in swinging his bat. A lump barrelled into him, he braced the bat across the lumps neck, but got a finger in his eye. Lofty crashed back but managed a sideswipe, as he rolled away. He got to his knees and wacked the lump on the head, lump went down. Lofty staggered to his feet rubbing his eye, blinded on his right side.

Djokovic charged out from behind the wardrobe, knife in hand, direct at Lofty's right side.

Scotch had stuck close behind Lofty, as he had barrelled through the flat, desperately trying to quell his fear. His anxiety levels had gone through the roof, he was struggling to keep control, not wanting to humiliate himself in front of his old comrades. Scotch took one look at Djokovic charging Lofty and before he could stop to think, he instinctively dived across Lofty's body. Time slowed, he floated in mid-air, heard the sucking noise, felt the cold slide of the knife entering his belly and then, fell to the floor in real time. All anxieties faded away.

Lofty, right eye streaming with tears, stumbled over Scotch, realising what had just gone down. With a cry of rage he grabbed Djokovic round the neck and wacked his head repeatedly against the wardrobe. Djokovic went limp. Lofty rolled off him and cradled Scotch's head in his arms.

'Delta three down, gut wound,' Lofty cried, and pulled the knife out and pressed down hard on the wound, to halt the flow of blood.

Jezzer dashed in, ripping a field dressing from his top pocket. 'I got this.' He tore Scotch's boiler suit open, stuck the dressing on the wound and wound tape around Scotch's body.

'"Way of the Wounded,"' Scotch looked up at Lofty and groaned.

'That's the best one yet Scotch.' Lofty chuckled, tears streaming from both eyes now. Scotch smiled and closed his eyes.

The rest of the lumps hadn't stood a chance. Djokovic was dragged into the front room, blood drying on his face, and heaved into an armchair, his hands lashed with plastic ties. The other lumps were tied back to back.

Eddie looked at Djokovic, not an ounce of mercy in his heart. A crash came from the small end bedroom, as the door flew in. 'Fucks sake!' came a shout from Spiky, who marched down the corridor. 'Sunray, he's got two girls chained up in there.'

'Shit. OK, tell them they're safe, said Eddie, 'Delta five and six take three to nearest A&E.' Fat Phil and Legal Evans picked up the corners of a coat with Scotch folded inside and carried him out.

'Take the van,' shouted Eddie, 'A&E Royal Free.'

'Fucker,' shouted, Lofty smacking Djokovic in the face.

Djokovic started babbling some shit about the Malones will kill them. Lofty ignored him and started searching a sturdy desk. He smashed the top-drawer open, fished out a bunch of keys and tossed them to Spiky, who started opening the other drawers.

'Hey that's my stuff, I got protection you fuckers,' shouted Djokovic.
Eddie smacked him, running out of patience with the prick.

'Look what I've got here.' Lofty whistled and turned holding Eddie's medal rack. Eddie gasped and took them.

'OK, lads, lash the lumps up and let's move out,' commanded Eddie. Jezzer and Lofty grabbed Djokovic, pulled a bag over his head lifted him off his feet, frog-marching him out the flat. Djokovic protested, wailing loudly.

'Were taking a ride.' Lofty smacked him around the back of his head.

Eddie looked in the small bedroom, two half-starved naked girls were chained to the radiator, terrified. 'Ops get a blanket for these girls, and bell Plod on the fucker's phone,'

'What shall I tell em' Sunray?' Eddie thought it through.

'OK, tell em' massive disturbance at this flat, women

screaming for help, an' all that shit.'

'Yeah Sunray roger that.' Spiky had found blankets and covered the girls. 'I'll do the Fire service an' all, they're quicker to the scene.'

They bundled Djokovic in the back of his Merc, between Jezzer and Lofty. Spiky climbed in the drivers seat.

'Drive easy now,' ordered Eddie, sitting in the passenger seat. The Range Rover followed, they worked their way to the North Circular and sped east.

The same old wharf east of the city, down river where the Thames became fat and slow fanning out into the estuary before embracing the sea. In times gone by it had been a hive of activity, hundreds of Dockers had swarmed over the jetties, unloading ships from the Indies, but now weeds poked through the concrete. It was just a forgotten industrial wasteland, stoically waiting its turn in the shadows for gentrification.

The glow of ambient light from the city reflected off the wide river, illuminating the dark crumbling wharf. Djokovic stood with his back to the river beside his Mercedes, the Range Rover pulled up, headlights casting flickering shadows over Eddie and the lads, standing in a semi circle around Djokovic. The headlights switched off.

'You guys in big trouble.' Djokovic stared defiantly in the gloom. 'I'm protected by the Malones. Yes fuckers.'

Lofty stormed forward, pickaxe handle in his right hand, grabbed Djokovic by his jacket and clipped him behind the knees with the handle, forcing him to slump down in a position of prayer.

'Let me take this vermin out Boss,' he appealed to Eddie, who shook his head and pulled his phone out.

'What you guys want?' Djokovic looked up at the grim faces, no sign of redemption and began to wheedle a way out. 'We can make a deal, yes?' He put his hands together praying. Look we all big men here.' He reached out and patted his Mercedes. 'You want money, I get you money big time.'

'I got a Mr. Djokovic here.' Eddie had the phone on loudspeaker. 'Mr. Malone, this fella says he's got a get out of jail card.'

'Hey Malone, tell these guys eh, they're in big trouble,' yelled Djokovic, summoning up his last reserves of defiance. 'They can't do this.' Memories of situations just like this played out in his mind, killings in Bosnia he'd presided over. 'This not right, eh Malone . . ?'

'Abracadabra . . .' Mental Mickey's tinny voice issued from the phone held high in the air by Eddie.

'All set Sunray.' Spiky climbed out of the other side of the Mercedes.

'Magic.' Eddie whispered in the phone, and gestured to Lofty. 'Put him in his car.'

Djokovic glared wide-eyed, thinking he was getting out of this nightmare. Lofty hauled him to his feet and smacked him across the wrists with the pickaxe handle. Djokovic cried out in pain. Lofty stuffed him in the driver seat.

'You fucker I take your other leg for this,' cried Djokovic.

Lofty slammed the door shut on Djokovic, who, swearing and cursing started the engine. Spiky fiddled with his handset, the Mercedes doors clicked and the back windows rolled halfway down. The Range Rover headlights switched on and growled forward. They could see Djokovic's head in the glare of headlights swivelled over his shoulder, looking out the back window, ready to reverse. The truck shunted forward, eased up to the boot of the Mercedes in a gentle kiss and pushed it to the end of the crumbling jetty overhanging the dark swirling waters of fat murky Thames. They could hear Djokovic screams over the wailing car alarm, as he realized what was happening. He hammered desperately at the locked door. The front of the car lurched out over the river and in slow motion it tipped and plunged, the ten-foot drop, face down into the river.

The Mercedes bobbled twice, the boot end sticking up out the river. Then a burst of bubbles, and the Merc sank, the wailing car alarm and Djokovic's screams cut off.

'Abra-fucking-cadabra.' Eddie threw his arms out wide.

'Don't like slave owners, don't know why,' Rum got out the Range Rover. 'Something in my coconut.' The mob cracked up laughing, frontline humour releasing the tension.

Eddie stared at the river, Rum walked up and stood by

him, as the lads sobered, shuffling on the old wharf, realising that they had just committed an execution. No one was sure what to do next

'What now Boss?' asked Lofty waving his hand indicating the lads.

'That was a bad business!' Eddie shrugged.

'Our business.' Lofty scratched his head.

'Good riddance to the evil fucker, chaining women up . . .' Spiky spat in the river.

'So, we in your world now?' Eddie looked at Rum.

'Well bro, I think you and your Mob just staked a claim in the Crim business of this fucked up town.' Rum lit a rolled joint, took a drag, blew a long plume of smoke and handed it to Eddie. Eddie took a pull to settle his jangling nerves.

'Mob chain of command, your call Eddie,' said Jezzer and reached over taking the spliff. Eddie stared upriver, the fuzzy glow of city lights reflected against the growing mass of roiling dark clouds. A storm was brewing.

'OK lads, that's the way you want it?' said Eddie, he looked the lads over, carefully, the execution was a heavy load to endure. They all took a moment to think, contemplate each other's resolve. 'We have just crossed a line, means we are back on active service, you OK with that?' asked Eddie.

'We are all either back in the Mob, or we are lost,' said Lofty.

'Well we're the other side of the Rubicon now right enough,' replied Jezzer.

'Copy that Sunray,' said Spiky.

Eddie shivered as a cold wind whipped off the river. 'OK, lads move out,' he said thinking, "it feels right somehow."

'Arigoto Boss,' Lofty flicked a salute.

Eddie nodded and got in the Range Rover, front seat, next to Rum. They drove out of the crumbling dockyard, headlights flicked over a road sign, "Central London".

'Rainbow City,' whispered Eddie.

The heavens' opened, a torrential rain fell, Rum put his foot down and they accelerated through the downpour, to London.

Chapter 61: Mental Calling

'Say the magic word for me.'

'Yeah, Abracadabra.'

'Nice one, Kushty.' Eddie could hear Delaney farting in the background. 'This me direct number, just don't save it under Mental, OK, haha.'

'I'll put you on speed dial, whatever number you like?' Eddie shook his head.

'Fucking seven, its the fourth prime number, that's fucking profound physics.'

'You wanna be seven or four?'

'Seven you fucking ale dancing Morris drinking idiot, I was just giving you context.' Mickey rang off, laughing high pitch.

Chapter 62: Sick Bay

Scotch flickered into consciousness and tried opening his eyes, to confirm whether he was alive or in some sort of afterlife. He was hoping for Valhalla, lots of drinking but the crud round his eyelids had glued them together. He was half wandering in a dream, he and Lofty sword fighting in a Kung-Fu type land. Just as he was giving up on thinking he was alive, he felt a hand on his brow, a damp cloth wiping his eyelids. He tried again and slowly blinked them open, a vision of Marigold swam into focus. Scotch thought he was still dreaming.

'You OK now, silly Scotch man,' Marigold's face beamed down at him, she dabbed his face with the cloth again. 'Me looking after you brave buoy.'

Scotch felt a deep warmth seep through him, he smiled back at Marigold. 'I was scared stiff.'

'You nothing to fear now honey, think you can eat some biscuits?' Marigold took hold of his hand.

Scotch laughed, coughed and felt whole again, for the first time in years.

A figure uncoiled itself from the chair beside the bed; Scotch craned his head trying to see. Lofty loomed over him.

'Brought you a bottle of Guinness mate, was going to bring you sushi.' He looked down at the dressing covering Scotch, and the pipes coming out his arm. 'But you know.'

'Aye, right you are,' croaked a weary Scotch. Marigold wiped his brow again. Scotch's smile split his rhubarb crumble face in two.

Lofty leaned in close whispering, 'the cops want a statement when you're up to it. The lads said they reported they found you staggering on the street.'

Scotch grunted, 'Aye, I'll tell 'em I was attacked by a mad fucker wearing a pink shirt and pin striped suit, so I will.' Lofty laughed and squeezed Scotch's hand.

Chapter 63: April Shopping

Harrods was packed. April grimaced, all these rich foreigners. The perfume counter girl asked her if she wanted the Paco Rabanne gift-wrapped. A hand took hold of her elbow. She turned.

'Buying me a present Showers?'

'Well well, our former employee Mister Conway.' April brought her surprise under control effortlessly.

Eddie mock bowed, he was enjoying the Mister these days. He reached for the Pacco; the counter girl let it go, captivated by a bit of live theatre livening up her shift, she leaned over the counter to listen. April gave her a "do you mind" look.

'Shall we walk Mister Conway, don't want to corrupt Goldilocks here.' They walked, Eddie held the Pacco.

'Your boss, Mr Agassi, he been pulled in yet?'

'No idea what you're talking about Eddie.' They strolled into menswear; everyone ignores each other in menswear and paused by a country squire dummy.

'But you know what I'm talking about?' April gave him the wide-eyed look.

Eddie fingered the tweed jacket on the dummy, 'Tweed - you think it would suit me, or is it just for the country set?' He said smiling, thinking of Lofty's bizarre dress sense.

'It wouldn't suit you Eddie, trust me.' They walked on, arm in arm.

'So how long you been a spook, recruited you at Cambridge did they?'

'Badminton Horse Trials, actually. April smiled at him. 'What a girl will do for a good ride.'

'Jesus it's like Tinker, Tailor, Soldier.' Eddie said abrasively, 'and the soldier is the last in the queue.'

'Really Eddie, they're just books.' April laughed it off. 'So are you here to shop?'

'No, just want to pass on a message.'

'Oh really Eddie, what message? From the poor Rainya to her father?' She picked up a bowtie, held it against his neck.

'This suits you, a dickie, yes Ahh ha.' April was getting turned on. Eddie could see the neon lights, glowing in the back of her eyes.

'Tell Colonel Henley-Rees when you see him down the Polo club, I got it all recorded.'

'You can't have!' April stood still, shocked.

'So, you know what I'm on about Showers? Very good quality, Spiky did a great job, the handover all recorded on four Go-Pros, good audio, be nice on YouTube. Madam Boss will be ever so pleased.'

'Look Eddie, don't play this game,' April continued the walk.

'Showers, certain Internet Wikileaks outfits will get a download if anything happens to me and my Mob,' Eddie gave her a wry smile, 'Tell Dame Winnie-the-Pooh stay away, we're off limits.'

'It's a nasty business Eddie.' April held Eddie's arm.

'So why are you in it?' Eddie looked at her puzzled.

'I'm not in it Eddie, I'm used by it.' April squeezed Eddie's hand. 'I only give the bastards so much, as you may have gathered. I prioritise myself in these games.'

'OK, so they got their claws into you somehow.' Eddie studied her face and decided she was telling the truth, as much trapped in the spider's web as he was. April nodded, went to say something, then paused and swallowed.

'Listen Eddie, Colonel Farouk Hakimi is in the wind, they let his boys out,' whispered April. 'A deal, I don't know what.'

Eddie halted surprised. 'That makes me a moving target,' he cursed.

'C'mon you love a battle.' Eddie shrugged in answer, April smiled affectionately and continued, 'well the Pacco will make you smell nice, let's just say I bought it for you.'

'Well that's nice of you.' Eddie hefted the Pacco in his hand. April pulled him by his arm.

'Another hotel, another time . . . ' she suggested.

'Yeah I know, of all the posh department stores you had to walk into this one.' Eddie smiled feeling balance restored;

some sort of deal was going down.

'We will always have the Waldorf,' she giggled.

Eddie smiled back. 'Bye bye April.'

'What happened to Showers? Eddie.'

'Yeah, it's May, April Showers has passed.'

They walked through the revolving doors and paused on the pavement. April kissed Eddie tenderly. 'Take care Eddie, watch your back.'

Eddie nodded. 'Will do.'

They walked in opposite directions. April hailed a taxi and Eddie headed for the Tube station.

His phone rang. 'Hey Jassi. What? No just out shopping,' he watched April get in the taxi, she waved goodbye. 'You know, men's things.'

Brigand
London

Brigand books can be purchased through our
website at **www.brigand.london**

My Eight Year War
Alfie Holland

This is the personal account of WW2 by an ordinary man, an airman in the RAF. Alfie Holland left school in Newmarket at the age of thirteen with no qualifications. In 1938 he joined the RAF, remaining in military service until 1946.

My Eight Year War is his memoir of the momentous events of which he was a small part like millions of others. This saw him in northern France, as part of the ill-fated British Expeditionary Force, mentioned in dispatches for shooting down enemy aircraft with an adapted Browning machine gun, a narrow escape through Boulogne in May 1940, the Battle of Britain, north Africa, the invasion of Italy at Salerno and year-long fight to capture Italy, Yugoslavia, Austria, then finally demobilisation and life in post-war London.

Alfie wrote this book in 1999 and died in 2004. It has been edited by his nephew Peter Holland.

Afterlives
Philip Tew

In 2014 shocked by the death of former friend, writer Sue Townsend, Jim Dent spontaneously decides he must complete his own novel. Afterlives focuses on a cast of eccentrics, creative people admired over the years, most lost due to premature death, their creativity frustrated. Professor of English Literature, numerous scholarly works published, Jim is still haunted by his failure to publish fiction. He doubts whether any of the rest really mattered. In Afterlives Jim faces his last challenge: will his ambition be thwarted, or, will he succeed in his lifelong aspiration?

Afterlives combines a novel with elements of memoir. Philip Tew knew Sue Townsend (1946-2014) from 1978 until he left Leicester in 1981, commissioning stories featuring Nigel (later Adrian) Mole for a short-lived local arts magazine. He met her again in Enfield in 1999. In 1980, he travelled through snowstorms to interview Modernist poet, Basil Bunting (1900-1985), accompanied by Leicester-based writer and poet Chris Challis (1946-1997). However, much of the rest is made up by the author, or so he says.

Philip Tew's book has been favourably received by established, award-winning novelists:

"The father's episode is a fine and moving piece of writing." Fay Weldon
"It certainly has the most alerting ending of any novel I've read." Jim Crace

Afterlives is to be officially released on 7th February January 2019, but advance copies may be obtained from 7th December 2018 via the Brigand Press website.

Barbary Slave
Peter Holland

Barbary Slave is Peter Holland's first novel, which was inspired by studies for his recently completed MA in Early Modern History (1500-1800).

The white slave trade was an essential part of the Ottoman Empire, which had an insatiable appetite for manpower, provided by seizing infidel non-believers. Between 1500 and 1800 it is estimated more than 1 million Christian Europeans were seized. Britain and Ireland were not as affected as Mediterranean European states, losing about 40,000 over the period, but it was increasingly a problem through the 17th and 18th centuries. Barbary Slave is set in 1631, the year of the notorious Sack of Baltimore, led by the infamous Murat Reis. All of the other characters in Barbary Slave are fictitious but the story of former Spanish Muslims known as Moriscos is true, as is the description of Algiers as a major centre for the holding and trading of European slaves. The story of Said, Khaled, Callum, Jack, Laura, Mary, Pedro, Oji, Anna, Mehmed and Madeline, is of lives entwined in this tumultuous year.

Peter is currently working on a sequel to Barbary Slave set in 1656, when England had been through a regicide revolution and was governed by Cromwell's Puritan republic. Throughout these momentous changes in England the problem of captives being taken to the Barbary Coast and sold into the Ottoman Empire persisted.